THE CARNATION COLLECTION

Edited by:

Victoria Holland

Brittany McMunn

Abigail Wild

Wild Ink Publishing LLC

wild-ink-publishing.com

My Thanks

As Wild Ink says, the anthologies we create are labors of love.

This collection is no exception.

To have the opportunity to help create something like this is a dream come true, to be honest. If you are a creative, *you know*. An opportunity like this is rare and wonderful. It gave me growth and fulfillment that was more satisfying to me than anything I've experienced before.

I got to use my lifelong love of fantasy and storytelling and expand my knowledge base of mythology. I got to use all my creative skills. I got to work alongside professionals and creatives with just as much passion as me. Usually, I'm a solitary creative. But with this project, I had to let go of the reins. There was more than one person in the driver's seat. We communicated and collaborated all in the service of creating something that, when I read it, shocks me with how *good* it is. These writers have such diverse, beautiful views, that when brought together become a collection that is so vulnerable and true. They are woven with myth and magic and they dance with the goddesses that unite them all together.

This collection is a *communal labor of love* and I got to be a part of it.

I want to thank my partners in crime: Brittany for being the best editor who ever edited and Abby for being the guide that I needed. Thank you Rose (@thepriestessrose) for

helping in the design of the carnation that this collection is named for. To my loved ones who supported Carnation. And to all the writers who took a chance on this project.
This collection was truly a taste of freedom.
I am so glad I got to be a part of it.

Thank you,
Victoria Holland

Dear Reader,

You have chosen to open this tome.

I am Hekate, the Goddess of Magic.

You should know that it is far from my nature to take a stand on anything.

Let me rephrase.

It is far from my nature to take a *moral* stand on anything. It is one of the reasons I am revered. And feared. However, I will break from this pattern once: This collection is filled with the words of incredible, imaginative, and courageous souls. *It is sacred.*

You would do well to remember that.

To gather all seven goddesses of this tome was no easy feat. To gather all the pieces within was almost just as hard. Yet, they came together when it came to the discussion of *divinity.*

Allow me to educate you: *Magic*—like nature or a knife—*is neutral.* It is not good or evil. It is not dark or light. It will bend only as the user sees fit. On some level, you all know this. Yet, it is still openly feared and misunderstood.

You can thank kind society for that mentality.

Yet, the souls contributing to this collection answered the call. The untold and unbridled truth that spills out in the private heart of an individual holds unlimited facets of beauty.

This anthology is overflowing with that beauty.

These goddesses are incredibly human in their

divinity. However, they also know that you are incredibly divine in your humanity. They have loved, just as you have loved. They have grieved, just as you have grieved. So, we offer our carnation as a promise:

Your *authenticity* and your *divinity* are the same.

I am of the mind that the souls who contributed to this collection know just that.

This collection is sacred.

Remember that.

Regards,
Hekate

TABLE OF CONTENTS

HERA
QUEEN OF THE GODS,
GODDESS OF MARRIAGE,
WOMEN, & FERTILITY

I am Queen. I am a daughter, a sister. I am a mother, a wife. I am a woman. I have been the scariest bitch in the heavens. I've been all over the map when it comes to privilege and oppression. So believe me when I tell you, there is no concept, thing, or person you should silence yourself for. Never.

HERA AND ME
Binod Dawadi

My goddess, Hera, where are you?
You are the goddess of
Marriage, women, and childbirth
With your powers, only the world
Exists. You give life to others
You want happiness of the world
I am 27 years old
As well, I am a single man
I cannot live my alone life
Happily, so my goddess

I would like to request you
To listen to my pains
To search me a beautiful fairy
From the heaven or from Earth
With your permission and powers
Please arrange my marriage with her
My goddess, my life is so much boring
As well as frustrated, this is because

No one does spiritual and
True love to me

I hope you know that
I hope you will give me a fairy
Which will be beautiful and
Kindhearted. Who
Does true love to me, as well as spiritual love
For forever
My goddess
You can give
A lot of blessings to me, my goddess
You are great, my goddess

From you, many people can get love
Many people do marriage
Many girls become mothers
Many girls can give birth
So, I also want to start a family
For that I need a beautiful lover
Who loves me so much
So, my godess, you are my inspiration and hope
I hope you will give me happiness
In my life for forever.

THE WOUNDED SKY
Briana Nicole F. Bautista
Lester N. Linsangan

They call me the jealous queen
The cruelest they have ever seen
Cursing all the innocent
Sitting on a throne so magnificent

Everyone is complaining
How I treat this illicit offspring
But no one ever cared
On what he and his numerous lovers dared

He gave me nothing but pain
Presumably the reason why I showed up as a villain
This is not what I envisioned it to be
When I swore myself to him

He gave me his solemn promises
As if his sinful eyes did not land on other goddesses
How can a man do this to me?
When all I did was to love him completely

All these years, I was hurt and betrayed
Fooling myself with our love that has decayed
I was forbidden to curse him to death
So, I ended up messing with his lovers' breath

I was blinded by love
As if it's the only thing I have
They'll see what they have caused me
And what betrayal made me do

My vengeance will burn like fire
Pride and dignity are my only desire
I am a goddess with great power and might
And when I sought revenge, I'll do it right

I'll be the nightmare to those who transgressed
Throw the feelings I struggled to suppress
Remind them that I am Hera, a goddess
Now you'll kneel and beg for my forgiveness;

THE TEARS OF THE LIFELESS GODDESS
Ma. Carmela S. Garcia
Lester N. Linsangan

To whom I owe my loyalty
To the man, I'll love for eternity
Our marriage is not far from vain
One of Why my heart is in pain

Whenever your lustful gaze laid on other deities
Thousands of needles perforate my psyche
I want to ask you, "Am I not enough?"
With other women, you smile and laugh

You mumbled things in your sleep
Names of women I want to rip
I was the one who stayed by your side
But your affection focused on other brides

I surmise that I live in your dream
A soul you forgot when lights go dim
These aching eyes become a stream
I'm doltish. I fall for your scheme

What happened to you
The love you had unexpectedly flew
How I wish I had a clue
Before I decided out of the blue

A love that cheats exists
And the love that heals exists
In the depths of our hearts
The romance feels the heat

As I unravel your past amours
I found secrets and many more
Every woman's heart you tore
Mine was the deepest you bore

You caused me heartbreak
Out of pain and heartache
I unleashed my inner fury
Battles? I wasn't a rookie

I'll make you fill the lake
I'll be present in your wake
The villainess is a Goddess
Be careful with whom you mess

"Zeus, the Incubus!» that's your name
To you, love is an elementary game
Poison my veins; it'll never be the same
Be ready; you played with a fiendish flame;

Hera—Queen of the Gods, Goddess of Marrraige, Women, and Children
Dana Hawkins

"Will you go to the Freshman homecoming dance with me?" The 14-year-old boy with ocean blue eyes and sandy blond hair asked me with a shaky voice.

He seemed nice, I thought, as I closed my locker door, leaving behind my New Kids on the Block shrine.

Twenty-five years later, I had his baby. But not in the way you might think.

Chad and I bonded over a shared a love of Doritos, Oprah, and Madonna. We swapped school lunch for burgers and fries at the local hot spot. We bought Orange Julius and pretzels at the mall and tried on clothes we couldn't afford. We hugged when he came out to me. We were inseparable.

During our early 20's, Chad and I first discussed surrogacy during a one-too-many margaritas and chips night. He threw something out like, "Would you ever be an oven for a bun?"

Pretty sure I said yes on the spot.

I had one child by then, a boy I had adopted at 21. I wanted more children, but surrogacy needed to wait until

I had my kiddos. Chad and his partner had been together for years, but gay marriage wasn't legal. We talked about surrogacy the same way people talk about "someday retiring in Mexico" or "I'm gonna save up and buy a Lambo." Surrogacy was a dream. A wish. Not an actionable plan.

One divorce for me and ten more years of our friendship passed. Chad and his partner had now been married for years. We (okay me, as he's always had freakishly good hair) got a little greyer, earned a few laugh lines around the edges, and added more years under our belt. The conversations about surrogacy ramped up.

After I had my daughter, I broached the subject with my husband. He was immediately supportive, even knowing it would change the dynamic of our family for at least a year. We decided that after we had our next, and final, child, I would be a surrogate.

Chad and my conversations went from hypothetical to serious. Chad inspired me with his desire and dedication for fatherhood. He was already a great uncle to my kids, a doting big brother to his much younger siblings, and a dog dad that any canine would envy. He had a natural caretaker ability, could make me laugh like no other, and was a born protector. There was no doubt in my mind he would be a perfect dad.

When my son was six months old, and I passed my mid-30s, I called Chad after weeks of heavy discussions. I'll never forget the two words I said to him:

"I'm in."

A copious amount of "Oh my god! I love you. I love you so much!" slammed into my ear and wrapped me in a dopamine-filled hug. I was about to embark on something huge with my person. My best friend. The shoulder I cried on through my divorce. My tipping partner at my first drag show. My snuggle buddy during messy high school drama.

Shit just got real.

We immediately went into business mode. Every possible scenario—we thought—was discussed. Do we need a lawyer? Will insurance cover it? Do we go through a clinic? Will the doctors sign off on it? And most importantly, how will I get pregnant?

Readers. Let's stop there and get that question out of the way.

IVF.

Cause, *ewww*. He's my best friend.

We agreed within the first ten minutes that we wouldn't use my egg. The idea of him and I having a genetic child felt like siblings pro-creating. And deep down, I wasn't sure I could emotionally disconnect from my pregnancy if it were my egg. Chad and his husband decided to go through a clinic to find an egg donor and coordinate the surrogacy process.

And so, it began.

I would love to say the process was smooth, that I had an easy labor, and gave birth to a healthy baby.

I had no idea the curveballs heading our way.

Surrogacy train. All aboard!

First stop. Find a lawyer.

We had a magical, fairy godmother in the beginning. A high school friend—now a lawyer—who provided pro-bono work for us and guided us on our journey. But within a short while, to avoid conflict of interest, the clinic required each family to retain a lawyer.

Let's get this next question out of the way because, for some reason, everyone was more curious about this than the conception. The dads paid for everything and gave me what I like to call "a Nordstrom clothes budget for someone who shops at Target." Lunches, dinners, spas, Chad paid for everything. And a mother of all gifts at the hospital, which will forever remain a secret between our families.

Next, we had to find lawyers who specialized in surrogacy. But not only surrogacy. We had to find lawyers willing to represent a pre-birth order—for the first time in the history of our Midwestern County.

What's a pre-birth order? Thanks for asking. It establishes parental rights prior to birth, so my name would never be on the birth certificate. A few raised eyebrows followed this request, accompanied by low mumblings of *who cares* and *it's just a piece of paper*. Even though Chad and his husband had been together for 15 years, Federal Gay Marriage was in its infancy. The dads wanted to protect their baby at all costs, which included not having an amended birth certificate.

Next stop. Exams. All the exams.

Countless medical exams were up next. And oof, these were not comfortable. Dyes in fallopian tubes. Internal Ultrasounds. Needles. The type of invasive questions that sent me blushing from head to toe. You get the picture.

The doctor gave my body the all-clear. But my head needed the same vote of confidence. Off to the psychologist we go.

The counseling appointment was no regular fifty-minute meeting to discuss feelings and dreams. Nope. This was a five-hour, intensive session, where all parties took a steroid version of the Meyers-Briggs-style personality test followed by an exhaustive conversation. Pretty sure by the end of the day, I'd given mental birth.

A million thoughts swirled in my brain as we strode into the office. But once I tip-toed through the door, I oddly fixated on only one thought: Where would everyone sit? The office contained exactly one chair and one couch.

A conundrum.

Should the three men sit on the couch and me on the chair? No.

Should I sit in between the dads, and my husband sit on the chair? Hmmm, that felt weird.

Should my husband and Chad sit next to each other, and Chad's husband in the chair? I didn't like that either.

Finally, after awkwardly standing there as everyone waited for me to lead the way, I sat in the middle with Chad and my husband on each side.

And I thought I resolved the most difficult decision I'd make that day.

Chad and I had spent close to 15 years talking about surrogacy. We talked about hospitals, birthing centers, hormone choices, taking time off work, and insurance. We thought we went through every possible scenario.

We were wrong.

"If Dana were to get in a car accident and be declared legally dead, does her husband consent to keeping her alive so the baby can grow?"

Holy. Crap.

"If the husbands choose not to keep the baby after you've given birth, do you consent not to seek custody?"

Yikes.

"Who has the right to terminate the pregnancy? It's Dana's body. It's the dad's baby."

Whoa.

For hours we talked about the most uncomfortable, awful scenarios that we hadn't even imagined. But we all, thankfully, agreed on everything with minimal discussion. Chad made one thing very clear from the beginning. Whatever I needed, I got. I had the final say over everything.

Feeling good about our progress, the doctor stood up, and vice-gripped a box behind her shelf with a stern look. Then she pulled out the needles. The first one was the same as an insulin needle.

I'm cocky.

I waved it off like it was no big deal.

My first husband was diabetic. Injections were a norm. I have tattoos all over my body. This tiny little needle? Piece of cake.

"No problem," I said with an over-satisfied smirk at my obvious bravery and strength.

"And this is the one that goes in your butt." She pulled out a needle that I swore was the size of a drumstick. My face went white. I swiped my sweating hands across my thighs. I stared at my husband, and the dads, and back at the doctor, wondering if it was a joke.

It was not a joke. Finally, I swallowed, and nodded.

Next stop. A massive setback.

Several months into our journey, the progression was promising. Legal papers signed. Egg donor search executed. The all-clear received from the medical and psychological exams. Should be smooth sailing from here on out, Chad

had said.

Famous last words.

The surrogacy coordinator failed to mention that Chad and his husband needed to quarantine a sperm sample from each of them for six months to see if HIV developed.

Six. Months.

The blow was tremendous. We were *right there*, at the finish line, so close to getting pregnant. Imagine being pregnant in your third trimester. A few weeks shy of your due date. You're tired. You're anxious. You have the crib set up and the hospital bag packed. And you go to a check-up, and the doctor says, "Oh, I'm so sorry. I miscalculated. You still have six months left in your pregnancy."

We cried. We begged. We filed appeals. I signed every waiver known to humankind. We yelled and threatened a lawsuit.

And they wouldn't budge. So, we waited.

For six months.

Next stop. Hormones.

With the journey back on track, the dads completed the egg donor search. Now, it was time to begin my shots.

At the appointment, the nurse explained to my husband how to inject me. Tiny one in the belly. Drumstick in the butt. She looked at us with all seriousness and said, "If you hit her nerve, she won't walk for months."

Dramatic? Perhaps. Effective? Absolutely.

She drew a circle on my outer butt/hip area with a sharpie and pointed. "Only in here. Got it?"

Got it.

Next stop. Pregnancy.

Of the entire process, this was the most uneventful. I loved being pregnant. Loved. It. Not surprising as I loved being pregnant with my other children. During pregnancy, I have self-diagnosed body dysphoria. In my non-pregnant state, I have a solid middle-aged mom wardrobe. Leggings. Baggy sweaters. Flowy skirts. During pregnancy, I'm convinced I'm the hottest woman alive. Cindy Crawford and Linda Evangelista (for the younger crowd, Bella Hadid and Kylie Jenner) could eat their hearts out. The tighter, the better. I carried that baby bump with pride.

Physically, I felt the same. Emotionally, totally different. During this pregnancy, I had no emotional connection to the baby. Sometimes I'd put my hand on my belly and say things like, "how ya doing, kiddo?" or "you hanging in there, little one?" But my focus was on my children, husband, and being an excellent hostess to the growing butterball in my belly.

Chad spent as much time as he could with me while respecting my life, children, and husband. We traded our quarterly drag show outings for take-out and movies. Conversations about work pressure or favorite shows turned to diapers and butt-rash creams. Chad researched like no other, digging to find the best monitor, crib, and organic cotton sheets.

Next stop. Fear.

My appointment was on a Wednesday. Thirty-five weeks along and feeling good. Vitals were great. Healthy, happy, had a respectable waddle, and frequent bathroom trips. On Saturday, I called Chad to chat. "Do you have your overnight bags packed yet? You never know when babies might surprise you."

He hadn't. We still had a few weeks, but he said he'd pack it that weekend. The purchased car seat was in the box, but his husband would assemble it in the next week or so. Good, I said. Cause babies don't care about our timelines.

I laid down after our call. My husband was out of town, and the kids and I were with my parents. Tired the last few days, I decided I needed a nap. Shifting to my side, I tapped my fingers to my belly. "Hey, little one, you doing okay in there?"

No response.

She always responded. A kick, a roll, bubbles. *Something.*

She's probably just sleeping, I thought. Man, I was so tired. And she was so quiet. And something didn't feel right.

But I tend to be anxious.

Some call it worst-case scenario planning or paranoid or over-active imagination. I often talk myself down (no, Dana, there is not a monster hiding under the bed ready to bite your ankles.) But I couldn't shake the doom.

Next stop. What's happening to my body?

I called labor and delivery and said that I didn't feel right. While on the phone, I noticed my swollen hands. Strange, I thought. They didn't look like that earlier. Or maybe they did, and I hadn't noticed. Hmm.

Sometimes I talk myself down to not appear "hysterical" or "dramatic." I was pregnant, hormonal, lacking sleep, and my husband was gone. I was probably overthinking this.

The L&D nurse asked about the baby's movements.

I said it didn't seem like a lot, but I had only started paying attention, so maybe she was active earlier without me noticing.

"Why don't you just come up anyway to check? Just to be safe."

That woman saved my life.

By the time I got to the hospital an hour later (no rush, I had thought, because I had kids to get dressed, cheerio bowls to clean, and a shower to take), my hands were sausages, and my ankles looked broken. And I was so very fatigued.

The nurse took my vitals, frowned, and retook them. I peed in a cup. They frowned again. The doctor came in. And frowned.

Next stop. HELLP!

"We need to remove your placenta. It's become toxic to you."

I thought about the doctor's words for several moments. "Okay," I finally said with a brave face and trembling insides. "So, what happens with the baby? Do you give me medicine or something?"

I didn't know. I wasn't thinking. And I was so, so tired.

"You've developed HELLP Syndrome."

Huh?

"We need to deliver the baby. Nurses, set her up in L&D."

I panicked. I was fine on Wednesday. *It's only Saturday!* How did this happen in less than 72 hours?

I looked at my mom with wide eyes. She returned a mirror image. I looked at the doctor.

And finally, I yelled, "Wait! I can't have the baby. I'm not the mom!"

Next stop. Chaos.

Changed from my clothes. Thrown into a gown. Monitors set up. I called Chad and hid my panic. "Ready to be a dad?"

"Yeah," he said, probably annoyed as he and his husband were shoveling the driveway, and I interrupted his work. He hated shoveling.

"Now, Chad. You're going to be a dad."

"Now? Now, now? Oh my god!" he screamed to his husband off the phone. "She's early? Are you okay? I love you!"

My husband was out of town. Chad was over two hours away. Excitement settled in because, well, I still didn't understand it. So, she was early. But it was a baby! How exciting! All these years later, it was finally happening.

And what the heck is HELLP syndrome anyway?

Blood pressure shot up at a bullet-speed rate. Medication turned my blood to lava. Seizure pads shoved around me. New medication, neon kaleidoscope hallucinations. Confusion. Tears. Vomit.

So. Much. Vomit.

I was so, so tired. I was never this tired with my other births.

And the severity of what was happening sunk into my soul.

I'm the person who nothing bad ever happens to. I don't even get sick. But my own mortality was shoved in my face for the first time in my life. And I was scared. I asked my mom to hold pictures of my kids in front of my face. If I go out, I want to go out looking at their faces, I said. I told her to call my husband and tell him I love him.

Chad entered with his husband. He held my hand. He gave me ice-cold towels. My flesh was burning; my insides were on fire. He was calm, but I saw the look in his eyes. My best friend was the goofiest person I knew. But I heard him whisper to the doctors and my mom. His hushed tone terrified me.

I closed my eyes.

Next stop. Is she breathing?

The baby was delivered. Chad and his husband cradled her for skin-on-skin. All this time, my only dream was to watch Chad hold his baby for the first time. But my eyelids were too heavy. My body was too weak. My mind was in a hazy purple space between reality and hallucination.

I heard my voice ask if she was okay. I heard whispers of oxygen level and breathing, unsure if they were talking about the baby or me. They whisked her to NICU. They whisked me to a different room.

Next stop. Recovery and a new normal.

What happened to the baby?

She needed to bake for a while longer. For the next month, she stayed in NICU to get her lungs in shape, and her body ready to face the world.

I pumped for the baby and brought tiny bits of breast milk every day I could for her. I still refused to hold her, worried I'd get attached. Besides, I loved watching Chad cuddle with her. When I finally held her, all my fears melted. It was the same sensation I had when I held my niece years ago.

Love.

But a different kind of love from my children.

What happened to me?

According to the Mayo Clinic website, HELLP (**H**emolysis, **E**levated **L**iver enzymes, and **L**ow **P**latelets) Syndrome is a severe form of preeclampsia that affects several organ systems. It is life-threatening to the mother and baby and may cause lifelong health problems for the mother.

It burst through like a freight train, hit me hard, and didn't let go.

"You'll have to be on blood pressure meds for a few weeks," they said.

No problem.

Six years later, I'm still on it.

Next Stop: Postpartum Anxiety & PTSD

Minus the blood pressure meds, life turned into a new normal. I could never get pregnant again, which worked in my life plan anyway. My family moved for a great job opportunity. Chad and I texted and called as we had in the past, but now our conversations were more "is this poop normal" versus "what did you do this weekend."

Everything returned to its previous state.

Until my husband took me to the ER, convinced I was dying.

Forty severe panic attacks in two months emotionally and physically exhausted me. I tried various meds. Therapy. Walks. Meditation. CBD. THC (don't worry readers—I live in Seattle where it's legal). I tried "bucking it up." Nothing worked. Exhausted, anxious, and tired, I was hopeless.

My anxiety was not due to missing the baby. It was due to the stark blackness of my mortality. It was being so grateful I called the hospital that day and didn't talk myself out of it or think I was being "too dramatic."

But surely, this meant that my body constantly sent me signs, right? And I needed to listen to each of them.

A tingle in my leg? Life-threatening blood clot. Arm sore? Heart attack. Stomachache? Tumor.

Because had I not listened to my body and instincts with the baby, I would have died. I promised never to ignore any signs again.

Next stop. It's a great life.

It took months, but the panic attacks faded. Chad sent weekly photos of the baby. I started a new job. My kids started a new daycare.

My "surrobabe" turned seven this year. This past summer, Chad and I left our husbands and took the kids for the weekend to an amusement park. I complained about my aching feet. Chad complained about his back. We both complained about how dizzy we got on the Ferris wheel. Yes, the Ferris wheel.

We also took over 100 photos. We let our kids eat too much ice cream. We pulled out old pictures of us as teens. My daughter pointed out how fabulously teal and puffy my homecoming dress was, and Chad's daughter said, "That's you, Daddy? No way!"

We told our kids about getting food poisoning on a camping trip our senior year. We talked about getting shakes and fries after school, the homework we'd do together, and how they'd never understand the joys of watching MTV on a Friday night.

We laughed at how much we had changed from Freshman year and wondered if our 14-year-old selves would be embarrassed by us.

Even though we live in different states, we plan multiple annual get-togethers. But now, our conversations are less "is this poop normal" and more about "have you read the headlines today," "when is the earliest we can retire," or "which college fund do you use."

So yes, my surrogacy journey was not as expected.

But if given the chance, I wouldn't change that ride for anything.

CITATION

"Preeclampsia." *Mayo Clinic*, Mayo Foundation for
      Medical Education and Research, 15 Apr.
      2022, https://www.mayoclinic.org/diseases-
      conditions/preeclampsia/symptoms-causes/syc-
      20355745#:~:text=HELLP%20syndrome.

GODDESS HERA RULES: MY PREGNANCIES ACROSS FOUR DECADES
Amy Nielsen

My husband jokes that I'm the Gordie Howe of childbirth. Gordie was a hockey player who competed across five full decades. I've given birth across four, so Gordie's got one up on me.

My first daughter was born in the 80s, my second in the 90s. My first son was born in the 2000s, my youngest in the 2010s. When the 2020 New Year's Eve ball dropped my heart sank with it. This would be the first decade in which I wouldn't welcome a new baby.

But the ringing in of that new decade invited me to reflect on the previous four. Medical and technological breakthroughs, fluid societal views, and my advancing age molded each pregnancy into a unique experience. So, jump in that DeLorean with Hera and me, and buckle up—we've fired up the flux capacitor and we're going back in time!

Push It, Push It Real Good—Eighties Baby!
Salt-N-Peppa circa 1986

Huddled in a laundromat restroom with my best friend, a pee-on-a-stick pregnancy test confirmed I'd be a mother before I crossed the threshold into adulthood. Seventeen and pregnant—not how I'd planned to spend my senior year.

Before the blue line appeared on the new-to-the-80s at-home pregnancy test, my parents split, my addict mother kicked me out, and I was living with an older boyfriend. I hid my pregnancy from him, and everyone else, until a bulging belly burst through too-tight Jordache jeans.

Living in ancient, pre-internet times, I didn't have the luxury of Google to secretly learn what was about to happen to me. My only resource was the high school library, and it held little to fill my growing curiosity and concern. Each new pregnancy symptom, from sore breasts to morning sickness, erupted with little warning and no explanation.

I was four months along before my first health department visit and terrifying physical exam. No stranger had ever touched me in those places before. But the kind nurses stuffed a folder with enough literature to fill the overwhelming gaps and sent me home.

Midway through my pregnancy, I had my only sonogram. A grainy screen revealed a healthy baby girl. For the first time, it felt real.

Not that I could have even articulated it, but no one asked me what type of birth experience I wanted. Pregnant women in the '80s had limited autonomy. Doctors and insurance companies made most of the decisions for us. And since I had no insurance, a lack of financial resources contributed to most of mine.

My pregnancy progressed in a silo—no Facebook groups or online communities existed. My only support came from other equally clueless girls in a teen pregnancy program I was forced into by my local high school.

Months later, when I arrived at the hospital in labor, a nurse administered an enema and ensured I was properly groomed in the correct area. Then she settled me into a large room of three other moaning women separated by thin curtains.

When it was time to give birth, a nurse rolled me into a bright, and cold delivery room hosted by a doctor I'd never met. They strapped my feet in stirrups, and the doctor used a pair of snippers to make his job easier, and my recovery harder.

After about an hour of pushing—my daughter cried. Fear fled, and love rushed in. But before I could imprint her image, a nurse whisked her away to display her behind nursery glass. I'd only see her every four hours for scheduled bottle feedings.

Plummeting breastfeeding rates over the last several decades meant nursing was rarely an option. During the 80s, most considered it barbaric, and healthcare providers rarely suggested it. Instead, professionals sent mothers home with a bottle of pills to prevent lactation and a referral for expensive formula.

The nurses didn't allow me to stand on my feet that night. If I needed to use the restroom, I had to call for a bedpan. The next morning one of them helped me into the shower. I finally got the first look at my sagging post-partum belly. No one told me I'd still look eight months pregnant after giving birth.

Once the twenty-four-hour post-partum mark hit— the allotted time welfare recipients were allowed to stay in the hospital after giving birth—my daughter and I were discharged with very little instruction. I remembered thinking the day we left: They just let anyone leave with a baby?

My only support was my unreliable mother's intuition and the minimal experiences of family members and friends.

But, despite the odds, we made it. That baby girl is now thirty-four, a Board-Certified Elder Law Attorney, and my best friend. And for the record, Fuck You 80s pregnancy and birth experience. Thanks to Goddess Hera, we nailed it anyway!

This Is How We Do It—Nineties Baby!
Montell Jordan circa 1994

By the 90s, I'd earned a college degree, a wedding ring circled my finger, and I yearned for another child. But month after month—nothing. After two years, my doctor prescribed Clomid, a fertility drug that prompted regular ovulation. That, coupled with Goddess Hera's divine intervention, made it happen.

Now a double-income family with good insurance, I had the financial means to pay for birthing classes and resources. I consumed everything about pregnancy I could get my hands on, including Heidi Murkoff's wildly popular What to Expect When You're Expecting. The more I learned, the more I craved a natural birth experience. So, I switched from my gynecologist to a midwifery center.

The visceral image of my first post-partum body motivated me to focus on exercise. In a Flashdance-inspired leotard, I held my own to Denise Austin in her VHS Pregnancy Plus Workout video.

The field of sonography exploded in the 90s. I had my first of many sonograms at the Southern Women's Show in Orlando. A couple of sonographers had set up shop in the exhibit hall offering $20.00 for gender reveals. I hopped on the table in the middle of the convention and exposed my round belly. When the sonographer announced I was having a girl, the room of strangers erupted in cheers.

First coined in the 80s, the Birth Plan spread widely in the 90s. Pregnant women were encouraged to write down what we wanted our birth experience to look like. This time, I was in charge.

My plan included being surrounded by family as I labored and delivered in the same private room with my midwife. I elected to forego pain medication and deliver my daughter naturally. The midwife placed her in my arms when she was born, and we bonded through skin-to-skin contact.

After delivery, I stayed in the hospital for several days to recover, and my daughter shared the room with me. By the time we were discharged, I was well-informed about breastfeeding and what to expect over the next few weeks with my newborn.

Big sister was eleven when little sister was born. She acted more like a second mom than a sister. The girls are now thirty-four and twenty-three, and nothing has changed!

Oops!...I Did It Again—2000s Baby!
Britney Spears – circa 2000

At thirty-one, the flu landed me dehydrated and in the hospital. Before taking a chest x-ray, a radiologist asked if I could be pregnant. The night before, in a feverish slumber, I'd fretted over the same question. *Maybe?*

A nurse drew blood. Minutes later, my doctor confirmed the test was positive. But a bleak report followed. He said the flu virus could cross the placenta. And at about only four weeks gestation, my baby would likely not make it.

But Goddess Hera had other plans.

The most notable difference during my 2000s pregnancy was the impact of technology. Websites for expectant moms popped up all over the internet. Instead of rereading *What to Expect When You're Expecting*, I followed their new digital platform. I signed up for regular emails that told me what size fruit I was carrying and what new symptoms to expect. But honestly, working full-time as a teacher, chasing a busy toddler, and soccer-moming a teenager, I hardly noticed any of them.

Instead of exercising with Denise during this pregnancy, I napped each afternoon with my toddler. Before we fell asleep, we watched two shows, Nick Jr's *Blue's Clues* and TLC's *A Baby Story*.

Back then, OG Steve was still skidoo-ing in his khakis with his dog Blue. Their kitchen friends, Mr. Salt and Mrs. Pepper, were expecting a spice baby. I connected the dots for my daughter that Mommy was having a baby just like Mrs. Pepper.

She learned her new sibling wouldn't be a spice jar through *A Baby Story*. Each episode featured a different couple in the late days of pregnancy, through non-graphic labor and delivery, followed by a quick check-in on life after the baby. Here my daughter could see real mommies have real babies. My toddler was as prepared and excited about our family's new upcoming arrival as I was!

Like my 90s birth plan, my 2000s birth plan included a midwife, and I also added a *doula* this time. Until 2004, the term doula wasn't even in the Merriam-Webster dictionary. Whereas the midwife provides the woman with medical care, a doula provides emotional support.

With the direction and supervision of the midwife, my son's father was able to deliver him. Yes, baby number three was my first boy.

Minutes after delivery, our family poured into my hospital room. Two proud sisters carried a blue cake topped with a zero candle. My son's family welcomed him into the world with a quiet rendition of Happy Birthday.

Once home, on my bulky desktop computer, I could look up anything I needed to know about caring for my newborn. Access to so much information was helpful but also scary. Dr. Google was often guilty of improper diagnoses, sending scared mothers rushing to the emergency room.

Once, my son bumped his head and grew a nasty goose egg. After a few minutes on the web, I rushed him to the hospital, concerned he might have a concussion. Thanks, Dr. Google — you could have told me he only needed an ice pack.

Now in my thirties, I felt more confident as a new mother. I nursed but also introduced a bottle earlier, so I had arms available for two other children. Being kid number three meant he had to often wait a little longer for his needs to be met than his earlier siblings. That benefited him. He's now twenty-one and kind and patient beyond his years. Growing up with two sisters, he has the utmost respect for women. As I am, I'm sure Goddess Hera is proud!

Can't Stop the Feeling—2010s Baby!
Justin Timberlake circa 2016

Fast-forward to the 2010s — I'm in my forties, divorced, and with a fast-approaching date for tubal ligation. During a trip to Key West, my new childless boyfriend asked if I'd do this baby thing one more time. The cocktails, blue water, and ocean breeze intoxicated me into a yes. Goddess Hera, we may have to talk at some point.

Due to my advanced maternal age (such a lovely term), In vitro Fertilization offered me the opportunity to defy ageism and join a growing statistic of older women pregnant past our prime.

With my previous three, I'd shared pregnancy alongside other women my age. We swapped maternity clothes and symptom remedies. But all my forty-ish friends were now welcoming grandchildren, not another baby of their own (shocker, I know).

I needed a new support system, so I joined an online mom's group. The April 2015 Moms (or A15s, as we like to call ourselves) were all due in the same month and year. Daily, we shared everything about our pregnancies.

With my first pregnancy, I gained twenty pounds, thirty with the second, and a whopping forty with the third. If this trend continued, I'd gain fifty with my fourth. Fortunately, the prenatal fitness industry boomed in the 2010s. I hired a prenatal fitness trainer and attended prenatal yoga classes. I kept the weight at a reasonable level; even better, being fit would help my stamina during labor.

I'd banked a ton of information about pregnancy during the decades that led to number four. I didn't need to seek answers to questions I didn't have. But I was delighted when *What to Expect When You're Expecting* was adapted as a RomCom film. The book and digital platform that had taught me so much during previous pregnancies now provided me with full-on belly laughs!

Like my 2000s Birth Plan, my 2010 included a midwife and doula, the new addition this time was hypnobirthing. Hypnobirthing is a combination of visualization, relaxation, and breathing techniques used to help manage pain. I brought my now husband to one session. I leaned comfortably back in a recliner, eyes closed, and manifested the peace in my doula's words. My husband shook his legs and fidgeted until he'd broken the arm of his chair. After that, I went alone!

My 2010s childbirth experience included laboring in a bathtub surrounded by candles and essential oils. When the time came, my midwife aided the process while my doula coached my husband and me. Seconds after birth, my other children burst into the room and welcomed their newest sibling with a birthday cake topped with a zero candle, just like we'd welcomed my oldest son years earlier.

Almost eight years later, the A15 moms and I are still friends. I may be the group's matriarch, but our same-age kiddos level the playing field of our friendships. Online communities now exist for nearly any commonality people could have. These women have been a lifeline for me through so many mothering ups and downs. Especially with my youngest son's autism diagnosis. I can't imagine how isolating raising him in the 80s would have been. Goddess Hera knew what she was doing when he was born last.

I don't know what Goddess Hera has planned next for our family. My oldest daughter is part of a growing number of professional women electing to freeze their eggs and delay parenthood a little longer. My youngest and her girlfriend hope to one-day experience motherhood via sperm donor. My oldest son and his girlfriend aren't sure they are having children. And for my youngest son, we aren't sure what adulthood will look like for him. But that's okay! I'm so blessed to be their mother. Thank you, Goddess Hera, for your influence and protection. I'll forever be grateful.

Future Nostalgia—Future Babies!
Dua Lipa circa 2020

I'm proud of my four decades of evolution from

a scared pregnant teen in the '80s, completely oblivious to what was happening to me, to a confident pregnant woman in her forties. But what's in pregnancy's future?

Egg and sperm donor banks and adoptable embryos offer a range of options for hopeful parents who would not have had such opportunities in previous decades.

Pregnancy and childbirth experiences now include things such as gender reveals, babymoons, and giving birth in chic birthing centers that often resemble spas more than medical facilities. Smartphones make it easier to record growing bellies, join online pregnancy and mom groups, and obsessively document our newborn's milestones.

But it's impossible to predict the future of pregnancy and childbirth, especially with a growing political movement determined to limit and, in some cases, eliminate reproductive rights. Goddess Hera, you've never been needed more than now.

I Don't Have Kids,
But I Have Nieces and Nephews
J.L. Jenson

I never wanted children. In fact, when I met my husband at age twenty-six and him thirty-three, I let him know. He was in complete agreement, and for eight years, I stood by this decision. I worked on building my career as a communications consultant while also being the sole caregiver for my severely disabled mother.

Then when I was thirty-four, my mother unexpectedly died at age fifty-eight. My father had been dead for seven years of a sudden heart attack at age fifty-two. My profound grief for my mother intensified as I realized the only person who would tell me they were proud of me was gone. I regretted not saving her random voicemails when she would call out of the blue. Also gone was the one person who needed me the most. I felt a loss for my mother, but also for the caregiver I had become. As hard as it was taking care of my mother, deep down, I liked being needed. I'm sure it wasn't healthy, but the urge to be needed and to take care of someone else was strong, and it quickly shifted into my desire to have a child.

I told my husband I wanted kids, and he suggested we wait a year. I was slow at reading his reluctance to discuss this topic and dutifully waited a year before I brought it up again. He suggested we look into adoption. I agreed, understanding that he was doing the best he could to accommodate me because I had changed my mind about kids, and he had no desire to father children of his own. Adoption also appealed to my altruistic side. My husband then suggested we adopt an older child instead of an infant. I figured this was a good compromise because he wouldn't have to "parent" for a full eighteen years.

Sure, I wondered what our biracial kids would look like. I imagined them being curly headed with their father's hazel eyes and my brown skin. I only allowed myself a few moments to ponder this before I plowed forward with signing us up for the foster to adopt program. I gathered all the information, filled in the paperwork, and paid the fifteen-hundred-dollar fee from my savings to the adoption agency. I had visions of filling the extra space in our four-bedroom colonial home, that was too big for the two of us, with our adopted children. I didn't ask my husband to do anything but provide his social security number for any background checks.

One or the Other

The adoption process took about two years, and we finally entered the last phase. One of the final requirements was for both of us to attend a two-day training seminar, which my husband did begrudgingly. He barely participated, and his attitude during the classes was that of a high school senior expected to sit through summer school to be eligible to graduate.

I ignored his behavior, but finally brought it up

the evening after our last class as we sat down to watch TV. I gushed about what we learned during the seminar as he prepared to navigate to the streaming app we would be watching that night.

"But you don't seem too excited about it?" I pressed.

I don't remember all we said, but remember I was sitting on one sofa, and my husband on another. At one point, he came over and sat on the floor, so he was looking up at me. He started to cry, something I'd only witnessed him do one other time, when he found out his ninety-something-year-old grandfather had died.

"I don't want a kid, but I'm afraid if I don't do this, you'll leave," he confessed.

As I pulled my husband to my middle to comfort him, I didn't feel a surge of love or warmth, but a dullness that shifted to a feeling of defeat. I didn't cry with him but instead stared over his head at the black mirror of the TV screen and our shadowy figures in it. That was the point I chose my husband over the child I didn't yet have.

DINKS

It took months for me to reach back out to the adoption agency to terminate our application. I didn't have the energy to go through the process of requesting my fifteen-hundred-dollar adoption fee back. Shortly after his confession that day, my husband supported my decision to leave my high-stress, high-paying corporate job. I became a classroom assistant in an elementary school and found being with the kids every day extremely fulfilling. I suppose allowing me to do this was my husband's tradeoff for not granting me children, even if it dropped us into a lower tax bracket. We were dual income, no kids, or DINKS after all, and didn't have to worry about putting food on the table for anyone besides ourselves.

Though I had mentally accepted I wouldn't have children, my body felt different. Crymaxing became a thing for me during intercourse with my husband, as I thought of all the wasted semen when he pulled out (yup, withdrawal was the birth control of choice for us educated idiots), and other sad stuff that came to the surface during those intimate times. There was a point when I asked him to not discharge on my back or breasts as he liked to do.

Or there would be times when I would see a small child, or baby, and feel an overwhelming longing toward them. My body ached, from a non-specific point, for something I couldn't give it. I also seemed to spend from age forty-one to forty-three in a constant state of arousal. If I had been a dog, I would've humped chair legs every time I entered a room. I wondered if, biologically, horniness was my body's final effort to urge me to go get pregnant.

I had a young, female doctor during my annual preventive care visit a year ago ask if I wanted to get pregnant.

I shook my head, and her response was, "Good."

Her reply was like a slap in the face as the realization struck me that I was now too old to have children, even if I wanted to. Now, forty-six, my mind and body seemed to be in sync as I accepted I wouldn't have children.

As a true-crime enthusiast, I told myself that maybe there's one less serial killer in the world because I didn't have a child. Don't mothers of killers muse about that, wondering what horrific crime could have been avoided if their kid hadn't been born? So, I found solace in thinking I'd somehow saved the world from a monster.

I Have Nieces and Nephews

When people ask me if I have kids, I always say, "I don't have kids, but I have nieces and nephews," all in one breath.

Because to me, my nieces and nephews are my kids. My older brother has two daughters, my sister has two boys and a girl. Though I'm not as close with my brother's girls, it's the complete opposite with my sister's kids.

When my first nephew, DL, was born to my sister sixteen years ago, I crossed the threshold into the hospital room, laid eyes on the little wrinkled being my sister held, and thought, "Oh, so this is what unconditional love feels like."

I had decided right then I would lay down my life for that little guy, no hesitation whatsoever, if it ever came to it. My sister was a single mom at the time DL was born and I had no problem stepping in as babysitter, or even second mom, to my nephew. Sometimes he did, in fact, slip up and call me 'mom.'

My devotion to my nephew hasn't changed since my sister got remarried and had two more kiddos—Junior (now age eight) and Kay (now age five). They live fifteen minutes away and my niece and nephews know they can ask me to help them with anything they can't get from their overworked, tired parents. They know I will come through and bring one-hundred and ten percent to whatever I do. This was evident when, two summers ago, I taught my then six-year-old nephew, Junior, how to ride a bike. I watched YouTube videos, took notes, and approached teaching him as I would any other project—with a dogged determination to succeed. When, after several wobbly attempts, we would make it to the end of the street, I would bark, "Again," as if we were in a dance studio and I was his ardent dance instructor. He eventually became frustrated, cried, and wanted to give up. I resisted the natural instinct to fold him into a hug and instead sternly explained that he had to work hard at the things he wanted in life. He eventually figured it out. His cries turned into gleeful whoops when he could ride his bike by himself for several feet as I clapped and jogged beside him.

Mom #2

One morning I was at the bus stop with the hordes of parents and kids from my sister's town house development. The bus stop was an introvert's worst nightmare, and I did my best to appear friendly, but not too friendly as to invite conversation. My five-year-old niece, Kay, wore a little denim jacket that would suffice during recess that afternoon, but wasn't warm enough for the chilly fall morning. She stood huddled against me, soaking in my body heat.

I nodded cordially at the mom of Junior's friend, and she called over, "Your daughter looks exactly like you!" I smiled and hugged my niece closer to me as I nodded my approval, not bothering to correct the woman.

One day, one mother will be more than enough, and I'm aware that my niece and nephews may not need me around as they get older.

"He doesn't talk to me," my sister said with a shrug when updating me about my 16-year-old nephew, DL. "But you can get more than short, mumbled responses out of him when he talks to you."

I didn't detect a hint of jealousy in this statement. My sister, who declared early on it would take a village to raise her children, was likely relieved there was another trusted adult her teen could turn to. In the end, that was one less kid she'd have to worry about in her already full day. As with many times before, I had no problem trying to fill her shoes as mom #2.

DL had already indicated he didn't need me as much, especially when I offered to teach him how to drive.

"I don't think that's a good mix," he said with a laugh in his baritone voice that I still couldn't get used to, even after two years.

He was old enough to join in on the ribbing I received from his mother and my other siblings about my horrible driving. He'd heard all the stories of how I would pop tires after hitting curbs and rip off rearview mirrors because I didn't pull into the garage straight enough. He would tell his own story of how I braked too hard, and he spilled soda all over his white T-shirt while sitting in the passenger seat. In my defense, I'd warned him about having open containers while I was driving.

I've concluded I wouldn't have nearly as much time or love to give my nieces and nephews if I had my own children. There's that old joke that having grandkids and nieces and nephews is great because you can give them back when you're tired of them. Sure, there are times after a long day of running DL to basketball practice, or going to the park with Junior and Kay, halting their bickering, and having dance parties in which I show them how awesome I am at the running man, that I'm happy to go home and sit quietly for the rest of the night. However, the next day, I will gladly get back up and do it all again.

A Beast with Black-Tipped Wings
E.L. Johnson

Mount Olympus, many years ago

My mistress, Hera, looked bored. I stood by, combing her silken blond hair, when she caught my wrist and pulled me around to face her, her round lips pursed in displeasure.

"Why are you combing my hair with this twig? This sapling?" she demanded.

I swallowed and my hands gave a traitorous tremble. The wooden comb I held was plain and simple but carved from a warm tree that bore fruit only rarely and blossomed with flowers once a year at the stroke of midnight. It was special. It would have fetched a good price back on the earthly plane, but to my mistress, it was lower than dirt.

"Where is it?" she demanded. "Where is my golden comb?"

None of the servants knew. I gazed around the room, Hera's cold hand still on my wrist. The room was hardly a room at all, for on Mount Olympus, Hera's throne room had an air of translucent being, with drifting clouds instead of wall hangings and tapestries, and bore a sunlight that warmed the soul but never stung the eye, until now. Muses who had stood playing the harp, drums, and lyre now froze. A muse with an artistic flair paused in her sketch of Hera's portrait, and others dance movements stilled and jokes faltered. No one knew. I looked back at her and met her unflinching gaze.

"How dare you soil my hair with this piece of trash. Do you remember who I am? Who do you serve?"

I stared at her golden sandaled feet.

"Look at me, Ris."

I raised my gaze.

The goddess herself was wondrous, with silky golden hair that trailed down to her waist, milky pale skin, so devoid of marks and scars it was like living marble, and dark eyes like chips of black agate that stared into me. "Did you take my comb?"

I shook my head.

"Well, it's missing. Where could it have gone?"

"I don't know."

"You know, Ris, as my friend, I expect you to tell me when something goes missing. I don't let just anyone touch my hair. I hope you realize what an honor it is that you've been given," Hera said.

I nodded.

"I didn't raise you up from the hordes of deserving servant girls just to be mute. Talk to me."

"I don't know where it is, mistress. There was that party yesterday. Perhaps it went missing then?"

"What are you suggesting? That one of my guests took it?" She glared at me, then tapped her chin with a flawless fingernail. "I hate to say it, but you could be right. Very well. To make up for your carelessness, go find out which one of my fellow ladies took my beautiful comb and bring it back."

"What ladies would those be, mistress?"

"Why, only the ladies of Olympus of course," she muttered darkly. "Those who bothered to show their faces anyway."

I looked at her with as blank a gaze as I could muster.

"Looking at you, Ris, is like looking into a mirror. I only see myself. You're a blank slate. There's no personality there at all."

I bowed my head.

"Anyway. Let's see. There was Athena, Persephone, Aphrodite, and Demeter. Artemis always has some other reason for missing my little parties, although Hestia kept herself away too, who knows why. Probably some field needed tending. . Those are the ladies who attended, so speak to them. One of them should let slip if she took it or not."

"Yes, mistress."

"I don't need to tell you, Ris, that if you don't come back with it, there's no point in you returning to my court at all. Do you understand?"

I nodded.

She chuckled and released my wrist. I clutched it gingerly and held it to my chest. She had squeezed it so tight, it felt like she'd dug her nails into my very veins to make a point.

But traveling from Mount Olympus was no easy feat. Artemis, the lady of the hunt, spoke, "At least give the girl some help to find them. A hound perhaps." She smiled affectionately at the bloodhound that sat curled up at her feet.

With a sound of exasperation and a touch of her fingertip to my shoulders, Hera whispered and gave me wings, soft, light, and fluttery. These grew to great large things that formed and grew like branches out of my shoulder blades, arcing outward and spreading to bloom into miniature feathers that grew.

I tested them experimentally. They rose and fell as simply as breathing, and in no time at all, they matched my ash blond hair, a similar shade of white and trimmed with gold. As I moved and flexed my wings, I caught the envious looks from many of those present.

"Don't forget, Ris, you are my champion. Someone has disrespected me, the queen of gods, by stealing. This is a grave insult," Hera said.

I bowed my head.

"Don't come back until you've found out who did it, and bring back my comb," Hera said, helping herself to a goblet of warm sweet wine.

"I will not disappoint you, mistress," I set aside the wooden comb and bowed, my wings echoing my movement like a shimmering white cloak.

"You waste your powers on trifles, Hera," Artemis said, scratching a hunting hound behind the ears. "A chariot would have done as much."

Hera locked eyes with the goddess and shrugged. "So what? They're my powers to give and use as I see fit. I don't see you helping anyone. But then you'd rather be out with the dogs, anyway, wouldn't you?"

The hound at Artemi's feet growled, and Artemis stood, slinging her bow and quiver of arrows over her shoulder. "Come," she said to me. "I will show you the way."

I followed her, stepping carefully as my wings were so full, they seemed to catch the air and want to glide. The feathers were so light, I could hardly tell I had them. The very muscles, like branches, that had grown from my shoulder blades now felt no more like minuscule twigs, and as a moved, hardly an afterthought. There was no weight at all. But when

I hesitantly stepped up, the air current caught me and threw me up, and my wings arched up wildly as I flapped, using too much force and power to try and regain my step.

Artemis surveyed me with amusement and waited for me to return to the platform. I tried to ignore the open laughter and snickers from those watching. I glanced back at Hera, who shook her head and smirked.

She and her hound led me from the shining glass platform that made up Hera's court and down a series of steps, leading to a smooth brick road of silvery cobblestones, that wound around curves and led away to a fork.

Artemis smoothed back a flyaway dark hair from her eyes and looked at me calmly. "Keep walking down and you will meet the earth, where the mortals live. Follow the fork to the left and you will find the lady of the fields. The goddess of love you may find in the ocean depths. The mistress of the lord of the dead dwells below ground, and Zeus's daughter you will find gracing the nearest battlefield." Her eyes narrowed at the sight of my wings.

"You do not like me," I observed.

"I do not like that Hera has chosen you to be a pawn in her latest scheme. She toys with us and uses you to do it."

"She is the queen of the gods and goddesses," I said.

"That may be, but no one said she was a good queen." Artemis surveyed me with a head of unruly dark hair clipped short, and a hunter's outfit of sturdy walking boots, loose trousers, and an archer's leather top and hooded jerkin, complete with stiff leather bracers covering her sleeves. She looked quite at home in the woods and looked at me with eyes that shone silvery like the moon.

I thought on this. "Did you see anyone take the comb?"

"No. But I wasn't paying attention. At the party,

your mistress was drinking with the lady of the fields and the lady of the underworld. The lady of love was admiring her reflection in a pool, whilst we began to race. I saw no comb, but you might ask the others."

"You were racing?"

"Zeus's daughter and I were racing chariots and betting on who would win. I have no time for trinkets or pawns and did not stay long thereafter." She looked at me. "Why do you serve her?"

"She is the highest and most powerful of all the goddesses. Whom else would I serve?"

"There are better masters and mistresses around. Why serve one who does not even address you by your full name?"

I reddened. "She's being affectionate. We are friends." She gave a petite snort. "The queen of gods and goddesses has no friends. Only those she tolerates and others to toy with. Take care, Eris. Do not harm yourself in fulfilling her little scheme. You may be a goddess but to her, you are little more than human."

I frowned. This was insulting. "May luck go with you, mistress of the hunt."

Artemis nodded and whistled, her hound trotting after her as she walked away.

I watched her go. I didn't like what she had said about Hera and my relationship. We were friends. She was the undoubted queen and I got to comb her hair. This was an important mission, finding out who took her golden comb. Would she have trusted such a task to a peon? Surely our friendship and my trustworthiness was proof enough of why I was chosen for this opportunity. Why else would she give me such beautiful wings?

As if thinking about them gave them life, my wings

rustled in the breeze and I sailed down to the earthly realm, where I spotted the lady of the fields standing by a freshly tilled field. My wings were full and caught the air, but I did not know how to land and spiraled down, landing in a heap of white feathers at her feet.

The lady of the fields laughed. "What an entrance." She wiped her tanned brow with her arm and smiled at me, despite the sweat and dust she had smeared across her heart-shaped face. A round woman with the look of a mother, with rosy cheeks and a warmth in her expression, she brushed back a sweaty blond hair from her eyes. "Welcome, young woman."

I accepted her proffered hand and got up, dusted myself off, and explained I was on a mission from the queen of goddesses.

"Hera sent you?"

"Her golden comb has gone missing."

"And she sent you to find it? What an odd choice."

"Rather…" I looked at the dirt and dug the tip of my dusty sandal into a spare patch.

"Ah, there is more. But you are delicately trying to find a way to say it. Speak up, child."

"My mistress worries that one of her guests at the party the other day may have misplaced her golden comb."

The goddess known as Demeter smiled. "I doubt your mistress has worried about anything in her life. More like she suspects one of us made off with it. And so, she sends you, a child with a new set of wings, to do her bidding."

"It is my honor to serve," I said, looking at my dusty sandals.

"Is it?" Demeter wondered. "Well, I can tell you I did not take her precious comb."

"How am I to determine who is telling the truth?"

She blinked. "You think I am lying?"

"No, mistress, not at all."

She took me by the arm and pointed. "Look there."

I followed her gaze and saw an ordinary field. The midday sun was harsh and beat down on us like strikes of a hammer, so bright it was, I shielded my eyes. The ground looked dry and cracked, having not had rain for some time. The very dirt seemed as if it might crumble beneath the smallest weight.

Demeter said, "The ground you are standing on is the field of a family, a father of three little girls, whose wife passed away from fever not long ago. He spends all his time looking after them, but he needs the money from the harvest, to feed and clothe his family. Without the grain it will provide, they will not survive the winter."

I glanced back at the simple hut and could picture the father and his girls inside. In the blink of an eye, I could see the snows fall, their clothes and faces grow worn and thin with hunger, and in no time at all, three little graves laid out behind the hut. The very sight made me shiver with cold, and then the image dispersed like vapor in the air.

"That is why I am here. To coax, grow and lend a helping hand. What use have I of combs when families like this need sunlight and a plow?" Demeter released my arm. "Do you see now, child?"

"Yes, mistress." I bowed my head. "I am sorry if I offended you."

"Not at all. But I do not like this work of hers, to send you about to cause trouble and ask questions. It can ruin relationships, asking too many questions."

"I'll keep that in mind."

"I hope you do. Fare thee well, daughter. I hope you find what you are looking for." Demeter waved as I struck the ground with my feet and flew. A white feather of mine fell in my wake, spiraling down to land at her feet. I tensed then and saw a black one take its place. For some reason that filled me with dread, but I couldn't say why.

The sounds of men's cries hit my ears. There was a battle taking place, and from the air I spied the lady of war's signature Athenian helmet, shining in the sun. I flew down to where she stood on the sidelines and earned a deadly-looking spearpoint aimed at my throat.

"Who are you and what do you want?" Athena asked.

"I'm on a wish from the queen of the gods. Her golden comb is missing, and she wants it back."

"And she thinks I took it? Hah! As if I'd need a trinket like that. What good is a comb when I need armies and men?" Athena lowered the spearpoint and gestured to the battlefield where a skirmish was happening.

Before our eyes, I could see the clash of shields, the battle cries and roars of men, and the crush of bodies that gave way to mud, fists, sweat, and blood in the air. Flies buzzed hungrily overhead, and buzzards and crows were not far behind, watching from their perches on Athenian rock.

She said, "These men are fighting for their honor, their chieftain, and their families. Whoever wins will change the course of history, in minor ways. I dare say this is of greater import than a comb."

"Not to my mistress," I said, "the lady of the hunt says you were both racing chariots at the part."

"We did. I won, but it was close. I must admit, I did not expect such scrutiny after a party. This comb must be of great import to her."

"It is."

"Then I wonder, why has she sent a servant to look for it? If it is so great, why not send a trusted lieutenant or general?" Athena glanced at me, taking in my silken wings, my ordinary sandaled feet, my ash-blond hair, and my long nose, with a simple coiled band in the shape of a snake around my good wrist. "She must value you highly."

"We are friends." My voice sounded unconvinced, even to me.

One of Athena's eyebrows rose. "I did not think the queen of goddesses had friends, only servants to do her bidding." She shrugged. "But perhaps I am wrong. It makes no difference to me, this business of lost combs. Soon this soft ground will be littered with shields and drenched in blood, and I have no more time for questions about this. If you must dally, speak with the lady of love. Artists have painted her in oyster shells and in the sea, and she has an eye for shiny trinkets." She cocked her head. "Were your feathers always black?"

I looked behind me. Not just one feather, like an idle black sheep in a crowd. Now the tips of all the feathers had dulled from gold to now freshly trimmed in stark black. "Odd. It must be from the flying."

"Yes, that must be it. Safe journey, Eris. Mind the waters when you visit the lady of love, she does not swim alone."

I set off, my wings sweeping away at the air currents until I rose to a great height. I hung in the air, searching, until I saw the glimmer of white, like a pearl in the ocean, that caught my eye. I flew down and saw her, a woman, dazzling and reclining on a large oyster shell, so big it could easily hold the body of a man.

But as I swooped, the blue-green glittering waters parted, and a giant fish breached the water, launching at me with a pale white fish belly, dark bull-like skin, and wide jaws that threatened to swallow me whole. The fish's jaws tore at my feathers and shed some into its mouth, but I escaped, with a shriek and pull of my wings. I cried out and flew upwards, keeping a great height.

The lady's light voice tittered and called, "You can come down now, they won't attack again."

I approached her large shell and beheld the lady of love. We spoke, but to say she was beautiful would be like calling a flower pretty. It doesn't begin to describe the simple loveliness of her curvy body, the tresses of golden hair that she hung around her like a garment, the rose color of her lips, or the light blush of her cheeks. Her eyes were mild, and she trailed a pale finger in the water, eyeing me. "You're nothing but a little bird in a goddess's body." She smirked.

I ignored her quips. "My mistress asks if you have seen her golden comb, that went missing the other day." But as I spoke the words, I felt ashamed to stand in her presence. She must have thought me an ugly thing.

She angled her head and arched her back as if posing for artists to sketch her., "No, I have not. The queen of us all wore it in her hair. If she was so careless as to lose it, I would not be surprised if some enterprising servant took it and sold it to make their fortune or treasured it as a gift from their mistress. Either way, I do not know who took it, or why they would bother."

"What do you mean?"

She turned her head, revealing a large, luscious pearl comb in her hair, that was as big as my fist and grander than gold. Light and iridescent, it caught the sunlight and shone like winking stars. "I have more than enough combs for my hair. Why should I stoop so low as to steal from my queen, when she is nothing but a spoiled royal harlot of feminine beauty?"

I blinked. "That is my mistress you are talking about."

"So, it is." Aphrodite's eyes challenged me. "What will you do? Tell her I spoke rudely? She wouldn't blame me. She would rather take you to task for repeating idle gossip in her court. You seem so fragile, little bird. Would you dare face her displeasure?"

I breathed in and let out a shaky breath. "The comb. She thinks one of her guests yesterday took it. I have spoken to the lady of war, the hunt, and the fields already."

She laughed, a light tinkling sound meant to charm the ears, but sounded almost mocking to me. "And you think I did it? Your investigative skills are subpar, dear girl. And I do not like your eyes, for they stare at me like I am a common criminal. They are as dark as your dirt-tipped wings. If you're looking for someone to blame, blame yourself for not looking after your mistress's things properly."

I balked.

Aphrodite smirked and said softly, "But then of course, you must do your mistress's bidding. Go to where it is dark and cold and see what the lady of the underworld does with her time. She may well take things that strike her fancy to keep her warm."

I bid her farewell and flew high and away, to a spot of ground out of her sight and away from any bodies of water that might contain hungry fish.

"To speak the name of a goddess aloud is to call her, and so I spoke a name to the ground, to find the way. 'Persephone, Persephone, Persephone,' I call thee."

Nothing happened.

I waited. There was a shudder and a shake. The ground trembled beneath me and opened up, and I fell down a hole, a deep dark one, that the ground swallowed up behind me as fast as mud falling.

I screamed and fell for I do not know how long, and

landed in a loud thump before the great dog Cerberus. If I had been human, my bones would have been dashed to pieces. The three-headed beast gave me a curious sniff, as the river master, Charon watched me from beside a rickety wooden boat. *Pay the fare*, his voice spoke within my head.

I had nothing but the last two white feathers in my wings. As I touched them, they fell like shedding hair and fluttered to rest in my hand. He took them and we set across the river Styx. I blinked back tears as I realized that now my feathers were all black. I was little more than a beast with black-tipped wings. How would I fit in with Hera's court now? She liked shining, beautiful, white, and golden things. I looked like I would better fit in here, with the dark rocky crags of the underworld.

The inside of Hell has been described as an ugly plane of hot, bubbling pits, liquid furnaces, and fires that rage from dawn to dusk and back again. But the artists and poets are wrong. It is quiet. The rock is dark and mountainous, and there are shadows and great curtains of stalagmites and stalactites that hang down from a ceiling so high, it made me think I had fallen to the very pit of the world.

The air was misty and cool, and the sound was of great sighs, like the whisper of weeping willows in the wind. The river itself flowed from an unseen source, and its murky water bubbled at times, as if heated from an underground stream, or if an underwater creature was about the break the surface.

I danced my fingers along the water, when I felt a tug, and a ghostly hand grasped my fingers, pulling. I shrieked and snatched my hand out with a splash, meeting Charon's disapproving glance. I swallowed fixed my gaze straight ahead. I could feel the hungry eyes of ghostly faces watching me.

Persephone sat on a stone throne, beside her doting husband. She welcomed me, wearing a girdle and shift the color of sun-bleached bone, both of which hung on her thin form like a shroud. Her cheeks were hollowed and her eyes sunken, but her smile was warm as she offered me wine and drink.

I refused, remembering how she had learned the dangers of accepting hospitality from the land of the dead.

Her grey eyes looked over my wings, so dark and black. "What has happened to you, child? Our queen does love a bit of gold, but you are not what I would have imagined as an emissary of her court. You were gold once, I think. But now…" Persephone looked at me thoughtfully. "What has she done to make you so? You are Nyx's child, are you not? A goddess."

"I am. But I do not feel very powerful." I bowed my head. My wings fluttered around me like a small black cape.

"You do not need to feel that way in order to be it. You simply are. It is a state of being," Persephone said, "I did not take your lady's comb. Will you not stay and keep me company? We do love it when people stay."

"Your wings are so dark, they are beautiful," The god Hades himself spoke, his words low and dull, but my mind they sounded like a whisper, smooth like silk. His black eyes reminded me of the flat look of a shark's gaze in those last moments before eating, and I shivered.

I begged my apologies, and his quiet mocking laughter filled my ears as I flew out and returned to Charon's side. I sat hunched in the boat, a failure. I had learnt nothing. Discovered nothing. I would return to Hera's court emptyhanded. What good was I?

As if he could hear my thoughts, Charon muttered, "The answer you seek lies in the beginning."

I looked at him in confusion. "What say you?"

But he stood as mute as before, using his long oar to coast along the depths of the river Styx.

It was not long before I stood before Hera again, my head bowed.

"So, you have returned. And looking much the worse for wear," she said, eyeing my dark wings with distaste. "Where is my comb?"

By a catch of the light, I observed it winking out of the pocket of her dress. "I believe it fell from your hair, mistress, and into your pocket." I pointed.

"What? You lie." She glanced down with a flash of anger. "So, it did." She picked it up and put it in her hair. "Oh well."

Her light-hearted tone annoyed me. "No one stole it."

She ignored me and examined her nails.

I took a step forward, bristling. "You made me go and accuse these women, these ladies of Olympus."

She snapped, "I never ordered you to accuse anyone."

What you did and said, you did yourself. And look what's happened."

My mouth opened in protest.

"Ris, come now," Hera said, "take your place and comb my hair."

The compulsion to follow her order was strong and it forced me to lift my sandaled foot, but then a beat passed, and I could not do it. I would not. My anger was too harsh a beast, and I put my foot back down. "You did this on purpose, sending me around on a fruitless mission. Why?"

"Is that what you're fretting about? It amused me. I am queen. That is enough." She touched her golden hair, motioning for a servant to bring forward a small hand mirror.

"Is that how a queen treats her friends?" I asked.

Her laughter pealed like warning bells around the court.

Everywhere, muses and servants stopped.

Her voice was mocking. "You think that because I called you friend and treat you kindly, you are on a level with me? You are not. And to even think it, is a gross misuse of your time. If I so wished it, I might bury you in the ground, between two sheets of rock, that people might never find you." She looked at my wings and wrinkled her nose at the sight. "You've ruined my gift. How did you get so filthy?"

"I did your dirty work, mistress." My voice held steel.

She shook her head. "No. You went out and accused my fellow ladies, and you've done nothing but cause trouble. You have damaged my name and reputation and now I have to repair the damage you've done. Get out of my court, and never come here again."

I stood, struck. Exiled?

She pulled her golden comb from her hair and tossed it at my feet. "Take it. You looked so hard for it, I don't want it anymore. Let it be a reminder to you of all you could have had if you had only served me well."

"But Hera, I–"

"Do not say my name," She hissed, "My name is sacred and shall not be spoken by the likes of you."

I instantly prostrated myself. Lying on the platform, I said to the glassy floor, "I only meant to serve–"

"What, by telling tales and trying to charm my other ladies into taking you into their realms? Please, little Ris. Even I know better than to trust one like you. You're no better than the dirt on your wings. I could take them from you, you know."

I stiffened. Take my wings? They felt like a part of me now. To lose them would be like losing two limbs, that I had grown to love dearly.

"But I won't," she said with a flick of her golden hair. "I can't be bothered with even coming near you. You disgust me. Your lies and half-truths, you're always stirring the pot, causing drama, making people turn on each other when really, all I wanted was a simple explanation. No, Ris. You are the problem."

"That is not my name." I looked up from the floor.

"What did you say to me?" she asked, her voice quiet.

"Ris is not my name. My name is Eris." My voice was cold but true. I stood before her, my wings now shedding all semblance of white and gold. In the brightness of Hera's court, their true color could finally be seen. They were a dingy charcoal grey, with shadows that played across the feathers, shining almost black as night.

"You look like your mother. If she were here, she would be ashamed of what you have become," Hera snapped.

"You are insulting my mother?" I asked, my voice almost a hiss.

"The lady of the night? No. I insult you, Eris. I do not like you, with all your questioning and insipid ways. I want you out. I would kill you, but you are of the blood, so I cannot. Get out of my court, and never return."

Her words spoke of banishment, like a brick wall. I felt the effects immediately. Like being ghosted, canceled, or shut in an asylum of my own making, I was exiled from the glittering beauty of Hera's court, with only the shocked and ashamed faces of muses to bid me farewell.

I do not know where I went, only that I wept silent tears and slunk in the shadows. I avoided battlefields. I stayed away from fields and kept my distance from waters that were filled with sharks, who gnashed their teeth if I was nearby. Any woods I approached looked dark and forbidden, and if I stepped inside, the yapping of hunting hounds soon warned me away. There was always a doorway to the underworld, but that frightened me. It would be so easy to eat, drink, and stay in Persephone's company, with the dead to talk to. The very idea of having corpses for company sent shivers down my spine.

All the goddesses had turned on me. I was nothing. I was a beast. I was a servant who had lost her mistress. I was punished.

I do not know how long I wandered, tearstreaked and alone. My black feathers shielded me from rain, sleet, and snow. My hair grew dirty and dingy, and the golden comb, now tarnished with my sweat and tears, was a constant reminder of the friendship I had strived for and all I had lost. I wore it in my hair as a symbol. *Here is one royal screw-up.*

At night I sang and cried beneath the blanket of my mother's night sky and felt the stars looking down on me with disappointment. Then it hit me.

I am a goddess. Hera may be the queen of the gods, but she cannot kill me. She could not destroy me.

She believed I was monstrous, a beast with black-tipped wings, not worth seeing at her court. I would get her attention in other ways.

It was through my pain and weakness that I realized just who and what I am. But it was not until I heard the first call for help, that I understood my true purpose.

The voice of a young woman, crying and in pain, awoke me from my misery. I walked, stumbling on air currents toward the sound.

The moon shone on her face, lighting up her tears as she called for help. I came to her side like a thief in the night, listening. She had thrown a party for her friends, only to overhear them slander her publicly, behind her back. She had briefly known such happiness, only to have her heart break from nastiness and jealousy.

A word in her ear, an idea in her mind, and I'd sent her off to do a little task that would reveal their two-faced natures or if not, at least get her the revenge she craved. She was the first but wasn't the last who called on me whilst in the depths of despair.

Today, when I look at my reflection in a pool, I am no longer meek, quiet, and hidden. My ash-blond hair has permanently darkened to match my midnight-black wings. Such a forbidding sight would have frightened me once, but now I take it as my due. It is a sign of my strength and resilience, this darkness.

I am the daughter of night but have no temples to my name. I am called, not by the chanting, ceremonies, or spilled blood of sacrificed bulls or rams, but by the cries of anger, outrage, and indignation of those who are treated unjustly, and want their sweet revenge.

Some may call me a cad, but I believe that true villains are not born, but made. We are the shell-shocked, heart-struck, emotionally scarred, beaten limpets of flesh and bone that are so desirable of love, like, acceptance, and to painstakingly belong that we will do anything to achieve it at the cost of our sanity and self-worth. We are the meek and quiet ones who are trodden on and left to mourn in private, quietly, and alone. Maybe we will regroup and become stronger through adversity; maybe we won't.

I used to wear red, a symbol of passion, strength, love, and even war. Now I wear black and lurk in the shadows, waiting for the next cry of pain.

For I am Eris, the goddess of discord.

And I will be heard.

Epilogue

I heard a whisper through the trees of an upcoming wedding to happen, where all of Olympus will be invited. All the goddesses would be there, including my former mistress. I of course would be overlooked for the guest list. But no matter. As I wandered through an apple orchard, trailing my hands along the decaying leaves of fruit trees, I wondered what would be a suitable gift to mark the occasion.

An apple, riper than the rest, dropped and fell at my feet. I split it open, its yellow skin so bright it was almost golden, and I got an idea.

I would bring a little gift to the goddesses, and make my presence known. For what harm could a golden apple do?

HESTIA
GODDESS OF HEARTH & HOME

I am the firstborn of Olympus. Mine is the hearth, where families gather for warmth. Mine is the home, where families love each other. Have you ever noticed that heart and hearth rhyme?

Both mean sanctuary.

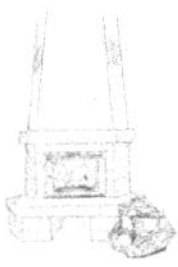

A HEARTFELT DEDICATION TO HESTIA
Danica Camille G. Manalastas
Lester N. Linsangan

A dreary goddess, as they presume
But veritably, a flower who's in bloom
The daughter of Cronus and Rhea
Oh, the Goddess that you are, Hestia

The fairest and most righteous of them all
Which led to mortals praying for you more
The peace, gentleness, and serenity you epitomized
Were the motive why your delicacy arise

Hestia, the Goddess of the hearth
Who seized Apollo and Poseidon's heart
War could start because of that
But chose to stray undefiled to avert the odds that may
uprise

The comfort in your flames
Can make every spirit vivacious
The goddess of the hearth, others may have devalued you
But thy legacy will never be thrown;

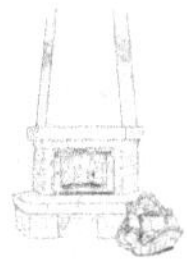

MODERN IMMORTALITY
Michele Barnett

My consciousness, roiling and trapped in the swirling vastness of entropy, forgotten and abandoned by the needs of this modern age, lost, alone, fading… ready to abandon the Sisyphean task that was given to me, to be the first… to be the last… to protect the home until innovation and industrialization have created a sterile, barren facility… my failure echoed in humanity's rise.

But there! A spark… A flicking dance of blinding light falling into the engulfing darkness lingered upon my faltering vision… My lethargic heart lurched to life in my chest and one thought reverberated through my being, "This one must be saved." I cannot let this effervescent soul be forever lost to the universe.

I reached out my hand, fingers outstretched, to gently guide this gleaming, glinting wisp of hope toward the safety of my presence. My lips parted to whisper a soft welcome to this scintillating stranger who had somehow stirred my soul anew.

The vivid incandescence moved to my chest, hovering over my heart, and descended into my being as if it had always belonged there. As the brightness of this beautiful, fragile, mortal blessing enveloped me, revived me, completed me, I felt myself renewed with a sense of new purpose!

I will fight to protect those who cannot protect themselves! I will fight to provide comfort to those who need it! I will fight to give others hope for the future! I will stand as a shield in the face of those who would harm those I love! I will not let hate win! I am the first! I am the last! I am Hestia and I will protect those I love, because they are my home!

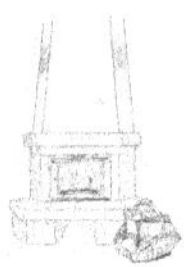

A MOTHER'S JOURNEY THROUGH ADDICTION
Little Flower

Anger. Sadness. Loss.

These are only just some of the feelings I went through when the phone call came. I spent so much time reliving the moments of his life. Trying to find that one moment when everything changed.

I looked over the many photographs and tried to find the one photo that showed me the change. I saw many things. Laughter. Love. Smiles. What I didn't see was the photo where I saw the change. The one photo that showed my beautiful, little boy becoming a drug addict.

ADDICT!

Say the word. Hear yourself saying it. Repeat it often and say it loud, is what I told myself. *Do not sit in silence and whisper it to yourself, because that will never save you or your child.*

I said, "Why me? Why my child?"

I believed God had a plan, and for some reason, my son's plan was to go through addiction. I had hoped to one day witness the reason and rejoice in his sober life.

***

My life was simple. I grew up in a rural community, on a back road in the middle of nowhere. Growing up in such a way truly made an impact on my life.

I grew up on a beautiful piece of property next door to my grandparents. An amazing place to grow up. My father was one child of ten, and my mother was the eldest child of thirteen. We were poor, but for some reason, I never knew that we were. Looking back on the time when I was young, I was incredibly rich. Times were simpler then.

My Mom didn't work and was a great Mom. I went to a small rural school in a very small town and was taught good values. How to be honest, respectful, and to know the importance of working hard. As a teen, I drank alcohol and went to parties. *I mean, who didn't?* There was always a party in a small town. Drugs scared me though, so I never tried those. Honestly, I never wanted to disappoint my parents. Although I did.

When I was eighteen, I was accepted into a small college about an hour from my home town. My parents were happy. It's a shame it was short-lived. I met a boy around that same time who was leaving for the military. Instead of going to that small college, I got married.

I thought I had all the answers.

The boy I met was part of a local family but had moved away when he was younger. I dated this boy for a short time before he asked me to marry him. Looking back, I wonder what the attraction was.

I had big dreams, and living in a small town influenced me greatly. After our wedding, we moved to a military base. It was then I realized I knew very little about my new husband. He was abused as a child and had a lot of demons and struggles of his own. The stress of the military, a new wife, and being far from home did not help his struggles.

The first time he was physically violent I was devastated. I felt bad for him. Telling myself what he endured as a child was the reason for his behavior. I avoided him and kept the abuse to myself.

I quickly learned my new husband had more problems that I realized and needed more help than I could give him. When I became pregnant I knew I couldn't allow the abuse any longer. Thankfully, his time in the military ended and we moved back to my hometown to be near family.

After our son was born I thought things would get better. It wasn't too long after that, me, and this young boy I met at such a young age, divorced.

When my son was four, I remarried, and we moved to a new town.

Our new home was wonderful. My new husband was amazing, a true partner and friend. The new home, this new town that I found for my son and myself was full of great people and had a fantastic school district.

To make things even better, after my third son was born, my Mom moved to our town to be close to us. At the time, she was living alone and battling a new diagnosis of cancer. She and my Father had divorced years prior, and she wanted to be close to my sons.

I was substitute teaching so I could be with my Mother during her cancer treatments and still work the days she didn't have appointments. We were happy, despite my Mom's cancer. Our home was full of laughter, love, and fun.

We went on family vacations, camping trips, backyard picnics, and attended all the neighborhood parties. My older boys were in Boy Scouts, and all three of them were so close. Even though my oldest son was from my first marriage, he was never treated as a stepbrother by my other two sons. When my oldest was twenty, our second son was fifteen, and our youngest was seven, my Mom's cancer became increasingly worse. She had been battling colorectal cancer for ten years at that point. It had spread to her lungs, her brain, and her bones.

She was so close with the boys. We all struggled so much with her diagnosis.

We were able to go on a "last wish" trip to Walt Disney World with her in June of that year. It was such a great trip, and even though she was on oxygen and had to be pushed in a wheelchair throughout Disney, she loved every minute of that trip.

It was a few months later she was hospitalized, and then moved to a rehabilitation center. My sister and I were with her almost daily, however, the cancer slowly robbed us of our Mother. When she was moved to a hospice house, we were told she was not expected to live throughout the week. Anyone who doesn't believe in Heaven or God has never sat with a loved one in their final days, hours, or minutes. Being so close to something so finite gives you a moment to question that higher power.

The hospice nurses helped us all to understand the stages of death. It was an experience I would never forget, but also one I never wanted to remember.

My Mother passed on the third of December.

I lost a part of my soul that day and I would never be the same again. We grieved as a family. My boys grieved hard. My Mother had meant the world to them. She had meant the world to all of us.

Even after such a huge loss, time moved on. Even though I didn't think it should. *How does someone so important and significant in your life die, but time keeps moving?*

Sometime later, a friend offered me a new job at a doctor's office. It was only a few days a week and I could still substitute teach at the school. It seemed perfect. However, my seven-year-old son started having difficulty in school. Calls were coming in almost every day.

He wasn't coping well with the death of my mother, or so I thought. I wasn't coping, so how could my children be coping?

A friend from the school district I worked in was a special education teacher. One afternoon, she handed me a book about Asperger's syndrome. I took it home and read the first paragraph. It hit me. I just knew my son was high-functioning Autistic.

My husband read the first paragraph and was also concerned. We started the long process of doctor appointments, and my son was finally diagnosed with High Functioning Asperger's (now known as Autism Spectrum Disorder) with High Anxiety.

I cried. I knew everything was falling apart because I didn't have my mom.

The same friend who gave me the book said to me, "You don't have time to feel sorry for yourself, your child needs you."

She was right. We began the long journey with our youngest son. We found a great group of doctors and a psychologist. Where that journey would take us was still unknown.

We were trying to grieve my mother, deal with this new diagnosis, and enjoy my second son's high school years. All of this was going on along with my oldest son's college years. But, there was so much ahead I could have never predicted.

I was happy with the choices I had made for my life and my family. When I look back now, I find myself trying to pinpoint the day. The one moment in time when I lost my oldest son.

I won't find it. I will instead make myself crazy trying.

Growing up, my oldest son had tons of friends in school. He was in the gifted and talented group, Boy Scouts, and he had a paper route. He always had after-school programs to attend and had summer jobs as a lifeguard, landscaper, caterer, and even worked at the local pizza shop. He loved history and talking to people. He would remember lines from movies and held conversations about Star Wars and the many different Marvel movies. He always wanted to be in business. He had the mind for it. His communication skills were so good he could convince anyone to do anything. My son was well-liked and always the life of the party. Now that I sit here and think about it, as a parent, I should have done things differently.

I know people say, "You are not responsible" or "You couldn't have changed things," but I wish I would have reacted differently to many situations.

Some of his friends' families were very wealthy. They were what most people in small towns would call, good people. I didn't realize at the time just how much he was experiencing by having these "friends". I was happy, if not thrilled that he had such fine, upstanding people in his life.

I knew they had weekend parties, but I drank in high school. *Wasn't that normal?*

My son was a great student, he was getting his Eagle Scout, and was a gorgeous kid. The truth was, he was drinking a lot, smoking marijuana, and experimenting with pills and cocaine.

My husband told me numerous times there was a problem. God, we argued so many times about it. I felt a little sad that my son had parents who were divorced.

I wanted my husband to be a great stepdad. I wanted

him and my son to get along well. I wish now I would have listened to my husband.

I did what a lot of parents do. I said, *Not my son. You are mistaken. You are picking on him because he is your stepson.*

It was years later, my son told me about the first time he tried marijuana. He was at the neighbor's house across the street from our home. They sat in the yard, and he could see me mowing our lawn. I never saw him. I never thought the neighbors, who were an amazing family, were not a safe place for him to be. The truth was it wasn't the neighbors. It wasn't their home, but it was the choices my son was making with their son.

Time passed and my son went off to college. I still didn't know about the addiction.

At college, my son was again very popular. But, college wasn't for him. He was not passing, he was on academic probation, and he had to change schools. After having such a difficult time, he decided to attend a small Community College near our home.

I realize now that all the trouble he was having at college, was due to the effect of the drugs and his growing addiction. At the time it was happening, I didn't see it. I didn't see the signs.

All of this was happening during the time my mom had just passed from cancer and my youngest son was diagnosed with Asperger's. *What else could go wrong?*

My oldest son started dating a girl. She was a single mother to a little boy. They seemed to make a nice couple. She had a good job working for her family business and she seemed to be a good mother. What we didn't know was she was also an addict.

Time passed on. She and my oldest son moved in together and things seemed great.

Until they weren't.

I received a call from her while I was on the way to my middle son's senior lacrosse game. She wanted to tell me that she and my son were both addicts. She had made the decision to leave the state and go live with her mother to try and kick her addiction. She wanted me to know my son needed help too. And, just like that, my world came crashing down.

What could she possibly be talking about?

What did she really know about my son?

She had to be wrong, maybe they had a fight.

I had to find my son and get to the bottom of this. I called my son's biological father and we met with him to talk. Denial! My son said he was fine, nothing was wrong, and he could handle it. That was what he said.

Things got worse.

He went missing, for hours at a time, and started to look awful. He was thin and wasn't taking care of himself.

Our family finally convinced him to go talk to a rehab center. Once we get there and start talking, we find out there are no beds available. He wasn't sick enough to qualify for a bed at the other facilities we talked with. He wasn't at risk of suicide. We couldn't find help anywhere.

Luckily the primary care physician I worked for took my son on as his patient and my son was admitted to the local hospital. The hospital had a rehabilitation center, and if this physician admitted him to the hospital, we could make sure he was transferred into the rehab center there. It was our only hope.

We sat in the emergency room and started the process. Our son lay in a fetal position on the floor. The withdrawals were now taking over. The emergency room physician admitted him to the cardiac floor because he had become so sick.

I remember the nurse pulling back the covers to show me his legs. They were thin and bony. My beautiful son who had always been so strong growing up was now weak and feeble.

The effects of drugs.

He was transferred to the drug rehab center within the next few days. No visitors for 5 days. When we were finally allowed to visit, we had to sit in a room with other families who were also visiting their loved ones. We all seemed to have the same look on our faces. We were lost. Now a part of a group we desperately did not want to belong to.

The visits continued each week. Some were good. Some were sad. Some were just visits. Hours spent going through a wide range of emotions.

When my son was released, we were filled with hope. We had gone through the worst, and we were on the road to recovery. Weren't we?

A good friend said to me, "This journey is only beginning."

Oh, how I wish her words weren't true. Time passed and my son was able to get a job. He seemed better. Was he better?

We tried outpatient counseling, but none of the therapists seemed to be the right fit. As a family, we had hoped things were better, but then things started going missing from the house.

They were small things at first. A video game. A hard drive he kept in his room. An extra ten-dollar bill I left on the table, maybe it was actually a twenty-dollar bill. I never had to watch my purse or my money. I had never dealt with an addict before.

My son wasn't himself.

He was gone for long periods of time. He looked different.

Was he sick again?

What was I missing?

The truth was, I wasn't missing anything except the strength to help my son. I was an enabler.

How can that be?

How was I enabling my son when I was trying to help him?

Why was this happening?

One of the counselors we went to said it was my fault because his parents were divorced. I was so mad. I knew addicts from homes that weren't broken. Addicts whose parents were wealthy, poor, good, bad, and sad. Well, if you are in a home with an addict, it truly is just that, sad. Every day passed with hope but attached to the fear of the unknown.

He didn't come home. Too much time passed that day since I last saw him.

Where could he be?

Who could he be with?

Someone saw him and called me. A mother of his friend whose son was also an addict. My son was at their house and not acting like himself. She thought I should come and attempt to talk with him. I got to their house, and he looked awful. I just knew it was starting again.

My son spent so much time in his room sleeping. My husband and I argued about what to do. None of us knew how to help him.

My ex-husband spent time on the phone trying to talk with him, to me, and nothing changed. But one day it did.

That week he was better. He looked better. He was

still working, although the jobs he was able to get were sporadic and seemed shady to me. But we still had hope. I was not willing to give up on my son.

People in our town knew. Of course, they did. Small towns always knew. Family who saw him at family gatherings knew. He was always so intelligent. Eagle Scout, good in school, could talk to anyone about history and loved to read. I felt they were all looking at me.

What was wrong with your parents?

Couldn't we see our son?

What were we doing to help him?

Time passed. I'm not sure how much time, but at least it passed without issue. I decided to go to a benefit in town. I would only be two blocks away from the house if there was a problem and anyone needed me. My youngest son would be alright to stay home with his brother. I would only be gone a short time. My husband was out of town for work and my other son was at a friend's for the night.

A short time after being at the benefit, I had a bad feeling in my gut. Something was wrong. I couldn't reach my oldest son on the phone. My youngest son didn't have a cell phone, and no one was answering the home phone.

I left the benefit quickly and went home to check on my boys. The house was eerily dark, and no one was there. My oldest son's car was gone. The terrible feeling from earlier still sinking lower in my gut. Finally, I received a text message that my oldest son went for a short drive to pick up a video game from a friend and took his younger brother with him.

I knew in my heart this was not a drive for a video game.

I started driving, just driving. I didn't know where I was going, but I knew I had to find them. I had to find my boys. Text messages kept coming, but each one was vaguer than the last. All they said was, *everything is fine.* They *would be right back home.* I *should not worry.*

I kept driving.

I went to the closest town where my oldest son's friends lived, trying to find his car. It was then I received a text saying they had made it home. Walking through my front door, I was mad, frantic, and upset. Accusations were made. There was a strict rule the younger boys were not to ride in the car with my oldest son due to the bad choices he had made.

Looking back, I wondered, *why did he even have a car?*

Well, because he had to go to work. He had to try and lead a normal life. However, there was nothing "normal" about this. My youngest son said it was all alright. He just waited in the car while his brother went into his friend's house and picked up a video game. My heart raced all night with thoughts about what could have happened.

My oldest son had always told us he thought he had seasonal depression. Every fall and winter he was so depressed and kept to himself. I saw this same depression every day now, no matter what the season was. It was sometime later that I realized he didn't have seasonal depression, it was just the effects of the drugs.

One afternoon my oldest son called me to let me know he was pulled over for driving under the influence. He was given a ticket and had to have a friend pick him up. My son had a prescription pill bottle with him. However, it wasn't labeled correctly. I don't think I ever got the right story about what happened.

Another afternoon he was at the house and not well. He was angry because we questioned him because he had a backpack with things in it he clearly did not want us to see. When we tried to stop him from leaving, he pushed me. My husband panicked and grabbed him. My son, my beautiful son was not himself. Everyone at home was upset. It was a mess.

My son left the house walking, and I just knew he was not in a good place.

I got a call from the insurance office on Main Street saying my son was in the office and was not acting himself. He had wandered in off the street and dropped pills from a pill bottle onto the office floor. The receptionist knew our family and called me. By the time I made it there, he was standing outside on the sidewalk. He didn't know who I was when I pulled up to the curb. He looked like he was a homeless person, but he wasn't. He was my son. My little boy!

What the hell happened to you?

Where was my son?

Where was my child?

I somehow managed to get him off the street and into the car. I called the same parent of his friend who also struggled with addiction and asked her to go with me to take my son to the hospital. I felt he needed to be examined and maybe admitted.

We drove and my son argued the entire way he was fine. He said, *I'm over 18 and you can't make me do anything I don't want to do.* At the hospital, he was examined and confirmed to be under the influence. Even though, he was not sick enough to be admitted. There was no medical reason to keep him, so he signed himself out.

As we drove home, my son showed some hope of wanting to get help. We agreed to call his Dad and he would stay there for a few days. I knew I could definitely use the break from constant worry with him at the house. I thought his Dad needed to help more with the situation anyway, so it served two purposes.

After my son's Dad picked him up, my husband and I decided to take the other two boys out to dinner. Make an attempt to have a normal, whatever that was, evening. My son realized his wallet was missing.

Could his brother have stolen his wallet?

One call to my ex-husband confirmed he had. As we drove to meet my oldest son and his dad to pick up the wallet, we all were so sad. Our family was being shattered and torn apart by this addiction.

Would we ever get through this?

But then the days got a little better. My oldest son seemed better. He looked better. He was just good at hiding the addiction.

Then the day came.

The person he had used drugs with. The girl who told us my son was an addict. She was back in town, and they were back together. They were moving into an apartment, my son, her, and her son. We weren't happy about the decision.

Had she really straightened her life out and got off all drugs?

My son was doing well, as well as could be expected. As well as a drug addict could do. At this point, I was only hoping I knew what "well" looked like.

My son spent his time between our home and the home he shared with this woman. Some days I thought maybe things were better. But as time passed, he was just getting deeper into the addiction. We started to see my son less. When we did see him, we knew he was not well. He was working at a temporary job, but at least he was working.

He called us one night to tell us his girlfriend was taken to the hospital. She had a seizure. He thought she had a bad case of the flu and that's what caused her seizure. My husband and I knew it sounded like a seizure from drugs.

I drove to their apartment to check things out and see for myself what might be happening. The apartment was dark. My son was there, and he looked awful. The apartment was dark and dingy, one lightbulb hung from the middle of the ceiling. I couldn't even believe my son was living in such a place. I wanted to take him home right then and there. To rewind the clock. I wanted to go back to the reality we once knew, but this was our new reality. My son was a drug addict living in a mess.

Days passed and things were not getting any better. I hadn't heard from my son. It was now spring, and his brother was playing in a sectional lacrosse game. I finished my day of substitute teaching and drove some other parents one afternoon after school. It was then my phone rang.

My heart sank.

My world shattered.

I was on autopilot as I listened to a friend who worked at the county police station tell me my son had been arrested. The girl he lived with was home alone with her son while my son had been at work. She had a drug dealer come over, and while her son slept in the other room, her dealer injected her with heroin. Bad heroin, and she overdosed. The dealer got scared, grabbed all of the drugs, and left. My son tried to reach her on the phone, and when she didn't answer, left work, and drove to the apartment.

He found her on the floor, started CPR, and called 911. By the time the police and the paramedics arrived, the girl's son had awoken from his nap and was in the apartment walking around witnessing the incredible disaster that was his life. The police thought my son had given his girlfriend the drugs, but then realized from the texts on her phone, that was not the case.

She was taken to the hospital and my son was arrested

because they were both in the home with a child where drug activity happened. My son was not charged with drug possession, but he was charged with endangering the welfare of a minor.

My friend explained it all to me while I listened, numbly. She told me I couldn't go to the jail where they were holding him, and that I should not go to the hospital. She said she would call me with any updates, but there was nothing I could do for him right then.

I was frozen.

My other son needed his mother at his game. He had worked so hard for this in his senior year. I just needed to go to the game and keep moving. I needed to keep doing normal things because if I stopped moving, I would fall apart.

My husband coached the lacrosse team my son played on, so he was already on the bus with the team. I couldn't call him and tell him something like that over the phone. I called my ex-husband and told him. He said he would try to get more information. I thought for a moment that I should call an attorney for him. To go to jail and try to help my son when I couldn't. I needed to drive the other parents to my son's game, just drive. I drove the two hours and never said a word to my friends about my son's arrest. I just stared at the road, smiled, and pretended everything was ok.

Nothing was ok.

Nothing could be further from ok, but what could I do?

What should I do?

I watched my son's game, spent a lot of time pacing the sidelines on the phone with my ex-husband, and the friend who called from the jail. The only good news was the girlfriend didn't die from the overdose. She was going to be fine and was also being arrested for child endangerment. I wanted to blame her so badly.

Why did she come back to town?

Why did she use drugs with my son?

The truth was, my son was using drugs long before she came into his life. I just wanted to be mad at someone, or something.

The next few days seemed a blur. I was unable to function and spent my days buried on the couch. My son could have visitors, but the thought of going to see him caused me to cringe. I couldn't possibly see my son in a jail cell. I was so mad at the situation, at him, at the world.

My mother-in-law was very close with my son and told me she wanted to be the one to visit him. She was a strong woman. She told me she would visit him and make sure he was ok for me. I think I spent hours holding my breath that day. My heart ached for him, my son, my little boy. Family and friends were supportive, but nothing helped my feelings of despair and pain. My mother-in-law thought my son was doing ok and said he was going to be entered into a drug court program. If he remained in the program for a year, he would have his charges removed from his record, and he could start his life over. While in the program he would be in a drug rehabilitation center, not a jail. The girlfriend took the same deal.

Every Tuesday, all of the participants would appear in court and speak with the judge to ensure they were moving in a good, beneficial direction. I was happy my son would now receive rehab. I hoped this would mean he could clean up his life. Maybe this would work. But maybe's are just that, maybe's.

I went to visit my son for the first time. He had moved to a rehab that was local. He looked good which made me hopeful.

Every Tuesday I would go to court and watch the proceedings. It was awful. My mother-in-law would go with me, and we would endure the metal detectors, waiting in the hall with the other families, knowing we all were dealing with the same hell. I watched my son enter the courtroom in handcuffs, an orange jumpsuit, and an officer who led him like he was a criminal. He was a criminal.

Where was I?

Was this even real?

Was this even happening?

I couldn't tell you how many times I wanted to run out of that courtroom and never return. I couldn't do that to my son. What I could do was face it. It would be ok. There had to be a reason this had happened.

Sometimes when he was in the courtroom, so was his girlfriend. I was so angry when I saw her.

I could go to the rehab centers and visit him on visiting days. We were making progress. The court had put me in touch with an Al-Anon parents group. They had meetings every Tuesday, so I started attending. The meetings were good, however, they were sad. There were so many parents going through what I was, and much more.

The rehab was going well for my son, or so I thought. He still didn't seem like himself. The girlfriend had been released from inpatient rehab and was allowed to stay in drug court if she went to outpatient rehab and continued to make good choices. Her son was sent to live with her mother out of state. I was happy because I wanted her to suffer. I wanted to blame her for everything, even though it wasn't right. But I was angry with her and my son for putting that child in such a horrible situation. That was an entirely different issue. The court advised her to stay away from my son during their recovery process.

It was a visitation day at the rehab center. As I entered the room, I saw her. The girlfriend.

What was happening?

She wasn't supposed to visit you.

She wasn't supposed to see my son.

I went to the counselor in charge and asked. They told me I was just being a mother who was upset, and I should not let it bother me. What? You bet I was an upset mother! My life was hell, my son was a drug addict living in hell, and it was not right.

I was sick to my stomach. I sat in the session they had for the family. I turned away from her as she sat there with my son like they were a couple. I wanted to vomit. I left and called the court to complain. I needed to save my son. I always felt like I needed to save him.

He called me that night from a strange number. She had taken a burner phone to him. Such a thing was strictly prohibited at the rehab center, but my son called to tell me it was all going to be ok.

Nothing was going to be ok!

Because of my complaint, he was moved to a new rehab center. It was temporary until he was sent upstate, about four hours away to a different facility. I was hopeful the new facility would be good for him and offer better recovery opportunities.

How was I to know, my son would never make it to that facility?

I remember that day. My youngest son and I drove to the rehab center to take my oldest son some books, money, and well wishes. I wanted him to have a few things for the transport to the new facility since I wouldn't be able to visit as often. When I got to the rehab, the receptionist asked me to wait in the lobby. I waited for a long time. Too long. Finally, she came and took us to her office to tell us my son was gone.

Gone where?

The transport already left?

He wasn't supposed to leave until the following day. The transport did not come early. My son was gone. He walked out of the facility on his own, which was impossible. I just spoke with him the day before and he was hopeful about the plan to go to the new facility. To get the help he needed.

Where was my son?

How could he just walk out of the facility?

The counselor told me they couldn't stop a patient from leaving, but once they do, they need to realize this removes them from the drug court program. The chance my son had to have his charges dropped, to become clean and sober, was now gone.

What was happening?

Where was my son?

Then the text came. As I drove away from the facility, a text message came to my phone. It was his girlfriend. She had picked him up from the facility.

I remember her words, "I will always control him. He is with me, and we will be together. No one can keep us apart."

My world stopped, again. What I texted back was harsh, frantic, crazy, and mean.

I hate her!

I hate addiction!

It didn't take long for the facility to report to the court my son had left the program. It was too late. My son was gone. They were on the run. There was now a warrant out for his arrest, his photo was in the paper, and I was in hell.

I couldn't eat, get off the couch, think, or even breathe. I slept a lot, all day. I could barely take care of my other two boys. Days passed and my son stayed missing.

Then the phone rang. It was my son. I will never know what happened between him and his girlfriend, but he told me they were over. He was no longer on the run with her, but he was now on the run alone. He knew there was a warrant out for his arrest, and he was scared. I tried to talk him into coming home, turning himself in. But he refused. He was a mess. I was a mess.

He begged me to meet him and bring clothes, a blanket, and food. My child was begging me for the normal necessities of life, and I said no.

How could I say no?

Because I needed to save him. I needed him to come home, to stop running.

Who was he?

My husband was an officer, we didn't run from the police. We are part of the law enforcement family.

How could any of this be happening?

More days passed. My son was still missing. I still couldn't get off the couch, still. I planned my son's funeral in my head over and over again.

Who would come?

Who would I allow to come?

No friends. No *drug* friends.

What would I say at the funeral?

How would I cope?

How would our family cope?

Our friend from the police department who called me when my son was arrested, called again, and offered her help. If he contacted me and I could convince him to turn himself into the police, she would help get him leniency.

Again, more days passed. The phone rang. He was scared, alone, tired, and ready to come in. I was scared for my son. Her son had been friends with him but was not a drug user. My son would listen to him, and he agreed to come with me and his mother to meet my son.

We met my son on a dark road in the middle of nowhere. He was so dirty, the soles of his shoes worn off. He got in the car with us, and we drove somewhere quiet to talk. We talked for a long time about every scenario. We discussed all the possibilities and choices he had. She made the call to the police station, and we headed that way.

We were able to enter through her office. My son was taken into custody in a calm manner while I waited there in her office. I remember feeling relieved, sad, nothing, dull to the pain of a mother losing her child to drugs.

What would become of my son?

Back to jail. My son was placed in county jail to await placement back in the drug court program. The judge would first have to agree to allow him back in the program and it was not going to be easy.

My son had other plans.

During a visit, he told me he made the decision not to go back into the drug court program. He felt being in an atmosphere with other drug users was not going to help him recover or make good choices. He had spent his recent time in jail in the law library and felt he wanted to defend himself. To take responsibility for his original child endangerment charge and serve his time. He was hopeful with time served he would be sentenced to six months in county jail.

I was devastated.

How could he decide to move forward without rehab? Without the chance to have his charges removed?

He insisted it was the only way he could beat his addiction and get out of the mess he created. The day he went before the judge as his own attorney and represented himself was incredibly scary for me. He was strong and full of determination. However, what did this decision mean for him? Again, my world fell apart.

If my world was falling apart, what was his world like at that point?

The judge sentenced him to exactly what my son knew he would. Six months in county jail. My life went on with the knowledge my son was in jail.

Who would keep him safe from the monsters of jail?

What would happen to my son?

I had to call and schedule the visits, but we visited every week. We would arrive at the jail, sign in, get a key for our locker to store our personal belongings, get searched, and walk through the metal detector. We had to open our mouths so we could be checked for whatever it is they check for, every week. We were put in a room with other visitors while waiting for our loved ones to walk down from their cells and visit with us for one hour. One hour a week to see with my own eyes my son was ok.

Were any of us really ok?

Time continued to pass. My middle son was now in college. Our home was sad, quiet. My youngest son was doing well with his Asperger's. My husband and I were well. Our relationship had survived, and we were strong together, thank God. Our families were supportive and kind.

My mother-in-law visited my son with me. She would take him books to read and make him laugh at our visits. He was better. He really looked and seemed to feel stronger. I still looked at the family photos of my son and wondered where the photo was that would show me his transformation into an addict. I would never find it because it was a collection of photos and moments I never saw.

There were other families I knew whose children had overdosed and died. I never knew what to say to them, so I would send a text or a card to let them know I understood how hard addiction was for a family. But I didn't know death from addiction, thankfully so. Although there were days I felt dead inside.

It was Thanksgiving, then Christmas. I always sent a photo card to family and friends.
What would I send this year?

I opted for a generic card with no photos. I hoped the next year would be different. My sons missed their brother terribly and we hoped he would be ok.

There was one visit where an altercation happened between the inmates and my son was hit in the head. He was ok, but I was scared.

What would happen to him in that place?

I would drive by the jail sometimes just to feel close to him. I would wonder what his days were like in there. Wonder if I should still plan his funeral.

What had happened to my beautiful son?

January was coming and so was my son's release date. I was scared, our family was scared. My husband wasn't sure if coming home was the right choice for him. We were all very concerned about the future. But the day came. I drove to pick him up and felt like a kid at Christmas. I was terrified, but I was so happy.

What did the future hold for him?

My son had spent time in jail studying in the law library. He needed to find a way to rebuild his life. Thankfully, the charges were a misdemeanor and not a felony. I hugged my son that day outside in the fresh air, with no supervising eyes, and no more sadness of having to say goodbye and leave him again in that horrible place.

I hugged him so tight, and we went home, together. Home?

That was a scary thought. How would he feel coming home, moving forward with his life?

Would he be ok?

While in jail, my son was able to get off the drugs and stay clean. He needed to continue moving in the right direction. While he was in jail I found out the girlfriend moved out of state and was rebuilding her life.

Could he do the same?

My son spent a lot of time in his room and kept to himself. He got a job and slowly, slowly rebuilt his life. It was hard, and it took a lot of patience. My son left his old circle of friends behind and realized his drinking days were over. It was a good thing. Every day he grew stronger. He was clean and sober. But it was hard work.

Days passed. Weeks passed. Months passed, and my son worked hard at staying sober. One of his physicians told us that his brain would have to be clean from all drugs for an entire year before we would see the old version of him again. We watched that happen.

My son would ask us questions about things that happened or that he remembered, but he didn't remember some of the things he did while under the influence of drugs.

I remember the day I realized only God knew how to save my son. God took my son and put him in what I thought was the worst place, jail. That's how God saved my son. I also knew I needed to forgive the girlfriend because God also used her to save my son. If she had not come into his life, we may have never known my son had a drug issue.

Would things have been worse?

I will never doubt God works in ways we will never understand. The times we thought were the worst times, that nothing could save us, are the times God worked to do just that, save us.

Jail and God saved my son.

I will never be able to explain why my son was saved from an overdose or death. I praised God every day for sparing him. God knew his story was only just beginning in his young life.

***

Ten Years Later

My son met the love of his life. She knows his past and loves him more because of it. He remains clean and sober. He was able to obtain multiple certifications for his job and is on an amazing career path using the knowledge he gained in the law library, working in litigation at his job. He married the love of his life, and they now live in the home they bought together. They have an amazing son. When I danced with my son at his wedding, he chose a song with lyrics that reminded him of his journey. Our journey together as mother and son, and how I never gave up on him. The lyrics are:

There's a ship out on the ocean at the mercy of the sea.
It's been tossed about, lost, and broken wandering aimlessly.
And God somehow you know that ship is me.
Cause there's a lighthouse, in a harbor shining faithfully
Pouring its light out, across the water, for this sinking soul to see.
That someone out there still believes in me.
On a prayer, in a song, I hear your voice, and it keeps me hanging on
Oh, raining down, against the wind, I'm reaching out,
Till we reach the circle's end. When you come back to me again.
There's a moment, we all come to. In our own time and in our own space.
For all that we've done, we can undo if our heart's in the right place

On a prayer, in a song, I hear your voice, and it keeps me hanging on
Oh, raining down, against the wind, I'm reaching out,
'Till we reach the circle's end. When you come back to me again
And again I see my yesterdays in front of me, unfolding like a mystery,
Your changing all that is and used to be
When you come back to me again.

We cried while we danced together. My son said, "Mom, we made it." I don't know why I was lucky enough to have that dance with my son when so many other mothers don't. They lose their children forever to drugs and addiction. I thank God every day for the blessings we have been given. I cherish continuous memories with my son, and now my beautiful grandson.

Watching my son raise his son is truly amazing. I know, one day, my son will have his own fears as a parent, watching his son grow. I know his experiences will impact those fears, and I hope he puts his trust in God to see him through those times, just as I did.

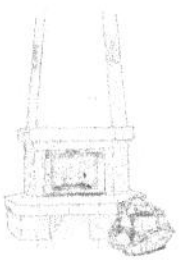

Dear New Homeowners— A Letter From Hestia: Goddess of Hearth and Home
Amy Nielsen

Dear New Homeowners,

Every home has a story—one overflowing with memories of firsts and lasts, of tears and laughs.

I'm Hestia—Goddess of Hearth and Home, and I'm here to tell your home's story—to share how its past prepared it to be your future.

A career opportunity lured a man from his country. He'd never been away from his birthland and family.

The man had one mission—to find a home, a place to begin his new life. He toured everything from sprawling lakefront estates to elder, well-loved cottages.

But nothing felt right until he stepped into a new build in its final stages.

It checked all his boxes—a large backyard, extra bedrooms for overnight guests, safe neighborhood. And for me, room for the family he unknowingly longed for.

With my secretive guidance, he picked the final touches—rich wooden cabinets, warm plank flooring, and cozy furniture.

He delighted in ending his workdays and coming home. His kitchen island was his favorite spot to prep evening meals. Weekends were spent floating in his pool and watching sports on his outdoor television.

He told his friends and family back home that it felt like a mini vacation each time he stepped outside. They couldn't wait to visit.

But it was a big house for a bachelor. The upstairs sat empty. He pondered long, lonely nights about what made a house a home. He didn't know it then, but he was praying to me, the Goddess of Hearth and Home.

Night after night, his heart grew heavy and sad. I had grown to love the man, just as he had grown to love the house. So, when his phone rang for a night out on the town, I made sure it was sitting on the kitchen island so he'd be able to answer the call.

At a local pub, one of his new friends spotted two women sitting at the bar and invited them over. He locked eyes with a petite brunette. With a little help from my friend Aphrodite—it was love at first sight.

The happy couple dated for a year before she and her teenagers moved in. He no longer prepped his meals alone. The teens kicked the quiet upstairs to the curb with guitar riffs, video game soundtracks, and pop music.

When I checked in, his bachelor pad had been transformed into a hub for a loving and energetic family— exactly what he and the house had been missing.

Another year passed, and with Hera's blessing, the couple made it official by saying "I Do" beneath an arch in the backyard. The oldest daughter officiated. The oldest son served as Best Man and the youngest daughter was her mother's Maid of Honor. Family flew in. In the home, there was room for all.

A few years later, we Goddesses collectively blessed the family once again—this time with a new baby. The couple created a cozy nursery downstairs. The parents spent many nights rocking their infant son to sleep in that room.

Soon, colorful toys littered the home, and a playground was erected in the backyard.

I took notes.

The little guy slept through the night for the first time in your new baby's nursery. He took his first steps in your new family room. And he learned to swim in your new pool.

All those firsts meant a lot to your home and its first family. And while I'm sad to see them go, I'm delighted to welcome your family to take root and experience many firsts with your new baby.

The first family loved your new home, and the home loved them back.

I'll never forget their beautiful memories, but I'm excited for the ones your family will make. When you get busy with life, I'll be watching.

If you ever pass your home to new owners, I'll share with them your history, just as I passed the history of your previous owners on to you.

Because, to me, a home's history is its heartbeat. And heartbeats are meant to live on.

Love,

Hestia — Goddess of Hearth and Home.

DEMETER
GODDESS OF THE HARVEST

As mother of the land, I tell you to remember that every mighty tree started as a small seed. Strength and wisdom come with time, patience, and experience. The rewards and obstacles of life will provide you with these traits as you go.

Go forth and grow, my saplings!

AMERICAN PRIESTESS
Amanda M. Hayden

swirled prayer lifts soft edge of bare feet
  weaving story and song through Demeter's forest
  mother-daughter-sister-goddess celestial phases
   of waxing, full, hard-won waning
    winding down to the creek and prairie
     to create ceremony of sweet alyssum, sage clary,
      lavender water, and woody ash
     to gently place lined palms to earth
   curving like willows seeking water, speaking to Her taproot
to heal wounds, unfurl knots
  untwist tangles of trauma
    banishing-the-invasive-which-tried-so-viciously-to-take-
    up-residence
      reclaim and sanctify multi-hued sacred dwellings
       ancestral villages, holy temples, feminine bodies
     built with strong, fortified bones
    weathered hands, hematite heart scars
  cedar sprig, thick braids and nectar
shapeshifters into alchemists

solstice trilling, h*old my hand, sisters, heal,*
and hold me
medicinal Midsummer bathed on
Persephone's tinctured tongue

More Than This
J.K. Raymond

"Welcome, welcome everyone!
It looks like we have a newcomer today!"
Demi immediately decided
this "new year, new me" was a bad idea...

"Would you like to introduce yourself to everyone?"
If by introducing, they meant vaporizing out of the room?
Then yes, she would like that very much.
But she knew she wouldn't leave the other women intact so…

"Hello," Demeter said, standing formally.
"I am Mother Nature; it is a pleasure."
She finished with a bit of a head tilt and modified mini curtsey.
Which induced a rather long pause, that sort of built camp there.

"Hi, I'm Dottie,"
The head woman in charge offered herself up
As if a knife to cut the silence.
Demeter immediately decided she liked her.

The rest of the women followed suit.
They too recognized the greatness in Dottie
"Do you by chance have a nickname Mother Nature?"
"Demi, will do." Yep, Dotty was a priestess in the making.

"O.k., let's start with a game.
Tell me what you're not.
This must be something you believe people perceive you to be.
I'll go first. I'm Dottie, and I'm not just a dishwasher."

"I'm Jane, and I am not a vacuum cleaner."

"I am Amanda, and I am not a wife."

That got Demi's attention fast.
Amanda was her daughter
Costume or not, Amanda was The Persephone.
And The Persephone was having marriage problems.

Demeter wanted to jump out of her chair,
But this was a fate line that once cut,
Would be gone forever. So, Demeter choose decorum,
Instead, which by any standard of measurement in this moment
Would be considered torture.

There was a shift of balances in the room at her acceptance
And with that, came shy, hurt, confused, upturned eyes
Eyes that landed directly on Demeter's,
Silence quieted the room for a second time
In just under sixty seconds.

FLOWER IN THE SUMMER
Danica Camille G. Manalastas
Lester N. Linsangan

Goddess of harvest, grain, and fertility
Demeter, I, for one, will always be astounded by your beauty
The role you played in Greek Mythology
was already part of the vast history

Truly prominent toward the farmers of Greece
Thy legacy will never come to cease
A delicate woman sitting upon her throne
Along with the crown you've always worn

Goddess of Harvest, the sovereignty you hold
Can alter the season into sunny and cold
Even the growth of plants you control
Oh, please bless our soul

Earned the name "Lady of the Golden Blade"
The lengthy, gold-colored steel in the battle you parade
Cultivation, you ruled
It was blue without you

Provider of good crops for food and survival
Thy goodness deserves to be carved in a mural
Demeter, Demeter, Demeter
Whose beauty is like a flower in the summer

THE WITHERED WOMB
Ma. Carmela S. Garcia
Lester N. Linsangan

You cannot conceal a mother's love
For it is golden and will fly like a dove
The warmth and comfort you always have
When your heart gets broken into halves

But now, her face filled with worry
Like a dog finding its puppy
Who would not feel uneasy
When your child gets lost in the city

When their loved ones went absent
No. Nothing could erase the sadness
Their soma will to be covered with coldness
Everything around them changes

Time flies while she hunts
Seven days turn into months
The search centered on hopelessness
Thinking that the operation is useless

River of tears come out of their hive
Reminiscing the moments when she was five
Her daughter waits for her to arrive
She hugged the child, and they then high-fived

For every mama, it was a nightmare
To lose any child under their care
For every touch, there was a flare
In every way, there was a bear

No! A parent won't accept defeat
She said, "No surrender, no retreat!"
She wouldn't sleep until it was complete
The day, the mother, and her child meet;

Too Beautiful a Creature
Shaelynn Long

Some say that to visit a graveyard at dusk is to court the darkness.

"Mon petit cœur, it is, you see, a welcoming in of ze blackness, oui? To ze—mmm, how do you say it?—ze âme! Ze soul!"

The words of my great-grandmother. A message. A cautioning. She swore that if a young witch with a broken heart spread her blood on the headstone of a grave no more than twelve hours old on the night of a blood moon, the Demon King would find her, raise her from the muck of humanity, and make her his queen.

But such a thing, I believed, was a mere tale told to children. At the very least, it was a warning from her not to thoughtlessly give my heart away.

I certainly never believed it could be true. But perhaps it may not have been a warning about giving my heart away—but a warning about what a loss like heartbreak might do to me. Bibiane Dandonneau

Summer

Bibiane strolled along the edge of the wheat field, trailing her long musician's fingers over the soft tops of the waist-high wheat stalks. She was careful not to trample any of the crops, knowing just a few damaged plants could be the difference between a much-needed loaf of bread come winter when the lands around her village were swept into an ice kingdom that only the gentle warmth of spring—or magic—could thaw.

Long tendrils of Bibi's dark hair, loosened from the braid that hung heavy down her back, swept upward in the wind. The same breeze carried the scent of Bibi's grandmother's mid-summer roses. The crimson and blush-colored flowers bloomed large and heavy at this time of year. In the village there were rumors that Madame Dandonneau's flowers were aided along by touches of the supernatural. Nothing so beautiful could be natural, it was said. Those same rumors typically died down after a tonic from that same Madame cured a burning fever, a body weakened by a wracking cough, or, Goddess forbid, a plague.

Bibiane, lost in dreamy, rose-scented summer thoughts, loosened her grip on her own magic. Its golden waves floated along the tops of the wheat fields, plumping the long yellow stalks from their very tips to where they rose up so royally from the soft dark earth. "I daresay the rumors must be true," a honeyed voice said in low tones.

Bibiane whipped around, leashing her hold on the magic so immediately she was almost taken to her knees with the sharpness of its return to her body. Lord Touissant's heir, Henri of Giverney, stepped forward from the trees. His wheat-colored hair fell to his shoulders in waves, surrounding a face Bibiane had tried not to think was beautiful.

But the blue of his eyes was like the sea. Her mother, Margaux, had already cautioned her against drowning in their depths, having seen Bibiane glance one too many times in the young man's direction. The Giverney family was titled.

No member of it was meant for a mere village girl–not even one as beautiful as a Dandonneau witch.

Those eyes raked over Bibiane, though, and she felt every second of the kind warmth she saw there. He did not look at her in fear. His eyes were alight with something else entirely. Desire, perhaps. But not fear–and that was the only thing Bibiane knew to watch for.

"My lord," Bibiane murmured, finally recollecting her manners, and dropped into a low curtsy.

"Rise, maiden, if that's what you are. Some magical sprite seems far more likely." Henry, shockingly, tilted his head in response to her pretty curtsy, showing her a deference she knew she did not deserve.

"You do me a great kindness, sir," Bibiane said as she rose and let her smile toy about her lips.

"I always thought society's rules about who bows to whom a bit tedious," Henri said with his own smile. "I'd much prefer if we showed deference only to those we feel deserve it."

"And I deserve your deference?" Bibiane asked, incredulous.

"Miss Dandonneau, the women of your family have saved this part of the country more times than I am certain anyone has dared to count."

Bibiane did not speak.

"I am speaking, of course, of the kindness and sympathy the Dandonneau women are known for," Henri continued.

She barely caught the wink, but it earned him a smile.

"I am to take it you will not admit to being a sprite?" he asked, maintaining his warm, teasing tone.

Bibi smiled but shook her head. "I'm afraid not, my lord."

"Henri, please."

Bibi's cheeks flushed at the requested familiarity. Henri came closer to her, though, And it was too easy to be distracted by his movement rather than his request.

"If not a sprite, surely you must be a mermaid," he teased.

"Sir, I am on land, am I not?" she laughed.

"Ah, 'tis so. Perhaps a fairy maiden?"

"Would I not have wings, my lord?" Bibi asked.

"Please, *mademoiselle fée*, call me Henri. Mayhaps you have hidden what must be beautiful gossamer wings," he suggested, holding out a hand and gesturing around her where the wings might be, were Bibi such a creature.

"Alas, *je ne suis pas une fée*," Bibi said sadly.

"*Mademoiselle*, surely you cannot be human, no? You are too beautiful a creature." He was before her, his seaglass eyes staring down into her dark chocolate ones as if they would memorize the sight of them. For the first time in her life, Bibiane did not feel a shudder pass through her at the use of the word "creature." His voice was too soft, too rich, too reverent. Henri did not wait for Bibi's response. He held out his arm for her to take, and with another soft smile, she placed her long fingers in the crook of it. She gazed up for just a moment through her dark lashes, so very pleased to discover that his curiosity was piqued and obvious in his heavy-lidded eyes. They continued along the path. Bibiane felt his eyes upon her for the duration and thought she might burst under such intense scrutiny.

"I will come for you tomorrow, and the day following that, and the next," Henri murmured over her hand before his lips pressed to her fingers.

Hope carried her over the stone path and into the house, not knowing the song she hummed made its way behind her and all the way to Henri, whose lips curled into a wondrous smile at the sound.

Fall

Henri had kept his promise, and each day Bibiane found him waiting for her at the gate to her family's cottage. Often, he held wildflowers out to her as she met him. Once he brought her a small square of chocolate and beamed radiantly at her as she let it melt on her tongue. "It is wonderful," she gasped.

"You are wonderful," he said quietly.

There was no charming smile, no wink. Just the words he allowed to sit in the silence around them. It was easy to trust him, then. Bibiane found Henri so guileless and so without pretense.

On a particularly crisp day with a wind that skittered dried leaves across the barren lands, he held out a gilded invitation. Bibiane had never seen anything so beautiful. "Lord Raoul and Lady Racquel Touissant of the House Giverney request the honour of your presence at a ball," Bibiane read, her words falling to a whisper before she reached the end. "Do not jest with me, my lord!" she cried, lightly tapping Henri's shoulder with the thick, gold—edged missive.

"I would not jest with you, mademoiselle. I told you I would waltz with you, and waltz with you I shall."

Henri gazed at Bibiane with such warmth and reverie. Bibiane's soft, round cheeks flushed pink as she glanced back down at the card in her fingers.

"Come and walk with me," Henri said gently, taking one of Bibi's hands. Bibiane tucked the beautiful paper into the pocket of her muslin day dress. She tried not to worry overmuch about what she might wear to such an event. Surely Maman or Grandmère would help her work over an old gown. She had nothing at present that was worth a village dance, let alone a ball at a lord's house.

"My father is worried about the late wheat yields," Henri said to her quietly as they meandered along the path on the edge of the forest.

"Surely things are not so dire," Bibiane replied, but she knew they very well might be.

"Already villagers are rationing their stores. Father is concerned there might be riots, especially with the impending ball."

"Not having a ball would not produce more wheat. There's no sense in thinking that," Bibiane said vehemently.

"You are quite sensible, mademoiselle, but not all the villagers are so."

"It is difficult to be sensible, I think, when logic leaves little room for hope." Henri was silent for so long Bibiane began to fear she had spoken out of turn. For all Henri's requests that they do away with the norms of society when it was just the two of them, he was still the son of a lord. She was a peasant. Lower, really. She was a witch, a daughter of a witch, a granddaughter of a witch. Just as her fretting reached its pinnacle and her lips parted to let an apology escape, Henri held a finger to her lips.

"You are wise, Bibi. You have given me much to consider."

The flush of embarrassment that had started to color her cheeks was the same pink of pleasure.

"I must go, I am afraid. My father's house is in shambles in preparation for the ball, but more than ever, Miss Dandonneau, I look forward to our waltz."

Henri bent over her hand and pressed a kiss to her fingers before he took his leave. Bibiane was left to daydream of the ball on her way back to the cottage.

A few weeks later, that innocent kiss–the simple warmth of his lips against her fingers– made it possible for her to endure the stares of the titled ladies and gentlemen and the whispers that arose from those same crowds as she glided about the room in the arms of Henri. Lord and Lady Touissant had been most welcoming, and surely that was all that mattered.

"I would waltz with you all night if I could, *mon chére*," Henri whispered to her as they took the night air out in Lady Touissant's fragrant gardens.

"But you cannot," Bibiane chided.

"Alas, I cannot," he admitted. "Even if I dared, I would not subject you to any more whispers and stares. The people–they do not understand you. I am sorry for it." He pressed his lips to her cheek, promising her he would see her the next day. Bibiane watched him return to the ballroom. The reality settled over her then. She was absolutely, irrevocably in love with Henri. With that knowledge clutched tight within her, she wound her way to the garden gate and walked home. Without the possibility of dancing with Henri, the ball no longer held any interest for her.

The next day, Bibiane was surprised to find Henri at the gate, just in time for her morning walk. He looked fatigued, and Bibiane could not help but inquire.

"I will not trouble you with it, Bibi," he said as he gave her a smile and walked with her toward the fields.

Once there, though, Henri paused and turned to look down at Bibiane. She felt the heavy weight of his gaze and enjoyed the warmth she saw in those now—so—familiar eyes. His long, tanned fingers reached out and took her more delicate ones, and he held them softly in his grasp.

"If there was just one thing you might do for me, *mon chére*, it would be this." Bibiane's gut tightened. She wished she did not know of what he spoke of. They had never said a word to one another about what Henri had seen that day amongst the stalks of wheat. As each day passed and he did not mention it, Bibiane could only assume she had been mistaken. But these words–they confirmed he had seen her bless the fields with her magic.

"I do not ask it for myself or my family. But the children in the village… already they do not have enough to eat. The yields are not good, and I–I am afraid, *mon cheri.*" Bibiane knew that horrible truth. Her mother and grandmother often left loaves of bread or baskets of vegetables from their gardens on doorsteps. The villagers knew who it came from, but it did not smart their pride to take things that had been so willingly left. She could do her part by fulfilling this one request from Henri.

He led her to the fields and watched in wide-eyed amazement as her golden magic spread out over the fields, bringing dying and even dead plants back to life.

"It will not last more than a single harvest," she warned.

"It is more than enough, *mon chéri*. You are such a beautiful creature."

Henri lowered his mouth to Bibiane's, and for the first time she felt in all reality what she had only been able to imagine. She knew they ought not to be sharing such a moment, but surely Henri was overcome in the moment.

Winter

It had been many weeks since the ball, and still Henri did not come. Bibiane, though, could hardly take notice of the heaviness that settled in her heart. There was a well-worn path from the village to the Dandonneau cottage. The once-proud villagers now openly begged for tonics, vegetables, bread, and even watered-down broth.

"*S'il vous plaît, c'est pour mon fils,*" Bibiane heard more than once.

Maman and Grandmère took turns answering the door and traipsing out into the frigid winds to follow a villager back to town in an attempt to nurse a family member back to health. "How dare he, that scoundrel!" Maman cried out as she unwrapped a long woolen scarf from around her head and neck.

"What is it, *mon cher?*" Grandmère asked, her tone low and concerned.

"Lord Touissant, that scoundrel, that monster–he is charging triple for the wheat." "For the wheat? From the last harvest? Surely it was not so much," Grandmère said. Bibiane sank to the floor.

"Mon cher, what is it?" Maman asked her, abandoning her rage and dropping to her knees before her daughter.

And in quiet, low tones, Bibiane confessed to the magic she had performed for Henri. Maman sat back on her heels and stared at her mother, whose soft, wrinkled features held a sudden and violent rage.

"I am so sorry," Bibi whispered.

"It is not your fault, *mon cher,*" Grandmère bit out.

"I do not believe Henri knew what his father meant to do," Bibi continued. "We shall certainly find out," Maman said as she rose to her feet.

Bibiane shot to hers, as well. She held out one hand to stop her family.

"No. 'Tis mine to deal with."

Spring

The fields would not yield to the plows. Machinery broke, was repaired, and then broke again. Horses neighed and bucked and refused to go near any bit of dirt that had been previously used for crops. It was as if the soil had turned to poisoned rock with the changing of the seasons. Money was offered and doubled, but not a soul in the village would take a cent. Lord Touissant sent his son into the village to inquire but he received cut direct after cut direct. It was not to be born, Touissant declared. Henri quietly exited his family manor and made his way toward the Dandonneau cottage.

"Bibiane, what have you done?" he asked when he came upon her sitting near the river.   "My lord, I know not of what you speak."

"You are vexed, and I am most sorry. My father sent me away unexpectedly." "And with the post so difficult to handle," Bibiane sniffed.

Henri sighed.

"I deserved that. I should have sent you a letter."

Bibi did not respond. Henri moved closer.

"You beautiful creature," he whispered.

Bibiane's eyes blazed as they met his, but Henri, to his credit, did not cower. "I am a creature, and you would best remember that," Bibi hissed as she moved to stand in front of the boy she'd thought she loved.

"Please believe me that I had no knowledge of what my father would do. I am ashamed," he whispered as his head hung low.

Bibi remained silent, and Henri continued. "I truly did not know, *mon coeur.*" "If I was your heart, you would be more careful with me," Bibiane said quietly. "But you are my heart, Bibiane, you must know that."

His lips met hers tenderly, as if he was not sure of the response he would receive. But Bibi thought she heard truth in his words and sank into his kiss. She could not believe he would have asked her to knowingly harm her village.

"Those in the village, though, you must know they will turn on you the moment my father discovers what they want."

"They want to feed their families through the winter, Henri. Surely that is not so much to ask."

"I believe my father has learned his lesson. But have they, Bibiane? Have the villagers truly embraced your family, knowing what you are?"

His somber gaze made her uncomfortable.

"They know—the villagers know of your witchcraft. It is only while it is useful to them that they will ignore it."

Bibiane would not say anything, but deep down, she knew he was right. The villagers, the townsfolk, even the lords and ladies knew what the Dandonneaus were.

Summer

Even Maman and Grandmère had to admit they eagerly awaited an offer of marriage for Bibiane from Henri Touissant. But he seemed in no rush toward an altar, and Bibiane was content to spend her quiet afternoons with him picking flowers and herbs for the tonics and medicines that the villagers still requested from them.

One afternoon they lay on Henri's cloak, spread over the warm grass, and lounged in the hot rays of sunlight. They were well away from the shadows of the trees and even a potential breeze from the river. Bibiane fanned herself with the delicate fan Henri had brought to her from his last trip to Paris.

"All the titled ladies have them," he'd insisted as he'd pressed it into her hands. "I am no titled lady!" Bibi had laughed.

"You are better," he said before he kissed her.

Yes, Bibi was content with her sunny afternoons

in Henri's arms. Soon, though, Lord Touissant had his son traveling once again. This time, however, there were letters. They were scarce and often short, but Bibi treasured them more than her memories of their ballroom waltz. He signed each one, "Forever yours."

Fall

Bibiane did not want to hear that another match could be made for her. She was inconsolable, much to the chagrin of both Maman and Grandmère. She had loved Henri with the blind passion that only the young are capable of. When Henri's betrothal to a titled lady, Florine de Jordain, was announced, Bibi refused to believe it. Henri was hers and hers alone. Henri's whispers of love and fidelity had found their home in her heart, and she would hear no one who spoke to her of either of them marrying another.

As Bibi crept from her warm bed and into the chilled night air, she knew she could yet turn back. The raised gooseflesh of her arms was yet another warning that she ignored, however. Over her nightdress, Bibi pulled on a thick, black cloak and grasped the candle she had not blown out for the evening.

With just a single glance back at the sleeping forms of her mother and grandmother, Bibi rushed from their small cottage and fled into the darkness and toward the old graveyard. As he'd promised, Henri was waiting for her. She fell to her knees and let the tears fall from her eyes.

"How could you?" she whispered.

"I had no choice."

"We all have choices, Henri."

Henri refused to look at her, and Bibiane's sorrow began its transformation into hot and violent rage.

"You called me your heart. You said I was beautiful."

Henri's eyes met hers then.

"I said you were a beautiful creature. I thought you understood. We could never be, you and I. I am a titled lord's son. You are a witch."

Bibi turned from him and fled.

Winter

The days grew shorter, and the nights were frigid. Fires burned as often as all could allow them to. Even Grandmère could not recall such a harsh winter.

Bibi loved it. The world, like her heart, was ice.

Maman sent Bibi to the village to purchase some things. As she walked along the dirt streets, she noted the drastic changes that had taken place while she had grieved the loss of her love.

"Mademoiselle, can you spare a coin? Please. The baker is charging so much these days," a thin woman begged.

Her skin had a frozen tint to it, and her clothes hung like rags on sticks. Bibiane was horrified, and she felt that horror in the tingling of her arms and legs. She thought she might be sick.

"Here you go," Bibiane said, pressing several coins into the woman's hands. The Dandonneau women did not have much, but Maman and Grandmère would surely understand. The woman, bowed in stature, limped away through the frozen muck, and Bibiane made her way to the bakery.

What she discovered there was treachery. The cost of the wheat, the baker cried, was too much. He could only minimize his own profits so much so as not to beggar his own family. He was already donating day-old bread to the villagers when he could.

Bibiane knew what had happened.

Henri caught her before she managed to get too far onto the Touissant lands. Someone must have alerted him to her presence.

"Your father," Bibiane spat. "He charges again for the wheat. The villagers are starving." "We need the money," Henri said.

"For what?" Bibi cried. "For nicer clothes? For more horses? What does your family want for that it is right for you to take advantage of these poor souls?"

But she knew then that there was no reason Henri could give her. As he spoke, she turned away.

There was no love for him anymore within her. There was only rage against what he was allowing his family to do to people who'd asked for nothing more than to survive.

***

Bibi crept through the overgrown grass of the headstones with a hairpin as her only weapon. She was headed for the gravesite of a young village boy who had succumbed to a fever and had been buried just that afternoon. She knelt on the overturned earth and breathed in the heavy scent of fresh dirt.

She found she needed more than a few steadying breaths to calm herself from her frantic run through the village. She had been so afraid that someone might see her. She had no fear of a drunken villager or any wild animal, though. Being kept from performing this ritual was the worst outcome she could imagine.

Bibi plunged the tip of the hairpin into the fleshy part of her thumb and gasped. The pain was sharp, but she delighted in it. After weeks of despair, it felt good to feel something else. The hairpin was abandoned to the grass and forgotten as Bibi watched the blood well up.

With a silent whisper of something akin to a prayer, her blood was smeared across the headstone. With only the moonlight overhead, the blood shone wet and black on the stone. Bibi bowed her head and listened.

And then he was before her. Resplendent in clothes dark as midnight with waves of hair just as black, his lithe body leaned against a headstone in the next row in a manner of nonchalance Bibi had never seen.

"You're here," Bibi breathed.

He smiled and came toward her then.

"Did you not call me here, little one?" he mused, his posed question not really a question at all.

Bibiane flushed with anger.

"You are mistaken, sir. I am already one and twenty."

"That is still quite young to me," he said with a mischievous grin.

He bowed low over Bibi's proffered hand and then pressed cool lips to her fingers. "You may call me Duval," he told her, his breath like ice against her skin. "I am Bibiane Dandonneau."

"Miss Dandonneau, have you not been told what happens to young girls with broken hearts who seek me out?"

His grin was dark and mischievous, and that small flame that had gone out when Henri had so callously broken her heart suddenly flickered to life.

"I have. Why else would I be here at such a time and performing such an act?" she asked pertly, gesturing toward the dark smear of blood on Tobias Silvine's headstone. Duval threw his head back and laughed.

"Is it true, then, that I will be your queen?" Bibi asked.

"Perhaps, my dear, but it is not as simple as the stories

might lead you to believe. You have spilled your own blood, but will you shy away from spilling the blood of others?"

"What must I do?"

Duval smiled wickedly before he leaned down and whispered in her ear.

"You must bring me the heart of the one who wronged you."

Bibi gasped.

"So perhaps you will not be my queen, after all."

This was her only chance. Henri had wronged her, and she knew now that he had done so with eyes wide open. He knew he was to marry a titled lady and still he had pursued her. He had knowingly asked her to use her magic so that his family could fill their own coffers.

Duval pulled from his pocket a long chain with a dark red crystal hanging from it. He motioned for her to turn, and so Bibi did. She lifted her hair and sighed as the cool metal settled itself around her neck.

"With my jewel around your neck, you may go wherever you wish to. And when you are ready, you will sprinkle this dust on the palm of your hand, whisper the spell, and then take his heart."

"Give me the spell."

And Duval did.

Later, Bibi looked down at Henri's sleeping form. It had been easy enough to get inside with Duval's dark crystal. A black fringe of lashes fluttered against the white skin of Henri's cheeks. His beauty was incomparable. If those eyes opened, she knew they would be the brightest blue. They had stared down at her so often these last few months. Those lashes had fluttered against her cheek as Henri had whispered promises into her ear. And there were his lips—so pink and perfect. Those lips that had lied to her with such ease.

Bibi carefully sprinkled the black dust from Duval's velvet pouch into the palm of her hand and whispered the phrase he had taught her. As Henri exhaled, Bibi plunged her hand into his chest and grasped his still-beating heart.

Those blue eyes flew open as she squeezed, and his mouth opened and closed—rather like a pathetic fish—as he tried to get air into his lungs.

"I loved you," Bibi said quietly.

She kissed his cheek and pulled her hand from his chest. The trail of blood followed her from the manor house and through the village to the graveyard.

Bibi placed the heart, red and bloody and still warm, on the stone in front of Duval. "Here is the heart of the one who wronged me."

Duval smiled wide.

"So it is, my dear. So it is. And would you care to know what I plan to do with it?" Bibi shrugged. It truly did not matter to her. Henri was her past. She said as much. "I am meant for bigger things," she said.

The heart vanished, and Duval held out his hand.

"Come, my dear. We have a coronation to plan."

And so it was that Bibiane Dandonneau became the Queen of the Shadowland, forever to remain at the side of Duval, King of Demons.

You, dear reader, may know Bibiane by her title: the Lilith. There are many stories of her, but few with even a grain of truth.

Summer Love Spell
S.E. Reed

Jaelynn Kent grew up in Seattle under an oppressive gray drizzle. She longed for sunshine and other like-minded people who enjoyed nouveau art, sustainable farming, and good wine. So when Jaelynn saw a flier hanging up on the community board of her condo complex, inviting recent college graduates to participate in a summer internship in the California wine country, she jumped at the chance. With her poignant essay on the antiseptic quality of red wine, she was approved in the first round of applicants to join the compound for the summer.

"Hey Tom! What's next?" Jaelynn asked and wiped the sweat off her brow.

She stood proudly next to a long row of compost she'd spent several hours turning with a pitchfork. Her blond hair was pulled up into a messy bun and streaks of dirt smeared her perfect complexion. It was only the first week and she was already thriving.

"Wow! Great work Greenhorn!" Tom, a senior staffer at Vineyard Farms, genuinely complimented her hard work. "Why don't you head to the Old Daniel's Barn— there's a bunch of stuff that needs to be sorted for the annual Midsummer Night's Festival. Stuff that can be used as decorations or sold and repurposed needs to be put out front for the guys to pick up in the truck."

"Sure thing!" She answered without question.

As an Art History major, this was exactly the kind of project in her wheelhouse. She took off running between the grapevines towards the edge of the massive property. She'd memorized the map of the eight-hundred-acre vineyard her first night. The old barn sat cushioned in a grove of hundred-year-old California oak trees. The wood on the barn was faded and matched the surrounding woody landscape. She slowed her pace on the approach admiring the sunlight as it cascaded between the branches, casting strange halos and beams of light.

Something clattered inside the barn when she placed her hand on the rusty handle.

"Hello?" Jaelynn called out suspiciously. "Anyone there?"

She shoved open the heavy double doors and a cloud of dust swirled up. She started coughing and put her arm up to block her face. A pigeon flew out wildly from the rafters, swooping a few inches from her head and out through the open doors. Jaelynn screamed and her heart hit her ribcage. "Shit, that scared me."

There was a gentle laugh in the shadows.

Jaelynn waved her hand to clear the dust. "Hello? Who's there?" She called out, unsure if she actually heard laughter, or if her mind was just playing tricks on her.

"Don't mind the pigeons— here look."

A handsome young man stepped forward and approached her with something cradled in his hands. He was a SoCal surfer type with a dimple. He had on faded Levis, a tight white tee and worn-out work boots. Jaelynn hadn't seen him with the other summer interns. But after a week, she probably hadn't met everyone at the vineyard, she told herself.

He flashed a grin and held his cradled hands out towards her.

"What is that?" she asked cautiously. A bead of sweat dripped down the small of her back.

"It's a pigeon's nest. It must have fallen earlier." The mystery man smiled, then added, "I've been here working all day and they get startled anytime I move something."

"Whoa, they're so tiny," Jaelynn cooed as she peered into the bird's nest to admire the eggs. The tightness in her throat subsided and her shoulders relaxed, there was something about this guy that felt comforting. "You've been here all day by yourself? That stinks! Tom sent me to sort stuff for the festival, so now you've got some company."

"Oh really?" He asked and walked back into the shadows. Jaelynn watched curiously as he placed the nest up on a ledge. She knew the pigeons would never accept the eggs again, having human scent on them. But the gesture was still a sign of kindness by this mystery guy.

"I hope you don't mind my company," she said as she looked around the barn.

It was a lot bigger than it looked from the outside and there were tons of hidden treasures, now that the dust settled. She spotted a 1920's wine press and a row of mason jars filled with old corks. Those would be great for decorations.

"I'm happy to have the help," he said and surveyed the room with her. "We can start with that pile if you'd like." He pointed to a row of wine barrels that were stacked with junk. "My name is Zeke, by the way." He wiped his palm on the back of his tight jeans and offered out his hand.

"Hi Zeke! I'm Jaelynn." She smiled and took his hand. It felt strangely warm and inviting. He had a sturdy grip, but not to enforce his manliness, more like he was sharing his strength with her.

For the next few hours, Jaelynn and Zeke sorted the piles in the barn. Her impression was right– Zeke was strong enough to move anything they unburied in the mess with ease. She was able to point out interesting items that he passed over, not knowing their value.

"Zeke, can you squeeze behind that old pile of wooden pallets and grab that little metal thing?" She asked.

"I remember this, it's a piece of an old gate that used to be outside the big house. It had rose vines growing through it." Zeke lifted the wrought iron gate out and brushed the cobwebs from it– exposing delicate detailed scroll work along the edges.

Jaelynn beamed over the find and put a hand up to high-five.

Zeke cocked his head and smiled, before putting his hand up. She smacked it and they both laughed.

"You really have an eye for this, what else do you spy?" he grinned.

She narrowed her gaze and looked around the barn. "Oooh, what about that?" She spotted a steamer trunk on the far side and ran to check its contents. "Help me with the latch, Zeke!"

"You've got to push the little button, then it pops the mechanism." He rested his hand on hers, showing how to open the antique lock. Their fingers lingered, entwined together for a few moments before lifting up the lid.

It was full of old hats and vintage clothes. "Oh you've got to put this on," she laughed and held up a moth-eaten corduroy suit jacket. Zeke protested at first but obliged when she pretended to pout and fold her arms. He placed one of the hats on her head and touched the tip of her nose with his finger.

"Cute as a bunny."

Something about him was so endearing, she almost couldn't believe a guy this gorgeous and nice even existed. Never once did he get on his cell phone or bring up politics, which seemed to be the only thing anyone else in the outside world wanted to do anymore.

They laughed and teased, it truly felt like they'd known each other for a lifetime.

"How long have you worked at Vineyard Farm?" she asked when he told her he wasn't a summer intern, but a full-timer.

"Oh, a while," he replied and winked. "I was born not far from here, so I've pretty much spent my entire life on the Vineyard. I'm not interested in what else is out there, I guess. The world is a complicated place."

No wonder he was such a diamond in the rough! He had grown up here, away from the chaos of city life.

"I couldn't agree more! It's so hard to find genuine and nice people anymore. That's why I took this internship in the first place. So, I could meet people my age who long for a more sustainable lifestyle, you know, farming, wine, art."

"Yeah, I bet you wanted to get away from the constant screen time and dealing with traffic." He nodded as he spoke.

Another point for Zeke.

She worried for a brief second that he might be too good to be true. Maybe he already had a girlfriend? Jaelynn blinked a few times to settle her nerves.

"Have you ever been to Seattle?" she asked.

"No." Zeke shook his head. He lifted his old canteen

and took a swig of water and offered it to her.

"It's such a drag, all the growth from the tech industry, the lifestyle is horrible," she complained before taking a drink of his water.

"I'm glad you're here then, to get away from that life. You seem to really love it at the Vineyard," Zeke said and stepped close to her.

She could smell the sweat on his tan skin, it was musky with a hint of rosemary. He reached a hand up to her face and tucked a loose hair behind her ear. Her heart was pumping, and her breathing sped up.

BUZZZZZ!

Her phone started vibrating in her pocket, sending her back into reality. And after all her talk about getting away from screen time. How embarrassing!

"Hi Tom," she answered, seeing the name pop up. "Yes, okay, thank you." She put the phone back in her pocket. "Well, looks like it's chow time– do you want to walk back with me?" Jaelynn asked hopefully, staring into Zeke's gray eyes. There was something so interesting about him she still couldn't figure out.

"I think I better finish up. But–" he said softly, "There's something I want to ask you." Shivers ran up her spine. He was so close, was he going to kiss her? Her bottom lip quivered. "Would you go with me to the Midsummer Night's Festival?" He asked sheepishly.

Jaelynn didn't think twice. "YES!" she shouted, scaring a pigeon who'd decided to return to the barn. They both started laughing and she leapt forward to give him a hug. His embrace was like his handshake. Strong. Warm. Perfect. Just like the kiss he gave her. Their lips touched in the most delightful way, softer than a feather, yet there was more passion in that one kiss than she knew her body was capable of expression. The barn felt like it was spinning, her knees were weak. "Bye," she managed to croak as she love-drunk-stumbled out of the barn and back towards the mess hall.

A few days later, Jaelynn finished showering after another day of hard work. She hadn't seen Zeke again, but tonight was the Midsummer Night's Festival and he had invited her after all. When she walked into her room, she spotted a fancy white box on her bed wrapped carefully with a lavender bow.

"That came for you," her bunkmate Sarah said and raised an eyebrow at her.

"Really? I'm not expecting anything. I wonder what it is?" She sat down on the bed, anxious to open the surprise gift. She carefully unwrapped the bow and lifted the lid. She wracked her brain— maybe her Mother sent her a gift. It wasn't really her style, but who else would have sent her such a lavish boxed gift? Inside was something wrapped in tissue with a note and a single red rose.

Jaelynn,
I can't wait to see you tonight.
Zeke

"Oh my god! It's from Zeke, that guy I told you about!" Jaelynn squealed and lifted up the contents. It was an antique cream lace dress. She held it up to herself, admiring her reflection in the mirror. She twirled once, like she was a princess in a fairytale.

"Seriously— who is this guy?!" Sarah gawked.

"I really don't know, but I'm going to find out."

Jaelynn was a vision in the dress. It fit her like a glove, like it was made just for her. The thought of Zeke picking it out felt so intimate it made her entire body tingle. Maybe it was just this place, all the hard work and sunshine. Or watching the wine presses in action or the laughter with the interns on the veranda at night. But whatever it was, the usual alarms that might have sounded in her head back home with other guys were nowhere to be heard.

The summer interns and staff were in awe when she cascaded down the stairs. She'd never felt more beautiful than in that moment as the gentle sunlight of the California evening caressed her while she was wearing a dress given to her by her mystery man.

"Has anyone seen Zeke?" she asked while they walked toward the Vineyard's annual festival. The music was playing, and twinkle lights illuminated the path. There were hundreds of people wandering around sampling wine and children were running with cotton candy, heading for the ferris wheel.

It was the quintessential small-town event.

"Don't worry, you'll find him," Sarah said and offered an arm to Jaelynn.

"I hope so." Jaelynn forced a smile and linked arms with Sarah.

The bunkmates went from booth to booth and sampled food and wine and played games and laughed with the other summer interns. Jaelynn let herself relax and have fun, even if she couldn't find Zeke. He was probably helping in the back or running one of the booths. He was a regular employee, and not just an intern, she had to remind herself. But then, when she'd nearly given up hope that she might ever see him again, she spotted a familiar pair of Levis near the dunk tank.

"Zeke!" she exclaimed.

He turned to face her.

"Oh Jaelynn, you look more beautiful than I could have imagined." He had a halo of light over his head from the string of Edison bulbs crisscrossed down the lane.

"Where have you been all night?" Jaelynn asked. She wanted to add, *I thought you stood me up*, but thought that was silly– he'd sent her the dress after all. He was wearing work clothes again and smelled like he did when they'd been working in the barn. So, he must be on duty tonight and not free to wander the Midsummer Night's Festival with her.

Her heart sank.

"I'm so glad you found me." He took her hands and laced his fingers through them.

"Me too," she leaned in closer. "Thank you for the dress, it fits me beau–"

Zeke interrupted her and pressed his lips against hers, taking her breath away. Jaelynn wondered if she'd sampled too much wine with Sarah because the world around them faded away. She didn't know up from down, right from left or day from night.

If this wasn't love, she had no idea what was.

"I can't stay long," Zeke said when they finally came up for air. Jaeylnn blinked a few times and the festival materialized around her, bringing her back to reality.

"But— I thought we would spend all night together. You work so hard around here on the farm, you deserve a night off," she complained.

"Oh Jaelynn," Zeke whispered into her ear. "I wish I could spend the rest of the night with you. I don't ever want to leave your side. I want all of you, forever."

She tried to stop herself, but she couldn't. Images flashed in her mind faster than she had time to second guess her heart; a wedding, a home, children playing in the garden. She felt it stronger than any feeling she'd ever had, a powerful love designed for her and Zeke. They were living in a cute craftsman bungalow on the edge of the vineyard.

"I love you," she whispered.

"I love you too," his voice wrapped around her like an evening breeze and penetrated every fiber of her soul.

"JAELYNN!" Sarah shouted, breaking the love spell that had just swept over her and Zeke. "Hurry, the fireworks are starting!"

"Zeke, come with me, please! They can't expect you to work through the fireworks!" Jaelynn turned around expecting to see his perfect smile and dimple nodding.

But Zeke was gone.

An awful gnawing feeling clamped around her insides. He wasn't just gone. He was gone-gone. But she didn't care. She still searched frantically, not willing to accept it. Not willing to face the truth. She ran around to the other side of the dunk-tank as a ball hit the target. The water splashed up over the ledge, drenching her and the beautiful cream lace dress. "ZEKE!" she shouted. The antique lace was not meant to get wet, it started crumbling on her shoulder where the water touched its delicate structure. "ZEKE!" she yelled again.

"Jaelynn, are you okay?" Tom asked. He was taking the tickets at the dunk tank. "Who's Zeke? Did one of your friends come to town?"

"I uh—" she stuttered and stumbled to her knees.

"Whoa, here, let me help you up," Tom leaned down. But Sarah came running up beside them.

"Don't worry Tom, I've got her. Come on Jaelynn, let's get you back to bed. Too much fun at the festival." Sarah laughed and pulled her from the ground.

"I can't find Zeke. One second he was there, the next he's gone. And my dress, it's falling apart." She panted as her throat tightened up. People were crowding around them, trying to reach the field with the fireworks. The music was getting louder, more aggressive and everything around her felt out of place.

"Jaelynn, I think you're having a panic attack. I'm going to take you back to the bunkhouse–" Sarah put her arm around her and started guiding her through the festival and navigating the crowds. Jaelynn tried to breathe, but the light evening air had turned oppressive. She looked around and the colors of the booths and balloons were distorted. The children eating cotton candy looked like ghosts. They walked past the fun-house and her reflection was disgusting, it was her, without Zeke. An old maid. A shell of a person. She leaned over and vomited.

It was Sarah who found the vintage picture in one of the other bunkhouses. A handsome young man, with a dimple, dressed in denim.

1925 Ezekiel Daniels
Co-Founder of Vineyard Farms

Jaelynn rubbed the framed glass and stared at the faded picture. "Zeke," she finally whimpered. "Sarah, this is him. This is MY Zeke. I just don't understand how I could fall in-love with a ghost. I mean, we kissed! We connected! It's hard to explain, but he wasn't like any other guy I've ever met."

"Maybe it's his grandson or something. I mean, he told you he practically grew up here," Sarah suggested.

"Yeah, but Tom said he didn't know anyone named Zeke. Remember?" Jaelynn reminded her and paced around their room. She felt like she was going crazy!

"Don't give up so easily– if it's meant to be with this

guy, you'll find him."

It was those words that haunted her most… So, when she saw an ad for a little bungalow for sale in the town outside the vineyard, she put in an offer, which was accepted right away. Jaelynn was hired at a local art museum in town and kept herself busy. She spent years helping out with the summer intern program at the vineyard, training greenhorns and working hard to tend the land. She put her heart and soul into the earth, giving it as much love and attention as she would a family. She helped with the Midsummer Night's Festival and launched a successful artist initiative for the community. But most of all, she took long walks, searching for Zeke.

She imagined their life together.

She heard him laugh and remembered their kisses.

She longed to look as radiant as she had the night she wore the lace dress he gave her, to feel her heartbeat in love once again. "If it's meant to be, I'll find you Zeke," Jaelynn whispered into the breeze.

ATHENA
GODDESS OF WISDOM & WAR

My correction of Arachne's presumptuousness caused her to hang herself in shame. Turned out I could only restore her to life in the form of a spider; some powers are not unlimited.

A word from the wise, think before you act.

STORM
Shaelynn Long

You are a storm
an entire fucking whirlwind
that spirals
until you're broken down
breathing hard
and the tears come more slowly
   the rain drips more slowly

You are a storm
a creature of Mother Nature
designed
and deadly
but beautiful and spiritual
giving life to the earth
with your tears

But you are a storm
they'll hide and they'll cower
and they'll run from your destruction

—even if they prayed for the rain.

A LIFE TO REMEMBER
Tom Elmquist

From his new life, a man looks to the ashes of the old.
He rebuilt his life and builds dreams untold.
Looking at the past, he finds the ashes are not cold.

Sparks of memory flow to and from his weary mind.
Some memories are sweet, but many are unkind.
His question is, Why must I always look behind?

A voice comes to him and rings in his ears.
Look into those ashes and see what appears.
Look into those ashes, see your deepest fears.

The demons haunting your mind are still there.
Those demons are evil, wicked, and unfair.
They are vicious, cruel, and have little care.

Always remember that place from which you came.
Remember who you were. You are not the same.
You have rebuilt your heart, your life, and your name.

Remember those battles? What have you learned?
Were you deserving of the reputation you earned?
Or were you simply one of the ones that were burned?

Some say you were guilty of crimes. I say in part.
Blame was not solely yours. You needed a new start.
Then you needed time to mend your mind and heart.

You ask yourself why you must always look to the past.
To remember who you were when the dice were cast.
And also to remember how to make your new life last.

Tell me, have you wisdom from the battles fought?
Or do you wish to be in the past and with demons rot?
Or do you move on with the true life you have sought?

Tell me now and tell me quickly, my dear young friend.
Do you move on with the heart and life you did mend?
Or do you turn back to that life you sought to end?

His reply is simple, profound, and with all his heart.
I must remember that place. Remember my start.
Remember my lessons and remember to be smart.

I am not the man that people once hated and knew.
In myself, I will find meaning and something true.
I will live a life of happiness only known by a few.

GLISTENING SKIES ABOVE
THE BLOODY RIVER

Geraldine Athena F. Gomez
Lester N. Linsangan

Her armored heart, her vicious look
Triumph in every warfare
The dignity of power
The brains and the brawn

Audacious and intrepidity she illustrates
like her tapestries that glistened like a brilliant shade of gold
she is like a blood moon that arises at night
Dancing in the skies; the red in blood is seen from her eyes

She abstained to be the object of scorn
She had the adroitness of a God
As war cries echoed in her ears
A relentless warrior known is born

Befuddled by the dignity faith had given
Seeking the truth and the truth only
Her luminous gaze; with tears or blood

She was like a warrior driven by wisdom
Her jealousy rare, but well known
Punished by the Goddess of Wisdom
Different versions of the myth unfold
Is it to shield her or punish her

Conceived by heroism and dignity
Ought to slain, seeking vengeance
Consumed by lies, as she curses a sufferer of mischief
Executing judgment, with a doubtful advantage;

Cold Gaze

Briana Nicole F. Bautista
Lester N. Linsangan

I was once young and naive
Not until I learned to hate the sea
It was all about that deity
Athena, a Goddess with exceptional beauty

When that nightmare came into me
To throw all my innocence in the sea
That is where she found me
I'm on my knees, begging for her mercy

She plotted, in secret, and sly
To rid herself of this envy, oh so high
But no matter what guise she wore
Jealousy will always be at her door

Athena, I was once just like you
A graceful woman with dreams that shone true
But your jealousy took me to this place
A victim of betrayal, with a heart full of hate

Where did I go wrong
I was careful for so long
I opened my eyes and saw the curse you have blown
My gaze became cold, wherever it landed turned into stone;

Andy's Awakening
Tom Elmquist

"Fine! I don't need you," Carol screamed at Andy through the phone.

"Look, don't scream at me. We both knew this was coming," Andy said, trying to remain calm.

"I didn't. As far as I knew, everything was fine. I mean, sure, we've had our problems, but what couple doesn't?" she asked.

"I'm not saying….," Andy began.

"No, you want this? You've got it. I'm done!" She screamed at Andy cutting him off and then hung up.

Andy thought about it, there wasn't any one thing wrong with their relationship. It was a lot of little things and a few big things. The biggest being. He felt like they had grown apart as a couple, and they had changed as people. Looking at himself in the mirror, he didn't recognize who he had become. He felt that in both the literal and the figurative sense.

When they had met, it was the typical whirlwind romance. From the day they met a few years ago, Andy couldn't remember them being apart for more than a few days. They had all the same interests and shared just about everything. He had even thought about marrying her.

It wasn't until earlier this year that Andy felt a rift starting. It was small at first. She would make plans without him or cancel plans with him last minute. He didn't think anything of it at the time. Then things escalated. It felt like she was trying to start fights, and then he realized he was doing it too. They would fight, and then they would make up. Things would be better for a while, and then they would fall apart again. This cycle continued for a few months.

A few days ago, Andy suggested they take separate vacations to gain perspective. She thought that an excellent idea and went to the beach with her friends. Andy lied and said he was going up to the mountains to camp. He stayed home and worked. The break gave him perspective, indeed. He was able to focus on work and was able to draw for the first time in years. He found passion in things he had forgotten about when he was with her.

He realized that he had become someone he didn't like and felt like he needed to evolve. He also felt like she needed to grow and evolve as well.

That's what prompted the call tonight. He began to feel like it was a rash decision. Then he became angry.

"No! This is what you need, dammit!" he yelled to the ceiling.

He looked down at his art board and started to draw again. He drew furiously for what felt like hours. He drew until the drawing began to blur. Then he fell asleep on the artboard.

Andy woke up and looked out the window. "Dammit, I slept all day again."

He had forgotten about her and wanted just wanted

to see Chris and hang out. He got dressed and headed out.

Andy walked down the street toward the diner. It was just after sunset, and the moon was just starting to break through the clouds that lingered around all day. He kept his head down as he walked, trying not to draw attention to himself. That didn't mean he wasn't paying attention to everything around him. He looked down the alley to his right and saw the couple embracing. On closer inspection, anyone would see the trickle of blood flowing down the man's neck as he held on in ecstasy to the woman biting him.

In the park, he saw a circle of witches casting spells or summoning whatever pagan god they worshipped. In the flames, he saw what appeared to be a woman dancing in time with their rhythmic chants.

As he walked on, he saw a man cross the street. He looked like any other businessman you would see anywhere in the world. The only difference was you could see right through him as if he were smoke.

Andy muttered to himself, "Damn ghosts," and kept moving.

Sights like this didn't bother Andy too much because they had been happening more and more over the last five years. It was slow at first. You would hear about kids running around dressed up like werewolves. Only to find they weren't dressed up like werewolves, but they were real werewolves.

Nowadays, you could see fairies, gnomes, elves, and all manner of creatures that came from story books everywhere.

No one knew where or how it started, but scientists tried to figure it out. They ran tests on every creature they could get their hands on. It became so bad that people and creatures were rounded up by the thousands. That was until the scientists started to change themselves.

Pretty soon, the world just moved on as if it were all

normal. So, you got used to seeing the strange and unusual. What's more, the strange and unusual became commonplace, making what seemed normal five years ago stranger than the fiction surrounding him.

As he walked on, he saw a mother and a little girl walking toward him. Nothing strange about that, but they were preceded by what appeared to be a teddy bear wearing a knight's helmet made of cloth and carrying a little wooden sword under his left arm. The bear looked like he was missing one button eye and had stitches running up the front of him. He looked like a well-loved toy that a mother repaired instead of replacing when it got worn out.

When the bear saw Andy, he put one arm on the little girl as if to stop her. Both the mother and child stopped with a smile. The bear drew his sword from under his arm and pointed at Andy.

Andy stopped and smiled.

"That's enough, Sir Mikey. I don't think the nice man means any harm," the mother said.

"Yeah, he looks like a nice man," the little girl said.

"Sir Mikey, I salute you and beg your leave to pass," Andy said and snapped a little salute.

The bear returned his sword to its place under his arm and saluted back. The bear's salute was comical, to say the least. Watching a two-foot-tall bear with four-inch arms try to raise its arm to its head made all of them smile.

Andy dropped his salute, and the bear did the same. The humans passed each other with smiles, but the little guardian returned to looking about to ward off danger. Andy wondered as he continued down the street what would make a little bear come to life and what horror did the little girl need protection from. Andy shivered at that thought but smiled again when he thought of Sir Mikey's comical little salute.

Andy remembered something he saw in a picture once. It was a little child sleeping in bed and a bear, like Sir Mikey pointing a little wooden sword at a monster. He couldn't remember the caption, but that made him realize children needed to be protected from real and imaginary monsters.

Andy saw the light of the diner a short distance ahead, and he moved a little faster. He was hungry and wanted to see his friend. He also picked his pace up because he had the feeling he was being watched, and he was. He looked up at the streetlight and noticed four fairies sitting on top.

Little voices came to his ears, "Walking alone isn't a good idea. Would you like us to fly above you and warn you if anything nasty is coming your way?"

Knowing that fairies always wanted some kind of payment for their kindness, Andy said, "No, thank you, but if you come to the diner ahead, I'm sure I could get you some honey or strawberry jam." Andy also knew that fairies were skilled pickpockets, and if you didn't offer them something to pass, they would steal, at the very least, all the change in your pocket. People had been known to lose wallets, wigs, watches, car keys, and even phones around fairies. Oh, they would claim they had nothing to do with it, but they would also have nice new shinies or insulation for their homes.

As Andy walked on, he heard their wings above him, and their voices sang a song that Andy couldn't quite make out. It was a happy sound, so he didn't worry too much.

Sure enough, as he reached the diner, he saw the vending machine was stocked with all the nice sweets that fairies loved. He plunked two dollars' worth of coins into the machine and pulled out two small jars of honey and two small jars of strawberry jam.

In Andy's hand, the jars were small and unimpressive. To the fairies, the jars seemed massive. Several other fairies darted down and made off with the jars. The leader got about three inches from Andy's nose.

"Thank you, kind sir. You have fed my family for a month or more. If my family can ever do anything for you, just whisper my name," the fairy said.

Knowing his voice at this distance would certainly deafen the little man before him, he whispered, "And what is your name, good sir?"

"Morgain Rupert Smallwood," the fairy said.

"Thank you for your kindness as well, and when the weather turns cold, I have an attic that you and your family could nest in," Andy said, knowing the offer would never be taken but would be respected.

The three-inch man flitted away, and Andy started to go into the diner. He caught a glimpse of himself in the reflection from the glass. His deep green eyes looked tired, his hair had greyed almost to the point of being white, and his face was wrinkled from years of worry. Other than that, his reflection was that of a handsome gentleman in a dark blue blazer, white shirt, and jeans.

He stepped through the door, and the bell jingled, letting everyone know someone had just come in.

Ruby's Diner was like any other diner in the world. A few booths sat so that people could look out the window. Each had a mini jukebox connected to the big old-time jukebox in the corner.

A few tables were scattered about to fill the space more than anything else. They were covered in red and white tablecloths, and each had four place settings. No one really ever sat at them because most would sit in the booths or at the counter.

The counter had about twenty stools; sure enough, Chris was sitting at the one closest to the middle.

Chris was a heavy-set man. His hair had thinned to the point that he just shaved his head rather than fuss with any kind of hairpiece. His dark brown eyes told the story of a man who had been through many trials in life. His face was smooth and wrinkle-free compared to Andy's. He wore a black sweatshirt and jeans, which suited him and his casual nature.

He smiled as he turned, and it was a good smile full of warmth.

"Andy, how are you tonight, bud?" he asked with a strong voice.

"Tired, my friend. Very tired," Andy said with a dramatic sigh.

"Welcome to my world," Chris said back playfully. "See anything new and interesting today?"

"I did. I saw a teddy bear named Sir Mikey that walked around with a little sword and a helmet. He was protecting a little girl and her mother," Andy said.

"Ok, that sounds kinda cool. I took a walk down by the beach and saw mermaids. Not just one mermaid but like twenty of them," Chris said.

"Ok, you got me beat," Andy said.

This was a little game they had. They had to see who saw the most interesting thing. Sometimes Andy won, but it was less these days because he didn't go out as much. Chris wasn't the kind to shy away from the new world they lived in. He walked every day and engaged with anyone or anything he met.

Chris made the first move on a chess board he had set up and waiting for Andy. "Your move, sport."

"Damn, man. Can I at least get a cup of coffee before

you start?"

As if summoned by magic, the waitress set a hot cup of coffee in front of him.

"Now, listen here, boys, I am leaving early tonight because I want to get home before the moon fully rises. You know how crazy it can get on the night of a full moon. Cathee will take care of you for the rest of the night," the waitress said with a smile.

"Alright, Liz, you be safe," Chris said.

Andy and Chris played and drank coffee for about an hour. Their conversation was light and almost too polite. Both men had the same question on their minds, It was the question the whole world had on their minds, but neither man wanted to ask it, which made for an uneasy evening. Cathee poured them each another cup of coffee, and then she spoke. "You know they say the world has gone crazy, or that we are living in someone's crazy dream. You see things that didn't exist a few years ago, and they appeared all of the sudden. It was like every story I had ever heard, and every movie I had ever seen just came to life. No one knows how or why. They are just here now. I mean, maybe this is just how things are now, but what do you guys think caused it?"

With that, both men looked at Cathee for the first time. They really got a good look at her for once. She was beautiful. She had the kind of beauty that poets wrote about. Her long brown hair flowed down to her shoulders in waves. It seemed to shimmer in the light of the diner. Her skin was flawless, as if she had jumped off the canvas of some painting. Her eyes appeared to be violet in the light of the diner. Her smile lit up the room, and it was a genuine smile. Her smile was full of joy and laughter. She was statuesque with a down-to-earth quality as well.

Both men sat in stunned silence for a moment.

"Well?" she asked. Startling both men.

Then Andy started, "I've been thinking about that a lot lately."

Chris retorted, "I wondered what that smell was."

"Shut up and let me get this out because if I don't do it now, I may never say it out loud," Andy continued. "I mean, well," he stammered. Then you could see his resolve solidify in his eyes. "Cathee is right. Where did this all come from? How did it all begin?"

Chris said, "I've been thinking the same thing but is it a bad thing? I don't mind living in a world of walking, talking fairytales, but yeah, how did it start?"

The conversation continued with a lot of speculation. They talked about everything from aliens to portals from other dimensions. They had thoughts and ideas on every subject, but nothing seemed to answer all the questions.

Andy was the type of man who liked to see the beauty in the world. He liked to think that there was something beyond this world, painting each day more beautiful than the last. So, his prevailing theory was this.

"I think that there is some unseen presence in our world now. It wants to remake the world. So that the impossible is possible. It's using some kind of power on us to make our worst nightmares, or our happiest dreams come true."

"But there is nothing like that in the world," Chris began. "I think that somehow we did this. Somehow we created some kind of power with our minds to create these things."

"That's impossible. The human mind doesn't have the ability to change the fundamental laws of nature," Andy countered.

"Do you boys want some more coffee?" Cathee

asked.

Both men nodded.

"Do you mind if I weigh in on this discussion?" she asked.

"Sure," both men said in unison.

"What if you're both right? What if someone from another world or another plane of existence came to this world and gave us the power to make these things real? I'd like to think these things are part of what we really are."

Andy became angry, "People want to become, or are monsters somehow?"

Cathee asked in a soft, calm voice, "Do you see only monsters? What about the teddy bear you saw tonight?"

"I see, see those things, and I wonder what made the need for a teddy bear come to life. What horror did a child see to make that real? I mean, it's a nice thought, but I'm not sure it's all good."

"Ah, See, you know the child created it, though," Cathee said.

"I mean, yeah, but," Andy stammered.

"What if those things you see as monsters are just what part of someone's dream or what they want to be? Think about it. The teddy bear came to life to protect a little girl. What do teddy bears normally protect kids from?" she asked.

Chris said with excitement in his voice, "Bad dreams and to keep them safe in the dark."

"Right, What could a person dream of to become a vampire?" Cathee asked.

Andy started to look confused. "To drink blood?"

Chris said with even more excitement, "No. Immortality. They see vampires in movies and want immortality. Then somehow, it becomes real. The fairies are people who want to live a different type of life. Like something from their childhood. Something magical."

"What about the ghosts?" Andy asked.

"What if ghosts are people who lost something inside and became a shadow of their former selves?" Cathee asked.

"Explain werewolves and mermaids," Andy said, feeling even angrier.

Cathee said again, in a soft, calm voice, "Simple. The werewolves and other werecreatures are people who wanted something of the wild to live inside them. They wanted to have an animal that their spirit felt close to as a part of them. The mermaids are people who wanted to live as one with the ocean or possibly something magical."

"But people can't just become these things. This isn't magic," Andy said in a near scream.

"Isn't it?" Chris asked. "Then you tell me another word that fits. What logical explanation fits all of this?" He point outside and continues.

"Seriously I watch a coven of witches summon visions of their ancestors for guidance. I have seen a little boy wish for a puppy with all his heart, and it appeared right in front of him."

He looked down at his coffee, "Sure, I have also seen the darker side of things because people in this world also have dark desires."

He slammed a fist down on the counter and looked up. "But I have seen an overwhelming amount of good in this world. I have seen things that can only be explained if there is magic in the world. You used to see it too."

Andy started to become uncomfortable and took his blazer off. "Is it getting hot in here?"

"No, not at all," Cathee said.

"Nope, not at all. In fact, I feel a little bit chilly," Chris said.

Cathee looked at Andy, and her eyes seemed to sparkle, almost like there were galaxies in her eyes. "Look at me and tell me what made you like this? What made you who you are?"

"It wasn't any one thing," Andy started.

"Tell us," Cathee commanded.

"When I was a boy, my father went away. He left my mother and me alone. That Christmas, there were no lights around the house, no tree, and no presents because my mother couldn't afford them. That's when I learned that there was no Santa Claus. I also learned that I had to grow up. So that my mother didn't have to worry so much about me. My mother fell in love with another man who did nothing but hurt us. So, I learned to hide my pain away. She then fell in love with a man who loved her but hated me. They had kids together. So, I became the outsider. There is so much more, though."

"I know there was. All of it made you who you are today. What did it teach you? Part of you still sees beauty in the world. Why" Cathee asked.

"Because I want there to be more in this world," Andy said.

"Exactly," Cathee said softly. She looked at Chris. "What about you? You see the world with some wonder, but something also broke you."

"I've been through a lot, but I always rebuild," he said.

"Yes, but with each rebuild, you've lost something. Tell us."

"I had a daughter who died when she was very young. I think that was the first time my world was really shattered. So, I rebuilt who I was. Then I fell in love again. She was my everything, but I discovered she didn't love me. She wanted to be with me for what I could do for her, and then she left me for another guy. So, my world shattered again. So, I rebuilt. I will always rebuild. Every time my world burns down to ash, I pull myself up and remake myself."

"You rebuild yourself, but I like the ash metaphor. Instead of building yourself, what do you really do? Hmmmm? Tell me," Cathee said.

"I have always said I rise like a phoenix from the ashes," he said. "I have always thought I had the spirit of a phoenix."

"Think about that for a while," she said and turned back to Andy. He was sweating so badly that his shirt was now soaked through.

"Here, you look like you could use this." She set a glass of ice water in front of him.

"Thank you. I didn't see you even get it but thank you," Andy said and took a big gulp of water.

"Just because you didn't notice that I got it for you, did it make you any less thankful?"

"No. Not at all. I just don't understand where it came from," Andy said as he started to feel anxious. At that moment, Andy wanted to leave and never come back. He was unable to move, though.

"In fact, it was very welcome. Like you, something else you would welcome back into your life. You want the wonder and awe you felt as a child back. You want to be the person you have always dreamed of being. You want to be able to feel magic, or maybe you want to be something else. What could that be?" Cathee said as her voice took on an almost musical tone.

"I need to go home, Chris said. "I need to really go home. Like right now." The excitement in his voice became an almost physical thing in the room.

"Then go. You know what you need to do," Cathee said.

"Andy, I hope you figure out what you need. I know what I want and what I need. I need to remake myself again, but this time I need to embrace it with everything I am.

Chris ran out the door and into the middle of the street. As soon as he did, there was an explosion, but it had no sound. What Andy saw as he watched his friend amazed him. His friend had been engulfed in flame. From those flames, Andy saw a beautiful flaming bird fly skyward.

"I knew he had it in him. He just needed to find himself," Cathee said.

"What the hell just happened?" Andy asked as he turned back to Cathee.

Cathee's eyes locked with his. Her hair seemed to lift from her as if blown by the wind, but there was no wind. Her eyes seemed to glow. She was more beautiful than any woman he had ever seen. He was helpless.

"Now hear me and hear me well. He found what he wanted to be. What do you want to be? Do you want to be stuck in a place with someone you can't evolve with? Or do you want to be like your friend and be more than what you are? Are you going to learn from what you recently discovered? Will you gain the wisdom to move on, or do you become like those ghosts you see? Those people who have no vision. They just exist," Cathee said and held Andy with an unseen force.

"I don't know, I'm afraid." Andy said in a meek voice.

"WHAT DO YOU WANT?" Cathee yelled and grabbed him by the throat. "Do you want to live or exist?"

"I want to live."

"You have finally learned. You have the wisdom you

need. Now make something of yourself. Do like your friend and rebuild yourself." Cathee said with a smile but dropped Andy.

Andy fell into nothingness. The diner was gone, the world was gone, and there was nothing but space around Andy. He fell through stars and galaxies. It felt like he fell for an eternity until he started to fall into a star. It became brighter and brighter as he fell towards it. It became blinding and began to scream.

"I want to live!" Andy screamed as he woke up. He realized it had all been a dream. He fell asleep on his artboard, and the light he saw was that of the sun coming through his window. Andy felt different somehow. He felt lighter and stronger. He looked at his phone. He had five missed calls and fifteen text messages. He cleared everything.

"I gotta move on. I have to live for myself," he whispered.

Andy heard Cathee's voice in his mind, "You're learning."

ATHENA'S LESSON: THE STORY OF MEDUSA
Luna Silverwood

Present Day- Rosie's Bedroom

"Rosie…"

"Rosie…"

"ROSIE! WAKE UP!!!"

The young woman, Rosie, awoke with a start.

"HUH? What? Who's there?" Rosie questioned.

"Really, Rosie. Are you so out of it you can't recognize me?" A woman's voice chuckled.

Rosie whipped her head around to stare at the being of divine grace and beauty. Her hair was dark as the night sky with skin that glowed as bright white as the full moon that shone through Rosie's bedroom window. The being was clad in a flowing, white chiffon dress cinched at the waist by a silver belt. Rosie knew this being. She was none other than her chosen goddess, Selene.

Rosie bowed her head to Selene.

"My lady. Not to be rude, but what are you doing here so late?"

Selene smiled, "No offense taken, my dear. I know that it is late, but I have a visitor who insisted she see you now."

At Selene's words, another divine being appeared. This individual also had dark hair, but her skin was a sun-kissed golden color. She was in an armored battle dress of bronze and steel. Rosie observed this new arrival with curiosity before turning her attention back to the Lady Selene with a questioning look.

"Rosie, please allow me to introduce to you Lady Athena, goddess of Wisdom and Strategies."

Rosie's eyes widened as her gaze returned to the newly identified Athena. "Well met, Lady Athena. What do you require of me this night?"

Athena sighed, "I have come hoping that you will spread the truth of a wrong that has been told throughout history. I have come to tell you the true story of Medusa."

While Rosie was surprised by the statement, she nodded. Settling in against her pillows, "Ok, milady. I'm listening."

Athena took a deep breath and began, "Back in the times of ancient Greece…"

1000 B.C.- The streets of Libya

Medusa, a devoted priestess to Lady Athena, was a woman of unparalleled beauty among mere mortals. Her hair flowed down her back like waves of spun gold, her skin glowed a healthy white like the sands of the finest beaches, and her eyes glowed a spring green of new leaves. Unfortunately, great beauty came with unwanted attention.

Medusa was on her way to tend to Athena's temple when she was stopped. A surge of power swept over her along with the sounds of crashing waves. Before her stood a god, for that was all the entity could be. The god was tall, standing at over six feet in height. His stormy, gray-black hair curled around his ears. His skin was a weathered, golden color of someone who spent their time in the sun and at sea. However, the god's most striking feature was his swirling sea blue eyes that made one think of deep oceans. The god's eyes gave away their identity to Medusa. This was Poseidon, God of the Seas and Earthquakes and Father of all horses.

"Lord Poseidon," Medusa greeted the god with a bow of her head.

Poseidon gave Medusa a slight smirk, "I'm honored that a maiden of such fine beauty is able to see past my mortal shell. May I ask the fair maiden's name?"

"My name is Medusa. How can I assist you?" she asked.

"I'm so glad that you asked. Medusa, I would like to inform you I have chosen you as my new lover."

Medusa stared at Poseidon in shock. "My lord, I'm flattered, but I have to decline your kind offer. I'm a devout priestess of Athena and have taken her vow of celibacy. Now, please excuse me for I have to tend to my goddess."

With a quick bow to the God of the Seas, Medusa made to move past when Poseidon grabbed her arm. Medusa glazed up at Poseidon in alarm.

"Please let go of me. I'm not interested," she pleaded.

It was NOT making a request!" Poseidon snarled, "I will have you!"

"Please, don't do this." Medusa begged. But, she could see that her words had fallen on deaf ears.

1000 B.C.- Athena's Temple

Tears streamed down her face as Medusa ran into her goddess's Temple.

"My lady Athena, please hear my pleas! I need your help!" Medusa cried out.

"I'm here!" Athena said as she appeared before Medusa. Athena took in Medusa's disheveled appearance, torn dress, and tear-stained face before turning to Poseidon who had followed her into the temple. "*WHAT DID YOU DO?*" Athena growled at Poseidon with her power glowing around her form.

Poseidon sauntered forward, hands outstretched in a placating gesture. "I did nothing! Your priestess just broke her vow of celibacy. I was coming to inform you," Poseidon answered.

Athena whirled around to face Medusa. "Is this true?" Athena demanded.

"NO!" Medusa cried. "He took advantage of me when I refused his advances. I would never betray my vows to you, my Lady! Please believe me!"

"She is obviously lying to avoid punishment!" Poseidon objected.

"SILENCE!" Athena yelled with a glare at Poseidon. Turning to Medusa, "I believe you. However, I am bound by ancient laws to punish your perceived betrayal regardless of the circumstances. I'm sorry, but please trust me!"

"Please!" Medusa cried, "I have done nothing wrong.."

"*I NEED YOU TO TRUST ME!*" Athena interrupted. "Don't be afraid. It will all be well."

Medusa closed her eyes with resignation, feeling Lady Athena's power expand before exploding around her.

She could feel her Lady's power flow through her, warm and comforting, while it changed her very being. Her long golden hair changed to a mass of twisting black and green serpents while her once glowing, white skin turned a deep stone-colored gray, her eyes dulled to a green-tinted white.

"No one will harm you ever again," Athena murmured to Medusa. "To those who cross you, turn them to stone!"

Medusa, feeling her newly given powers flow through her, began to cry at the feet of her goddess with relief.

Athena smiled down at her priestess before turning to Poseidon with a glare. "I'm sure that your wife would love to hear about this crime that you have committed!" Athena sneered.

Present Day- Rosie's Bedroom

"After I informed Lady Amphitrite of Poseidon's transgressions, I whisked Medusa away to the island of Sarpedon to recover and relax from her ordeal," Athena explained. "Medusa chose to stay on the island, to protect herself and others. However, a mortal is not meant to live an immortal life unless their minds are expanded into that of god or goddess. The weight of Medusa's powers drove her to madness and changed her into a true monster. When Perseus was sent by King Polydectes to slay Medusa, I helped by gifting him with a shield that helped him end her life. I gave her kindness and mercy, not cruelty and vengeance like the current myths depict. Please, help me correct this injustice to Medusa's memory!"

"Thank you for telling me Medusa's true story, Lady Athena." Rosie breathed, "I will do my best to spread the truth of Medusa to the world. You have my word!"

"Thank you," Athena sighed with relief. "Selene was right in having me come to you. For your help and aid, I bless you with wisdom in battle and in life. May your enemies tremble before you and your words be as sharp as your sword!" With her piece said, Athena departed.

Rosie turned to her goddess. "My Lady, how am I to spread the truth of Medusa's story where people will actually listen?" she questioned.

Selene smiled, "My dear Rosie, you are intelligent. I would not have brought Athena here if I did not believe you could successfully help her. I believe in you. Go forth with your task and know that I am always here to help and guide you." With her words of wisdom, Selene took her leave.

"What am I to do now?" Rosie complained to her now empty room. As she glazed around looking for inspiration, Rosie's eyes landed on her computer.

"Hmm…," Rosie hummed. "I have an idea!"

Knowing that sleep was a lost cause, Rosie rose from her bed, and sat at her desk. After turning it on, she opened a blank word document, and hummed to herself.

"Let's see. Where to begin…," she muttered to herself. "Oh, I know."

Rosie began to type, "Let me tell you a story that has been twisted through time and history…"

Brianna Raptor and the Halloween Problems
P. Carter

The moonlight beats in the house's windows like they're the party's heartbeat. I smile. The car and our campaign signs have been vibrating for blocks from the non-Halloween music thumping in the school auditorium, across the street from that house. But houses are built to insulate people from noise and its effects.

Also: Thank you, acoustics, for not being that *other* science. Even with my mother being less bad, I'd still rather go a year without sex than acknowledge …

I glance at my love, Samantha, who stuffed her radiant purple hair under a brown wig for our campaign's Halloween party and our ensuing trick-or-treating. Then I refocus on the road. And here's the parking lot. Finally, an event where we won't have to use our special favors: for me, furrowing my eyebrows to read people for trouble they think is problems and problems whose solutions inconvenience them; for her, communicating with animals.

I still have my sunglasses ready in case, though. I touch my pocket to reconfirm.

As Samantha takes a selfie of us to text her mother (I smile), she squeezes my hand, jamming her wedding ring into my finger, then releases. I grin. I love feeling the ring I put on her finger. I love that she trusts me enough not to ask if she squeezed too hard or if I remember when she accepted that pain doesn't always equal love.

I park near where I used to. Samantha yanks her hand away and becomes a green blur out of the car.

I don't.

I still struggle to believe she and I graduated fifteen months ago. To believe Devin's graduation'll be the last time I come here until our ten-year reunion or something.

Maybe a campaign event. Whatever. It won't be the same. My heart is hurting from it all, like I abandoned someone who did nothing wrong. But no high school has a thirteenth grade, and I've been ready for more since before my friends and I canceled Sinclair.

… the green beside me. Samantha. Right. I exhale school nostalgia, step into the cold and the harder thumping, and she's facing me, the moon shining in her eyes and on her three makeup freckles, which have risen past the bottom of her nose, she's beaming so hard. And the cold has reddened her cheeks. It's her favorite shade of blush: frigid air.

My heart fills. I love my girl.

She points behind me. "Two raccoons playing in the back," she says. Her buttery baritone melts me like I'm hearing it for the first time.

"Owls. Crickets, ladybugs. Snails," she says as she looks around us. Then she looks to me. She beams. "They all say everything's super fine. … well. *Technically*, they super loathe the noise. But …"

She squeezes my hands. I stand and lean in, touching my costumed chest to hers, my cheek to those freckles, and my lips to her ear.

I close my eyes and relish her heartbeat. Her warmth. The excitement of our hearts pounding harder as I move a hand to her hip.

Nongod, her hips. *H-o-w.*

… I'm salivating. I swallow.

"Your hips … are …"

She pants. Her pulse races under my fingers. She releases my other hand — it zips to her other hip like they're gay-magnetized for each other — and plants her hands over my repurposed fur-lined robe against the sides of my bra.

I grip her hips and nod. This isn't about to be sex — she needs other things, so I need them too — but a year of long distance with her was an agonizing lifetime, and eighteen months of sleeping next to her have flitted by in eighteen milliseconds.

She kisses her way toward that spot under my ear. Her cheek is hot against mine, her pulse thumping with the music.

My heartbeat quickens. I damn near rip her shorts unbuttoning and unzipping 'em. Then I nibble on her earlobe.

"I want a wifely favor, not a special favor."

"The music n'at now counts as the party," she whispers.

Her lips ki — touch that spot. And she taps on my bra clasps.

My heartbeat nears light speed. Finally, she's teasing me. I close my eyes, jam my fingers into the belt loops on her hips, and pull her into our thumping car.

She unhooks my bra and closes the door.

How? Whatever. She lowers her head to tease-kiss me.

… okay that was a fantastic five seconds of teasing,

but now I need to be fucked. I sink my hands into her hips and *pull*. She braces against me. She beams. Her eyes fill with mischief.

I let go of her hips and slide two f —

My phone buzzes with B's emergency chomp signal.

Fffuck. My jaw shakes, and I clench all five fingers into a fist and slam it against my seat. This had better be bigger than the fucking nuclear codes.

She shrugs. "We'll get through it together, love," she says as she offers a light squeeze of my fist on her way to my phone, which she pulls from my pocket and scans.

Better her than me. B's been my best friend since forever, but unless they or Howard are dying, sex with my wife trumps their every blah disappearing message app blah, aka chomps.

"A boy who has accepted the campaign's special favors deal wants you to do yours in Sinclair's old room. 'And yes, he knows,'" Samantha says as she chomps back. She glances at me. "I said we'd be a minute."

I fume. In a minute, I will feed that boy into a metaphorical woodchipper. I would furrow him out here, to confirm he's committing campaign suicide because he has minor trouble, but I don't want to think about emotionally immature man-children while my wife's straddling me and my bra's begging to be practically ripped off.

She slides my phone back in, then positions herself where my hands are. Her eyes meet mine. She bites her lip. "I was going to tease you down to your underguchies, love, but …" she shakes her head.

She lowers it until she's touching that spot.

Squeezes my hand.

Plants it on her hip.

"One minute."

We switch positions. I suck between her hips. She clutches my hair out of its bun as she pants. And she —

My alarm buzzes.

My alarm buzzes? How the fuck did —

She set it for one minute when she was chomping.

I rage-fix my hair.

She squeezes my hand. I look to her.

She blushes. "Do you like the confidence?"

I like*d* the getting-fucked part. But I smile as I squeeze her hand. I'm whole. I can wait. She …

"Love it. And you."

She kisses me. Slides inside me and *presses* and *Jesus fuck there's teasing and there's tormenting,* and I'm panting, my hips are pressing into her, and fuck we can spare *four minutes* I *can* get there that fast, and then we'll w —

She slides her fingers out.

I.

Suck.

In.

Air.

Samantha sniffs her fingers, grins at me, then grabs a cloth one of our friends invented and removes my scent from herself.

My heart breaks. My hips die. And I redress myself, shove on my FL-41 sunglasses on general principle and furrow my eyebrows. The boy who wants me to read him — who I am hereby naming Fuckface — wants face time. My mission in life is now to give him as little as possible. Fortunately, most of his situation is already obvious: In cashing in his Empathy Party volunteer hours tonight, he will be barred from all future party opportunities, which means he plans to rejoin his original political party. He didn't haggle on the matter, which tells me weak establish Democrat from a family whose political power has decayed for decades. It originated in … a military great-grandfather settling on Maryland's Eastern Shore. Democrats there care about the environment and crabs. But Democrats there haven't cared about him. He's torching his place in our party so he can return to them, so he wants something niche. Unreasonable. Pettiness-saturated. Privacy-invading. Now, in asking to meet in a place he "knows" my friends and I socially condemned, he's seeking shock value and importance. That means … surveillance outside a crab restaurant on the shore.

But the restaurant's safety isn't the thing. What is? … an emotional support object near it. To furrow out which, I'll have to do at least a quick, sunglass-free glance.

Samantha hands me our other cloth. I remove her scent from my mouth and fingers, and then she prances, and I fume into the night.

***

The purple, gleaming, ceramic Susannah-for-President jack-o'-lanterns framing the school's front doors can go fuck themselves.

Samantha prances between 'em on her way in, then beams at the purple Halloween/campaign decorations on the walls and waves at random campaign staff passing to or from the party.

I narrow my eyes and look to Sinclair's door. B is standing in front of it, cringing, in their purple 3 costume. We trade lone waves, and then they bolt for the party. Samantha and I reach the door and face it, and I … giggle. Fuckface has picked this room in which to castrate himself socially and professionally, deliciously disrupting Sinclair's villainous refusal to ever admit any guilt whatsoever.

I place my hand on the doorknob.

Samantha squeezes my other hand. … up and down.

I turn to her. She's crying.

I nod. And since she doesn't want more — doesn't want comfort from memories of Francis torturing her for thirteen consecutive Halloweens — I don't give it to her. Instead, I wait, and I type on my phone, then show her once she's done:

"This doesn't count as the party, love."

She grins. Wipes her eyes. Points at the door. "And neither does talking to the guy in there."

Fuck. My heart plummets, but I nod. My love has a thing for the wounded, so I'll do my pseudo-therapist thing.

I place my sunglasses in my robe pocket, open the door and furrow out Fuckface, who in the long term is hiding his problem under trouble he has shielded with light emotional inconvenience. In the short term, now that I've let the thumping music invade, he has clamped his hands over his ears and is cringing through the emotional immaturity of that imported self-importance. He is also manspreading in a blanket of a ratty green T-shirt that screams *I'm the reason you're here.* It's a keepsake from his grandparents. They had a favorite shore restaurant and a favorite bench outside it. When his grandmother died, his family bought naming rights to the bench. And he collapsed emotionally.

His twitching feet tell me he's a skater. He wants surveillance to catch other skaters violating an anti-skating ordinance in front of the bench, particularly if they're exposing their underwear, which his grandmother loathed. And he wants them to apologize, since fines don't work on beach bros. I ignore his hopelessly shouted complaints about the music volume, find him in the campaign directory, find the bench and the restaurant, then chomp him, Ted, and B using the regular notification:

Video surveillance enforcing a new ordinance requiring anyone caught skateboarding, particularly with their underwear exposed, in front of the Sophie and Thomas Smith Memorial Bench near Shakey's Crab Shack on the Talbot County boardwalk to apologize.

Samantha closes the door behind us, and as Fuckface bleats emotional immaturity, we sit on either side of him.

I look to him.

"When your grandmother died when you were eleven, you lost your Saturdays with her: on the boardwalk, at the restaurant, on the bench. As a typical cry for help processing the grief, you stopped maturing emotionally. But nobody offered help. The support structure your grandmother had raised you on failed you, so you awkwardly invaded the beach bro culture she had disdained, figuring someone there would at least react. But again, nobody came. As a last gasp, you joined the Empathy Party. Our people have cared about you, but we're not the Democrats your grandmother raised you on, so every time you've helped us, you've felt like you were betraying her."

Do I tell him about Grandma Amy? … no. He needs to heal a little first.

I glance at the door behind us, then return to him. "You picked this room because you wanted me to excoriate you for deliberately getting us so close to where Sinclair hurt all those girls. I'm not a therapist, but I can tell you need someone to talk to. Fortunately, once Susannah and everyone else is in office, we'll be passing Medicare for All, which'll make mental health carefree at the point of service. Will you be okay waiting that long?"

His problem floods his eyes. "First hundred days,

right?"

I nod.

He does too.

I smile. "I left the rest on your phone." As he looks, I get up, and Samantha dances us to the auditorium doors, where B and Howard are waiting. The four of us quick-hug, Samantha texts her mother another selfie and shows me the "lovely, sweetheart" response, and we all stroll into the party.

B and Howard peel off soon — I offer a wave in their direction — and then everyone else ignores me and Samantha as she prances us to the back corner. She sets her phone alarm, plants my hands on her hips and her hands a hair's breadth under my bra and pulls us as close as we were in the car.

My heart races. "Tease!" I shout in her ear as I heat up.

She nods, and her cheek and body burn against mine, and she slides her hands up my bra.

I quiver. *So* close. But I need to be able to stand, for her, so I endure the burning and heart racing, and we close our eyes and sway to the music, which is slow in the only place it has to be: our hearts.

And in this moment, I am not a senior adviser. I am not the person who furrows out everyone's problems. I am Notorious, I am Samantha Raptor's wife, and I am a face in a crowd.

Her phone vibrates near where her fingers were in the car. *Her alarm*, I realize as I quiver. She releases me and stops it, and suddenly I'm aching and shivering.

I need her.

But she needs trick-or-treating, and I'll survive the hour she needs of that, so as I put my sunglasses on again, she takes another selfie, shows me her mother's latest enthusiastic reaction, then squeezes my hand and walks me to the door as everyone else ignores us again.

****

She's clutching my hand as she hoots back at an owl, gushes over Ted's Halloween map on her phone for the billionth time, and prances down the steps and toward the car. The map's lavender petals are saturating my sunglasses and eyes, but I've raced down these steps too many times to mess 'em up this time.

She happy sighs. "All these nice Empathy Party supporters. All this candy." She points at a petal and looks to me. "Starting with Sherry Hammerstein."

Shit. My heart breaks, and tears threaten to flood my eyes. This is what I get for not furrowing out Ted. Sherry must have insisted that he put her first — and who can say no to their old, kindly first-grade teacher? Ten years ago, I blazed a trail to her place.

But ten years ago, she … remembered my name.

Samantha doesn't know about her.

We pass another row of cars.

Sherry stopped driving two years ago. I think she still tutors some, but … and now my tears are a hot flash flood down my cooling cheeks.

Cooling. Samantha cherishes the cold.

I want her to cherish her first safe Halloween in thirteen years, too, so I district myself gloriously with the night re-reddening her cheeks, the safety saturating her beaming smile, and the moon dotting her eyes like a refuge in that one dwarf star's brown storm. Give her a pastel dress and turn some of those digital lavender petals real and she could be a midnight winter wedding flower girl.

She prances us down an aisle that exists only in my head, chatting with her animals all the while, then settles into

-186-

the driver's seat, ending the imaginary wedding and the real conversation.

She squeezes my hand. Turns to me. "Did you want to talk about what's wrong, love?"

I nod, then dry my eyes. "Please don't correct Sherry."

"Okay," she says in her everything'll-be-okay-no-matter-what voice.

And she drives.

During the day, our campaign signs are an unobtrusive purple amid the blue and yellow and red here in our suburb and around the country. But at night, light transforms them into unobtrusive beacons of empathy — and, on this night, sugar. Soon Samantha is beaming as she nestles us in among other cars on the street beside Equality Park's parking lot, which probably filled before dark. She snatches her rainbow canvas bag and bounds toward Sherry's purple sign — and lavender house — like she's a little girl again and her birthday party starts there in five minutes.

As I work my way there and other kids walk toward the next house, shaking their heads at and re-enacting what they just saw, she brakes at Sherry's door. Her head snaps around, and she motions for me like if I don't teleport there, she won't get candy. I dash to her and slide my hand into hers, we do another selfie, she enjoys another reaction from her mother, and then she raps on Sherry's door.

I prepare to not cry.

"Just a second," Sherry says. Soon the door cracks open.

"Trick-or-treat! Hope your day's been sweet!" Samantha says.

Sherry glances at my face, then lingers on Samantha's, furrows, and returns to mine. Its comfort soothes her furrow, energizes her cheeks, and lights the dimming personality candle in her eyes and smile. "Brianna Carter and Notorious," she says. "Two of my favorite women."

My heart aches. Notorious died less than six weeks ago, and I haven't been Brianna Carter in eighteen months. I squeeze Samantha's hand to purge pain that must not — cannot — flood my face.

Sherry furrows again, then squints above us. Points. "Who raked the leaves? And what's that purple —"

Lady, you're killing my heart. "Empathy Party volunteers and yard sign," I say as I grip-clutch-torture my love's hand and force the joy of days past into my eyes and heart. "Our presidential nominee, Susannah Martinez, is queer and brown, and we have a whole slate running to save the planet and the peasants from the oligarchy."

She beams. "Excellent!" Curiosity fills her face, and she looks left. "We're voting for Susannah Martinez, right, uh …"

Anabel, I think as I look away and cough through anguish-saturated sobs.

"We voted early for the entire Empathy Party slate in your kitchen," Anabel says.

"Excellent!" Sherry says. "Does we have a chance?"

I dry my face on my sleeve and steel my heart against

—

"Ask Brianna. She's a senior adviser."

That.

Sherry turns to me. "I didn't vote for losers, did I?"

Ahhh. I laugh, and my heart heals a little. "You voted for winners my wife and I helped recruit, Sherry."

Sherry laughs. "Excellent." She grabs two candy six-packs from the bowl beside her. "Share with your mothers — we like these," she says as she drops a pack in each of our bags.

She looks to us and raises her eyebrows. "Now. Would you like to see a *brief, slightly* scary 'trick'?"

"Always, Sherry," I say as Samantha's eyes balloon.

Sherry smiles.

Her teeth transform into a fanged, jagged, bloody … and back into her regular teeth.

"Jesus fuck you're a shark," Samantha sputters as she pants like we're having sex and mangles my hand like she's terrorgasming.

Sherry cackles, and her eyes light up. "Excellent. Have a lovely rest of your night."

We wave goodbye.

"That was," Samantha pants as she loosens her grip, and we walk toward another supporter's house. "I don't *want* to talk to *that* animal."

I beam. "Last year, you would have jumped out of your underwear — and not in the sexy way."

Samantha snorts. "Still weird to hear underguchies called that."

I smile. You can take the girl out of Pittsburgh, but you can't take the Pittsburgh out of the girl.

The next house lacks shark faces. So do the next five, and the next twenty, and eventually Samantha is favoring her left side because our bags are getting heavy.

An owl hoots.

Samantha hoots back.

Side-eyes me.

Drops my hand and her bag.

"Boys. Trouble. Ahead."

She sprints for them, chirping and hooting and otherwise amassing her critter army along the way.

I grab her bag.

She slows to an angry trudge, then aims herself at a

tall bush. She isn't signaling to me, so I pocket my sunglasses, furrow, and tiptoe into the now-slightly-lighter darkness of a non-supporter's leafless lawn to help. And I furrow.

"Did they stop, captain?" asks a boy behind the bush. A follower.

"Doesn't matter, cadet," says a taller boy as he stays facing down a boy who's a head shorter. "The law is the law."

His dad's a cop.

Samantha stands tall, her cheeks red with justice. "No, yinz, *they* did not stop!"

That justice rages through my body. She can't go back in time to save herself, but she can save this kid. So, can I. I'm not a therapist, and I don't want to be one, but this is a problem, and I will solve it.

"Oh, shit," a third boy says. He and a fourth boy step onto the sidewalk, but I keep my eyes on the tall and short boys.

The shorter one's been taught by someone emotionally close to him — his mother — to let people hurt him so they'll finish and leave.

His face paint is smudged. It was white with black lettering, which is why the other boys' fingers are black and white. They torment him daily.

Samantha's animals speak to her. She shakes her head. "We're scaring predators and helping their victim."

The small boy's eyes flit left, like he was just granted a sliver of hope that someone might magically save him. … an older brother who can drive and isn't in college or busy.

I activate dark mode on my phone, then text B.

Shifty-seeming guy at the party, 16-17, has a younger brother who's here solo. Not by choice.

Samantha marches up to the tall boy with her army behind her like a force of nature waiting to swarm something and devour it whole.

"That's that animal whisperer chick from Susannah's campaign, Br — captain," a sidewalk boy says.

The fake captain — the tall boy — scoffs at his underling. "Animal tricks are a distraction, cadet. We will maintain law and order until they defund us." His father believes comforting lies about our call to defund people who "fear for their lives" when they see black construction paper, let alone a black person. So, whereas his pupils have dilated a quarter of an inch because he reveres Samantha's ability to talk to bears and whatnot, he's channeled that awe into disdain because he worships his father.

… don't need to know that. Do need to know about the small boy. I refocus on him. Beneath the customary layer of fear in his face is chronic and acute longing that says his father keeps not showing up — including tonight, when he was supposed to have custody. But as they were readying their costumes, he said something like *you don't need my help — look how good you've done on your own!* and then skipped out, yet again, so he could devote his whole night to getting high off smaller kids delighting in his costume: the Easter bunny.

Emotionally immature asshole.

Parents are divorced. Father is an extrovert. Travels for work.

Any younger siblings? … no guarded peace, no jealousy.

Two boys in the family. Mother has primary custody. Browbeats them when they want her attention. Older kid drove himself to the party. He's probably ducked out four times to guilt-check his phone.

Samantha steps in front of the fake captain and offers the small boy her hand. He stands there. Doesn't move. Because where will she be in two days when the tall boy and his followers are suddenly looming over him in some corner of the cafeteria the teachers can't see?

Temporary versus permanent solutions. One of the things trauma taught Samantha.

Her pets advance on the fake captain's fake cadets, whose eyes and shiftiness grow as their breathing shortens. The short boy is too busy showing the tall boy he fears him to bother.

… fear. I met Stanley Richardson and his mother, but never his father or brother. I check the campaign app. Jason, Stanley's younger brother, is gay, and his special favor is information recall. But how do I prove … hmm. The costume is … was lettering. Wing — no. A cardboard — the white of his face paint with a thin, gray border that's been torn away. Lettering … slanted, straight, slanted and straight … W. I. K? — oh. That's an information recall costume. I chomp Samantha his name. She checks her phone. Nods. Pockets it. Re-extends her hand.

"Hi, Jason. Sorry about your costume. Want help?"

He again is too scared to look. Reminds me of her before she chose to leave.

I resume texting B, and I add Stanley.

Samantha and I are helping Jason. Stanley, drive to one block shy of your house at 10.

We'll take him and Jason home, and I'll furrow out

and help their mother, who has problems. Now, the fake captain: He's peering down over Jason, his arms bent and his legs wide. Scraps of papers are strewn at their feet. He had his fake cadets rip up that part of Jason's costume.

His father has raised him to think he's untouchable. That's why he has a real-looking fake cop badge on his belt buckle, under his shirt.

I play a hunch and start recording on my phone.

"Move along, miss," the tall boy says as he sidesteps her and pulls his shirt hem left to reveal his badge — a toy — "or I'll have to command one of my cadets to —"

Samantha's fingers dance in and out of her pocket. Then she hoots.

Her owls divebomb his fake cadets.

They flee, screaming into the night.

The fake captain's eyes dart up and around briefly, and he shrinks a little and watches his fake cadets run as his arms tighten and his hands fly to his zipper.

But no owls are coming for him.

Yet.

He scoffs and attempts to dominate Samantha.

"Interfering with official police business. Section 3.2-6555. I'll write you up, then get this miscreant —" he points at Jason "— for accessory to littering."

Samantha's owls return and resume circling over her head. She shows him something on her phone.

He glances. Scoffs. Puffs out his chest. "*I might hurt him.*"

Jason cringes. Samantha offers a soft smile as she pockets her phone, then turns again to the fake captain and gestures at her army.

"From this day forward, when my animals sense you being unkind, they will come for you. Do you need proof? I gather from your 'animal whisperer chick' friend that yinz saw my special on the importance of respecting the destructive forces of nature."

He smirks. "Eagle News destroyed your 'special.' But that did sound like a terroristic threat, so I have no choice but to arrest —"

She jabs a finger at her pocket. "*Super* fake-arrest me while I record you committing multiple violations of 18.2-174. I'll send the video to the chief of police. He attended my wedding."

The fake captain pants, and his eyes balloon.

Samantha grins. "Now …"

She chirps.

Hoots.

Chitters.

Her owls divebomb him.

The rest of her army swarms his legs.

He swats and cowers.

Shrieks.

Kicks.

Falls.

Gets swarmed up to his neck.

Flaps and kicks.

Whimpers.

"Make it stooop!"

Samantha stands over him, lightning raging in her stormy brown eyes, and plants her fists on her hips.

"You first."

He pants. "Okay! Okay! I swear!"

She chirp-hoot-chitters her animals off. He scrambles up, bolts past streetlight after streetlight and becomes a silhouette.

She scowls and squints in his direction.

"Jagoff."

I squeeze her hand and gaze upon her justice-reddened cheeks. "Your compassion is unmatched, my love. You were spectacular. As you always are."

She shrugs. Gestures at Jason.

I nod, then look to him. His eyes stay on Samantha, like she's proved herself to him, but I haven't — even though he's seen me defeat political bully after bully on cable entertainment shows.

None of them were the fake captain. To prove myself to Jason, I need to do what he needs, not what the country needs.

I point at my bag, since Samantha long ago taught me traumatized people don't trust smiles. "I would love to help you enjoy the rest of your trick-or-treating. And then Stanley'll …"

His lips contract, then relax just as fast. He doesn't want me to know Stanley isn't what he's worried about.

He looks between us at the darkness the fake captain fled into.

Samantha nods. "Take as long as you need. Trusting safety can feel like trusting a bully who's suddenly being nice."

My heart breaks. I wish she didn't know this horrific stuff. I wish nobody did.

"Trust," he says like he's trying out the word. He walks toward where the fake captain disappeared. Jogs around that first streetlight. Stops in the relative darkness ahead.

Comes back to us.

His trust issues aren't as bad as Samantha's were, but he has a problem. I will start solving it tonight. I just need more infor —

"Please don't read me?" he asks like he's graduated from trying trust as a word to trying it as a concept.

I shove my sunglasses on.

"Thanks," he says. "If … I could ask for — and I know she already said no, but … read my mom?"

I nod. Samantha squeezes my hand. Jason offers a brief, slight smile, then looks to Samantha and shakes her hand.

And he starts wailing. He flings his arms around her and buries his face in her shirt like she did with me eighteen months ago. "There you go," she says as she nods, drops my hand, and strokes his back.

I stand there, preventing my breaking and soaring heart from violating their moment. Because right now, he needs the person he trusts to be the only thing happening to him, and she needs this person she helped to be the only thing happening to her. Because eighteen months ago, she started working on herself so she could be for other people what I was for her. And because every time she gets to be, she gets to help herself, too, because she's telling herself she's better.

Many minutes later, they let go of each other. He dries his fa — his face sinks into his hands. And he slides them down, exposing the second-most terror-saturated set of eyes I've ever witnessed.

"My mom can fix your shirt! Please! Pl —"

She smiles, and she pets his cheek. "Wanna watch my animals fix it — and your costume?"

His eyes grow like she just said she's going to fix all of his problems. He tucks his hands behind himself like he's making way for her animals, and she grins, then chirp-hoot-chitters.

Her ladybugs crawl onto her shirt, grab flecks of face paint, and give them to her raccoons. One of them jumps into Jason's arms and lets him pet it. The others clean the flecks, then give them back to her ladybugs, who crawl onto his face to reapply it. Snails crawl over the edges of the paper scraps, gluing them back together, and owls bite the corners of his posterboard, then flap them back into place. The job done, her animals settle behind her, leaving him to enjoy.

He nods. Feels around. Offers a smile. "Solid." … that's emotionally limited. Why? I lower my head, elevate my gaze and furrow.

He doesn't have a phone. His mother won't let him have one because she insists he's not mature enough, so he can't see that Samantha's animals fixed the costume he spent an hour doing in his father's bathroom mirror. I give him my phone, and as he looks at and feels for everything, and nods as he confirms he's good as new, his offered smile grows into a Jason-healing beam.

"Didn't belittle me or skip out early," he whispers.

Yes, indeed, I am going to fix this *set* of problems.

He takes a selfie of us all, then sends it to Samantha, who shows us her mother reacting. And she pets his cheek again. "How about a physical treat?" She points at me. "I love holding her hand, but I'm feeling like something else right now. Wanna?"

She holds her hand out.

He fixates on it and clutches it like it's going to fix his problems.

Then he beams at me.

"You furrowed out who I was and chomped Samantha my name, right? That's the power Linda and Jo gave you? Because otherwise, that was something out of Athena's playbook."

Athena? Samantha and I trade puzzled looks.

Jason laughs. "Greek goddess of wisdom."

I shrug. Smile. "Okay." Remembering that stuff is

Lucy's job, not mine, but he doesn't need to be shot down.

He looks at her owls. "Might be wise to bring along some striges. That's the plural of strix, which is Latin for owl."

I shrug and smile again. Samantha communicates to her animals, who amass behind and above him. His eyes balloon, and he struts, with Samantha, toward the next house. I walk beside them.

He knocks on the door. Someone answers. "Trick *and* treat!" he says.

"… *and?*" the homeowner asks.

He nods. "You give me a noun. I make a fact sheet about it for you. You give me candy."

"Hmm. … Halloween," the homeowner says.

Soon we have candy, and the homeowner has a fact sheet. The next homeowner asks about kidney beans, and the one after about dogs, and so on.

Soon my alarm dings. We turn left, walk a few blocks, and there's Stanley, dressed as the socialist prisoner who ran for president over and over. He trudges toward us, his face long and low and his bag of candy almost dragging on the sidewalk.

We reach each other. He holds the bag out for Jason. "Sorry. This is for you."

"No thank you." Jason leans in, and his jaw and cheeks move. Stanley's eyebrows shoot up. Then they plummet, and he whispers back.

This is a family of problems. I will solve them.

They hold our hands, and we walk toward the next house. Stanley turns to Jason. "Anyone ask for a dog fact sheet?"

Jason nods. "Three."

Ooh. That … I look to Samantha. "Can you get

something for the boys? I'll arrange for everything, and it'll take you out of their mother's line of fire."

She nods. Clutches my hand like I'll flee if she doesn't. I chomp her, then B. And then Daddy.

****

Leafless lawn, but no sign.

Control.

Jason and Stanley take off their shoes and walk past the bag of candy their mother, Tina, has left out.

Pre-compliance with a shoe policy. In the cold. And dark.

Stanley opens the door.

"Shoes, damnit!" Tina hollers as he and Jason deposit their shoes in a padded bin by the door.

They bolt upstairs … silently.

I deposit my rainbow boots in the bin, pocket my sunglasses and close the door.

"Mind if I furrow?" I ask as I take in the lemony scent and social media-worthy decor.

And all. These. Photographs.

"I … guess not," Tina says like she just got caught.

Emotional maturity. Good. There's hope. Now, what do the photographs say?

The oldest, on the living room's near wall, are a foursome of her and Stanley the day she gave birth to him. She's glowing, exhausted, and elated. Across from them, on the mantle, is a picture from six months later.

She's a mess.

… no. Mom is a mess in our six-month photos. Tina is a set of symptoms. Subsequent photos show symptoms worsening until Jason's third birthday party. Then, on his fourth birthday party, she's only a mess. I research on my phone to confirm postpartum depression.

My heart sinks. I hate being right about awful things.

"Stanley, help Jason at least *try* to wash his face! Please!" Tina hollers at her sons as she scrubs the sliding glass back door in her bathrobe. She looks at me, then refocuses on where her sons went. "And put on some music so Bianca and I can talk — in *private*."

I'll correct the name later. For now, the stairs. Twenty-one photos of her sons' birthday parties. They're trophies, but she doesn't understand why.

Music that combines classical and hard rock starts playing upstairs.

Now, again: the photos. They display pristine tablecloths, gorgeous cakes, perfectly arranged spreads, her immaculate living room, and neither symptomatic eyes nor birthday boys. The point is *look at how clean and perfect this party was*, not *look how happy everyone is*.

… she's eying at me as she scrubs. I turn to her. She stops scrubbing and allows a partial smile. Sighs. "Your special was impressive."

She's still terrified.

I smile. "Thank you. We'll start with help for you. And praise."

Her lips tighten, and her eyes narrow.

"Praise."

She doesn't trust me.

She gets back to scrubbing, and I get back to her photographs.

The photos framing the lowest stairs give way to graduation photos, a few photos from work, one with her in jeans with her sons, and — the lone image by her bedroom door — one of her in those jeans with a guy in a hiding spot in daylight. After she took that, they kissed. The picture from after that kiss is on her phone, but any thought of dating him is neutered by her self-medicating tight grip on her life.

… where are her wedding photos? Not here, not on the fridge, not in the living room. She's buried them in a place only she can access.

But her ex didn't cheat on her. He's an extrovert. When she had postpartum depression, he saw her struggling and combined both of their needs by getting a job at a baby product company.

But she didn't need advice or prototypes. She needed *him*.

He was laser-focused on Stanley.

She saw that. Got pregnant again so he'd laser-focus on her. And he did. But the second she gave birth, he laser-focused on the new baby. She ran herself ragged caring for a baby and trying to wrest his attention away from it, but it and work were letting him binge energy, so her postpartum depression issued him an ultimatum: work or home.

Twelve years later, he still chooses work. She still chooses home. And she revels in the fact that he has abandoned any pretense of choosing home: He uses a cleaning service, and he misses some visitation weekends to attend trade shows. She, on the other hand, spends her nonwork time cleaning and doing other boring things for her sons, and she feels superior to him.

That dates back to when she accidented into self-medicating with cleaning because the laundry piles were epic. As her brain healed, she found power and control in cleaning and furnishing. Today, she has a hospital room-worthy glass door and a social media-worthy everything else, including the dining room's gleaming mahogany table and chairs and the kitchen's stainless-steel fridge, whose magnets bear four Mother's Day art projects from between when she stopped being sick and when her kids stopped using construction paper in art class. Every project is colorful, intact, and flawless, and every project helps her maintain a fantasy in which her children are young. Cute. Guided.

Immature.

They took their shoes off before they entered the house, but she was expecting them to mess that up. She was also expecting them to mess up face washing. And she didn't ask how trick-or-treating went — doing so would have given them a chance to talk about something they did well, even if she wasn't there to see it.

She's stunting them emotionally and socially because she sees her ex-husband's energy in the carefree, energetic things they do, and she can't punish him, so she's punishing them. They probably hole up in their rooms unless they're eating, and they don't clean up after — she'd browbeat them if they offered or tried. The only cleaning she trusts is the cleaning she does.

She cleans this house like it's her third — and only obedient — child. Everything is in its place, from the chairs to the construction paper to the trash can, which is tucked in a cabinet a carpenter built for her a decade ago.

That was his second job in this house.

Okay. That's this part of the house. Now I head down the two stairs to the living room. Leather sofas that look like they were delivered today frame a gleaming mahogany coffee table with no shelves for books or games. On its near side, two padded chairs are jammed between the sofas, and at the far side, a loveseat is jammed against the sofas.

The seating arrangement is for looking at, not using. There's no television, no gaming system, no bookcases, only brick wall. And to inhibit snacking, the kitchen is largely walled off. She sits alone on the near sofa sometimes, looking at the mantle and her most haggard photos, reburying herself in her trauma and her victory.

Right now, though, she's scrubbing that door with a blue sponge on a gray stick. Her hair's in a towel, and she's enveloped herself in a bathrobe with tightened sleeves. Her phone is in her right pocket, but that pocket doesn't look baggy. It looks new.

Her whole robe does.

Every Mother's Day since Jason was four, she has dumped her kids at her mom's house and gone to her emotional support home goods store, communed with the products in its cleaning aisle — her safe space — and then gone to the bathrobe aisle to pick her new second skin. She's had the sleeves tightened for cleaning, then collected her kids and gone home. No celebratory meal, no flowers, nothing else.

Lonely.

But the alternative is to trust. The closest she gets too trusting is her not-boyfriend. She has her phone there in case he chomps. She humblebrags to him about her house in chomps and on two social media platforms, on which they share their love privately. At her request, he chomps suggestively about "cleaning up" the results of him thinking about her at the same time every night, after the boys are in bed and before she's too tired to get what she wants as a result. I'm thinking 11:37.

… I think I have enough. We'll talk about all her problems: postpartum depression, her sons' responsibility, therapy with so-much-not-me. And I'll modify the dog thing. I chomp Samantha, and we're set.

I look to Tina.

She sighs, places her sponge stick in her cleaning bucket, and gestures at the love seat, her eyes filling with dread.

"It's not that I don't trust you. It's that …"

I nod. She places herself on the love seat. I join her. She glances at me.

"Not to curry favor — which I probably can't — but your Notorious costume is amazing. The look's the thing. 'I dissent. In your face. With a flamethrower.'"

We chuckle. I've went as Notorious for Halloween since I was six, so that makes sense. Mom was upset, but that prize-winning mother-daughter chemist duo's dissent game is weak.

Tina sighs like I'm about to say she overcleans. "I should have put our Susannah sign out. Just … cleaning and …"

I nod. I gesture at her house. "Amazing. Immaculate. Which social media brands have featured it?"

She beams. Exhales. "I have photos of the stories in my bedroom."

I grin.

She sighs again, and her shoulders fall. Reminds me of Mom pre-therapy. "But they're lifestyle brands, not parenting magazines."

I nod. "Not your fault. You —"

She blinks.

Hard.

"Not my fault."

I gesture to the mantle. "Grab the photos of you from when Stanley was one, from when Jason was one, and from when Jason was four."

She groans as she gets up. Then she places the photographs on the coffee table and places herself beside me again.

I point to spots in the photos. "Hopelessness." She nods and sighs. I point to more spots. "Feelings of inadequacy." She nods and sighs again. And more spots. "Withdrawing from your children. Loss of appetite. And more." Then I show her the postpartum depression page in my browser app.

She exhales. Bites her lips. Furrows her eyebrows. Looks to me.

"I had that?"

I pocket my phone and look in her eyes, and we clutch hands.

"Both times. You self-medicated with cleaning. You deserve help. Therapy. Because …"

She smiles.

Chuckles.

Gestures at the photos and laughs.

Looks at me and guffaws.

Looks to the ceiling, pumps her fists and cackles.

Looks to me again. Clasps her hands so hard she claps. And oh, the life in her eyes.

"I even saw a doctor. Old white guy. 'Mrs. Richardson, this is just baby blues. Now, how are your children?'"

We hug. My heart fills. "I'm so happy I could help," I say.

Her cheek rubs against mine as she nods. "So much."

She lets go. Looks at me. Lips tight. Eyes lifeless. A sighs. "And now … the real reason you're h —"

She gasps.

Her eyes grow.

She lunges for her photos.

"Oh God!"

Zips to the mantle putting them back.

Straightens them.

Wipes them with a cloth.

Then her shoulders fall, and she trudges back to me

and collapses on the love seat. "Destroy me."

I smile sadly at her, and I hold her hands. "You don't let your sons clean, argue — anything. You've stunted their emotional growth because you disdain trusting them. You three need therapy and better coping mechanisms. That sounds like 'You're a bad mother,' but it's actually good news: You …"

But she's smiling through fury that's fomenting in her eyes.

It subsides.

"My sons *can't* clean. I will acknowledge you helped me with postpartum depression just now, but … I'm *good* at cleaning, and it … makes me happy."

I grin. "So does the guy you made that video for."

She fights a smile. And loses. And doesn't care. And is now beaming.

"He is *scorching*," she says as her eyes light up and she checks her phone for chomps. "And totally onboard with my cleaning."

My heart plummets. Fuck codependence.

She sighs and pockets her phone. "He's everything Richard isn't. Everything my boys aren't. Reliable. Clean. … *boring*."

I nod through her binary and inaccurate view — Jason and Stanley are reliable, but saying so won't help right now. Instead …

"How about a positivity-based trust exercise with them? Not cleaning. Thanking each other for something, and saying you're welcome, with emotional support items to purge your feelings into." I gesture around the seating area. "How about here?"

Her lips tighten. She sighs. And in her eyes, her insistence that her part-Richard sons can't be trusted battles her acceptance that she needs to raise her sons, not stunt them.

I wait. I trust emotionally mature people to make good long-term decisions when they know they have support.

Her eyes quiet, her lips relax, and she sighs and nods. "We can try."

I nod. "I'll ask them," I say as I walk toward the music. I invite them to turn it off, Jason tells Stanley he can trust me, and soon the house is quiet and they're placing themselves on the couch opposite their mother, who is slumped facing away from the haggard photos and looking like she hasn't cleaned in a week.

I sit in the love seat and look to them all. One low-stakes way to identify trust issues is to have people pick a number, so we'll do that on our way to the higher-stakes trust exercise. "I'm thinking of a number between one and ten. Closest goes first. If there's a tie, I'll pick someone."

Tina's emotional support pocket shifts, and she side-eyes Jason, then refocuses on me. "What if one of us knows the most common number?" Her face sours. "And —"

She points at him like he just sprayed mud on her trophy photos. "See? I can't get out two senten —"

Stop her, then assess.

"Do you want your sons to be healthy?" I ask as I fold my hands in my lap and smile at her. "Yes or no."

… some of her anger is new. So is Jason's emotional support pocket. She saw it shift, felt guilty, had no space to process her guilt, and flash-pressurized it into anger before she could stop herself.

Meanwhile, her sons are inert. Therapy will give them confidence.

Tina scowls and sighs, and she folds her arms across her chest. "Of c —"

Defensive rage fills her eyes, and she points at Jason like he's Richard. "He was up five hours past bedtime one night reading 'number facts.'"

"*Yes or no:* Do you want your sons to be healthy?"

She slumps, and her arms fall to her sides, and she rolls her now-resigned eyes and sighs. "Obv —"

"Yes or no."

Her lips tighten. She sighs, and she squeezes her emotional support pocket.

"Yes."

"Thank you. Pick a number."

"Two."

"Does mistrusting your sons make them healthy."

Her defensive rage returns. "Fine." She sighs. "Fine." She squeezes again. "Five. Or I —"

I turn to Jason. "Pick a number."

He looks down and away like that fake captain is here. "Nine."

Tina scoffs. Rolls her eyes. "Far as you can get from the others." She pushes herself upright. "You three can do your trust thing," she says as she walks toward her bucket, "but I have a *lot* of cleaning —"

"You're cleaning to self-medicate after you risked trusting your sons and you feel they betrayed that trust. Please sit down."

She stops. Loneliness floods her eyes.

"I hurt."

I nod, then look to Jason, who is still looking away. "What's the most common number picked between one and ten?"

"Seven," he offers in that small voice.

Tina sighs, and her shoulders fall, and her face looks like Mom's when she accidentally hurts me. "Fuck me. You *wanted* to tie. I'm sorry, Jason. You deserved better. Thank you for trying to avoid conflict." She trudges back to her seat, then collapses in it and faces him.

I look to him. His emotional support pocket has shifted, and tears are pooling on his eyelids. And he's looking at her.

"You're welcome," he says in a bigger voice.

I smile at everyone. "Want to keep going like this?"

They nod. My heart fills. We progress, and they squeeze their pockets less. After we finish, I smile. "Good job. Be proud of yourselves. Follow up with a therapist. And … my wife and I'll be getting a second dog. Jason, Stanley, you're welcome over after school and on weekends. I wanted —"

Stanley and Jason turn to each other. Whisper. Nod. Turn to me. "Tomorrow is the weekend."

I look to Tina. "Coordinate with Richard? Our place, a dog park, …"

Her lips tighten, then relax, and she emits a light sigh. "I will ask."

"Thank you," her sons and I say.

She smiles. "You're … welcome. I'm n — no. You're welcome."

She pushes herself upright and power-walks to her room.

Her sons and I grab our shoes. "You'll meet the dog tonight," I say as we go outside, "and tomorrow, you can stay until your father's ready to leave."

I chomp Samantha. Soon she stops by with Sparky, our new dog. He and the boys bound around as Samantha and I hold hands and watch. A few trick-or-treaters happen by.

"They look happy," Tina says. "The nearest shelter's

five miles away. Special favors?"

We nod.

Soon her phone dings. The boys cry as they tell Sparky they'll see him tomorrow, and with their mother now standing in the doorway, they walk toward the house.

Stanley stops in the doorway. Turns to her.

"Thanks for …"

She nods. "Y …"

They hug like they haven't in years, and her weeping swallows the rest of her words. Jason flings his arms around them both, and Tina moves an arm around him. Now they're having the healing moment they need.

Samantha squeezes my hand. "Mention therapy, love," she whispers.

I wait for them to finish, then smile and walk up to them.

"Good job."

They look to me, their faces saturated in healing and pain, and they smile and sniff.

Tina doesn't sigh.

I nod. "Weekly therapy. The back door will survive. We'll use subsequent dog visits as a reward in a system you work out with a therapist."

Samantha nods. "Yinz are welcome to come down the hahs."

The boys beam. Tina furrows. "Yin … Pittsburgh? Richard does some conference there every April."

Samantha beams. "Super! Does he ever talk about that restaur —"

Tina cringes. Sighs. "Sorry. I'm not usually focused on … anyway. Visits would be good. And I hope therapy'll help me trust my boys to … not let a dog destroy my house."

She looks at them. "Jason, you've memorized

everything about dogs. Stanley, you've volunteered hundreds of hours for the campaign. You deserve trust. You deserve better."

The three of them smile at each other, then wave goodbye to us three, walk inside, and shut the door. I chomp Daddy again, and we three drive off.

****

Samantha thousand-yard-stares at her phone. I squeeze her hand, but she shakes her head, so I let go. Soon I'm grabbing bags of rainbow candy from Linda and Jo's gate knob basket, near their purple sign. Two houses and purple signs later, we pull into my old driveway, I put on my sunglasses, and Samantha spies Madison in the doorway dressed as someone to dream of.

Devin, beside Madison as *the* computer guy, offers a wave. "You good? Cold tonight."

Madison glances at him and chuckles. "You're wearing a sweater." She points to her top. "This stopped being warm in August."

I grab our bags and escort Sparky and my gawking love to Madison, whose eyes are sparkling with the mischief of the anticipated question. "Now, who are you going as?"

"Tihatee, hoyodehbesee," Samantha says. "Youah seh pee theeah eh see."

I grin. Madison blushes and beams, and her eyes dart to Devin, then back to Samantha. "Thank you. Again. It's …"

Devin puts his arm around Madison and offers a few words. She leans into him and looks at him like Sa — like I helped Samantha find the safety to look at me.

Daddy walks in behind Devin and Madison and smiles. "Hey, honey."

Samantha bawls.

Dashes to him.

Collapses into him.

Wails into his shirt.

Squeezes him like he'll flee if she doesn't.

But he has wrapped his arms around her, and even if he hadn't, he wasn't going *anywhere*.

He strokes her back. "I heard about how you helped Jason. I am so proud of you."

She wails so hard I'd worry a neighbor was going to call the cops if that police chief hadn't told them better. (Still waiting for his "wisdom" to backfire.)

Samantha's wailing steadies, and she turns to Mom.

And it's my turn with Daddy. "I'm always proud of you, honey," he whispers as he strokes my back and Mom and Samantha talk chemistry research. Something clicks behind me. Probably the door.

I nod. I squeeze him. "Miss you," I whisper. "I love privacy, and Samantha, but …"

I give him a hard squeeze, then let go.

And now Mom. "Halloween article doing well?"

She smiles. "Yup." She puts a chocolate-and-peanut-butter cup in her mouth.

Sherry's. I grab her six-pack from my bag and toss it at her. We do a brief hug, and then —

"Hug for me now?" Madison asks. "Theme of the night other than can …"

Samantha spins around like Madison is her true north, then darts to her and hugs her. They whisper whatever. Eventually Madison lets go and hugs me. I mention her vibrating windows. She chuckles. "She might keep 'em. The other night at dinner, instead of listening to her one financial podcast, mother put on music. It was ancient, but —"

Samantha squeezes my hand. Hoots. "I think Bailie

needs us."

My heart pounds, and my legs quiver. She's probably lying, but as Daddy and the others offer concern, I speed us out and home anyway. We and Sparky greet Bailie as we zip to bed, Sparky and Bailie bound outside, and Samantha slides my clothes off like they were greased.

And *gawks* at me.

"You are so super-gorgeous."

I blush, and I ache. "Only for you, love."

She beams. I strip her. Lay her on the bed. Park between her hips until she needs a break. It's not enough — nothing'll ever be enough — but it's a great start. Her cheeks are red, and she's sweaty everywhere she's squishy, which is everywhere. We snuggle and kiss.

Then she turns my head.

Yes. My heart flutters. That tease.

She kisses my cheek.

Yes yes.

Kisses between it and my ear.

Yes yes yes.

Kisses my ear.

Yes yes yes yes.

Kisses that spot under my ear.

Yes yes yes yes yes.

Sucks on it.

Yes yes yes yes yes yes. My heart races and I plant my back on the bed and clutch her hair and we do everything I've been craving for three hours.

Ahhh. Animal communication is her power, but touching me is such a close second.

She lies beside me. Smiles. I smile back. She squeezes my hand.

"Jason and Sparky … filled me in a way you can't.

I want to start trying to get pregnant — and I know I still super need tons more therapy. But I need a baby too."

I nod. "We're ready enough." She could be pregnant in our first year of college. If it's a girl, my grandmother's legacy might live on. But that's a then thought. I want a now thought.

I dive back between her hips.

****

She nudges me awake. "Tina texted you. 'I have a date with Lucas. The boys'll be by at 9 with Richard. Maybe after the election, you can help me talk to him. Most women adore what they think he is, but you'll see right through him.'"

I chuckle. "Give her the autofill."

She types it. "Worked. She says, 'Thanks for the referral.'"

She puts my phone down, and we cuddle. She pets my face. Squeezes my hand.

"You want to be a therapist. Deep down. And I super yearn to help you. I refuse to let more kids suffer like I did."

I clutch her hand. I hate this, but … she's not wrong. Is she ready, though?

"Can you handle me dumping patient trauma on you?"

She laughs. Pets my hand. "You mean, can *you* handle dumping on me." She gestures toward the yard. "Our lavender bottles-turned-planters?" She points at her phone. "The app's lavender flowers? I didn't tell a single oil joke. I'm better, love."

I sigh. Chuckle. Squeeze her hand. "I need to see you as strong, not just stronger."

She grins. "Gotta be super strong to have a baby."

I exhale. "I'll talk to HR after the election. And … we can do a session with your therapist."

She squeezes my hand. We kiss.

She gets up to feed and commune with the dogs. I get up to make breakfast. And I text Richard:

Breakfast/snack: beef with broccoli. And a conversation until after the newness of me wears off :)

ATHENA'S ENCOMIUM
Glenda Darusow

Athena once stood at the peak of Olympus during the "Golden Age" of ancient Greece. That age was very different from what we experience today. It was a time when both gods and goddesses continually garnered great fascination, adulation, and worship. Her father, Zeus, and his whole Pantheon were in their heyday. The glitz and glamor of Olympus basked in endless idolization. Athena had taken her rightful place as one of these twelve immortal beings. She was the true goddess of wisdom, warfare, and handicrafts. A being who was worshipped in her own right. Athena stood out among them. Her commitment to integrity, fairness, and her natural grace made her a favorite of mortals all over the Greek countryside. Her life was to be inexorably tied to those who idolized and worshipped her. She gave back to them all she could, but it was not always the easiest journey.

Athena did not have the greatest relationship with her father. He could be a difficult entity to deal with, even during the best of times. Leading the Pantheon, and relentlessly pursuing females, was a full-time job that left him little time for any meaningful relationship with Athena. Zeus established a Patriarchy that restrained all the goddesses at Olympus. Athena was no exception. She was a goddess existing in a god's world.

Athena was the daughter from Zeus's first marriage to Metis. This had a profound impact on Athena. When Zeus remarried to Hera, everything changed. Athena found that this made her relationship with her father much worse. Hera was a demanding goddess who was full of false personas and subtle manipulations. She so busied herself with Pantheonic intrigue that she and Athena never developed much of a personal relationship at all.

It is not widely known by the general public, but Athena was a victim of rape by her half-brother Hephaestus. These types of stories have become almost common place in today's media, but it was not so in Athena's time. Goddesses have come forward with their stories raising the light of truth, but this was not how the press treated this topic in Athena's time. Goddesses were expected to smile and keep quiet. The fact this rape was a product of incest made Athena's situation even more taboo.

Very few of her fans and worshippers ever knew, but a child came from that unfortunate union. Athena, due to her station as a goddess, had no choice but to raise her son Erichthonius in secret. Life is hard enough for single mothers, even in the best of situations, but imagine raising a child that is a product of rape in an environment of shame and persistent, harsh, societal scorn.

Adding to this harsh social environment, Erichthonius was plagued with a plethora of health problems that started when he was an infant and carried into his adulthood. He was unable to walk for most of his life and usually needed a special chariot to get around. Athena never wavered in her dedication to her child. With great patience, and great perseverance, she cared for him. After some time, he grew up to be elected king of the Athenian City State.

While raising her child in secret, Athena served as the goddess of war during a time when the act of war was almost exclusively a mortal man's domain. There were Amazons to be sure, but they made up a very small percentage of combatants and worshipers. It has often been reported that Athena was the first goddess to be the purveyor of battlefields. This is simply not true. There were many goddesses of war that appeared on the stage before, and after, Athena's time. Ishtar in Mesopotamia, Bast in Egypt, Freya in Scandinavia, Morrigan in Ireland; the list goes on and on.

In ancient Greece the field was quite crowded with lesser female war deities. Nike was worshipped for victory in battle. Eris was the goddess of conflict. Enyo was the goddess of battle lust. Athena was perennially on the A-List when it came to being a goddess. All the other goddesses paled in comparison to Athena in terms of popularity and station, but it is important to note the level of competition she faced when it came to worshippers before, during, and after a war. Out of all these lesser goddesses mentioned, Enyo was a deity of note because she was the consort of Athena's true Olympian nemesis, Ares, god of war.

If dealing with Zeus's patriarchal leadership was not hard enough, Athena also had to contend with a god of war who was markedly less popular than she. The jealousy and emulous felt by Ares towards Athena was legendary. It was said that Zeus himself had to separate them when he held court on Olympus because their rancor had such a negative influence on the entire Pantheon.

Ares loved physical strength and combat, but his narrow range ended there. He was always bested by Athena because she understood there were other things that go into fighting a war besides physical strength and combat. Athena understood such concepts as battlefield logistics. It was not important to only have an army in the field. They must have things like food and weapons in order to fight. Athena understood strategy. Just running an army straight at their enemies in an open field was not always the best idea. Athena also understood the value of battlefield diplomacy. Why fight and have soldier's die if you can talk things out instead? It was this full understanding of all battlefield endeavors that made her popular over Ares as a war deity.

Even the Spartans, a city state that dedicated themselves to constantly making war upon their neighbors, worshipped Athena six to one over Ares. Those numbers have long been confirmed and makes for a wide margin when it comes to followers. Zeus favored Ares as part of his patriarchal control. He was continually propping Ares up despite his low ratings. When one goes back and looks at the actual worship numbers, Athena was far more popular among the all-important "common soldier's demographic" than Ares could ever hoped to have been.

As one could certainly imagine, Ares's poor performances, and his rivalry with Athena, lead to a lot of rumors and innuendos being generated to denigrate and slander her. This is the kind of thing some Olympians would do. They would manufacture a story about another god or goddess and spread it out amongst the mortals who would repeat it as fact. Even when these lies and fabrications were exposed by scholarly initiatives for what they were, the original manufactured stories persist even today in public consciousness.

One of the best examples of this behavior was the pack of lies about Athena turning Medusa into a horrible monster with snakes for hair. Everyone has heard this story in one version or another. This tale has been researched and investigated by classical scholars and there are simply no solid facts behind it to back it up. In a tell-all published by Homer, that was later noted to be in clear violation of a non-disclosure agreement, he stated the following: Medusa and Poseidon did go into Athena's temple to make love. That part of the story has never been in dispute, however, as incredible as it may sound, Poseidon was having trouble performing in a public place. Instead of acknowledging that he had been battling this very selective form of E.D., he instead blamed his lack of erective response on Medusa. He body shamed her. He said it was her ugliness that prevented him from performing. To underscore his point, and to keep Medusa quiet, he made Medusa so ugly she could turn mortal men into stone. There was no doubt that Ares and his cronies were the ones that circulated the story blaming Medusa's disfigurement upon Athena. Athena was upset about the defilement of her temple, but that was the extent of it. She did not deface Medusa in a fit of jealousy. That was simply not in her character.

Athena was by all accounts a trailblazer as a goddess. In the face of great patriarchal opposition, she alone held her ground as an individual. Since the end of the "Golden Age" in ancient Greece she has not only been credited as the founder for the capital city of Athens, but also as the modern symbol of democracy itself. Athena has always been a shining symbol of empowerment for all women. She held her head high in the face of devastating adversities and weathered each personal storm with grace, strength, and intellect. She is a true warrior who would be a staunch protector of all the fragile treasures that lie deep within in the heart of every woman.

ARTEMIS
GODDESS OF THE MOON, THE WILDS, & THE HUNT

You are wild and I am wild. Life is so complex, yet nature is the wildest thing I know and she has no such complexities.. You can choose whatever path you want, I don't care. But if you are pretending to be anyone other than your wild, authentic self, what are you even doing?

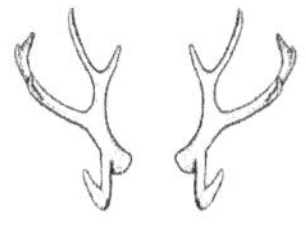

HOPE
Emily Reed

So, I'm supposed to be answering who I am
Or at least who I think I am
But asking who I am is like asking what's in the air we breathe
I know it had to be something like atoms or particles, but I'm
still a topic I don't understand Beyond the bare shell of it, I
still don't know what the atoms or particles are

I can take some classes or do some soul searching, but that
will take up time
I'll probably forget what I am here for
My thoughts are as spaced as the gaps in my memories.
The fog lingering
An all-too-familiar feeling of hands around my neck

For so long, I fought just to get through, to survive
I never took time to sit and think about what could be
The future always a big question
Like a canvas, I never know what color to pick
While other people paint and plan, I am too busy

Dressed in an apron I always expect the mess
Too busy tiptoeing around the thorns I never smell the rose

There are no threats, the sky isn't falling, and my boat isn't
filling with water
Those are the slowest points of my life
I spent my whole life swinging this avenging sword, I feel
empty without its heavy weight
What do I do?

I float through days like I'm lost at sea on my raft
Maybe I'll eat some fruit, but what can you do?
There's nothing for my mind to focus on.
All I can see is calm waters, but all I can do is wait for the
storm.

This chaos has become my regular, my comfort zone a
hurricane
I know what I'm supposed to do
Stay away from windows, hide in my basement, and cover
my head
Even so, this disorder isn't an amenity

I've done all I can to win the war
But now I want to experience all I've lost
I want to be everything I couldn't be,
So loud that I can't not be heard
Run until I can't, just because I can
Laugh in ways I haven't in years

Be able to ask questions and learn those things I was denied
Have people I can grow close to, more significant
connections, and stability

Someone I can call home
Experience the small things
Coffee in the mornings
A book before bed, without worrying about the nightmares
that used to come after

So, maybe I don't know who I am
All I can tell you is who I want to be
But this is my life
And I've fought hard for it
I will live it.

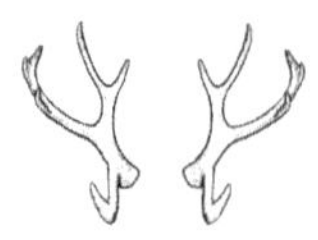

I Am Stardust
J.K. Raymond

I will follow my path.
The path that's true
And kind and good.

Older than the oldest tree in the wood,
I am stardust given breath,
What choice have I but to shine?

So worry not for me.
I have learned to translate the winds
That whisper in my ear.

A whisper that said,
"You are my daughter, timid child.
Draw your courage from natural things,
Things wild and legend and free.

For the words and laws of man
Will hold no power over thee."

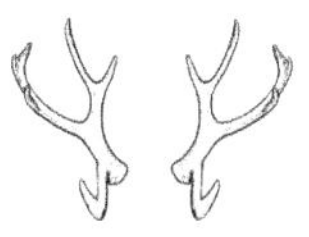

THE WATCHER
Lacraecia

I'm a dragon of the night.
A watcher from the shadows.
Within the silence I tread
and slip in and out of sight.

This forest is my life.
A home, a family, my friends.
And such it is dear to me
and so I guard it from strife.

Long ago I made an oath
to myself and to the wilds I love.
When the outside sends its threats
I tear them to shreds, no questions asked.

It starts out innocent, a quest for knowledge.
It's just for discovery, for science.
But then you come with your weapons, gun, knives
all for your selfishness and pride.

But don't think me cruel or unkind.
I don't want to hurt the denizens of the outside.
I'd rather you live, so keep to the path
and I indeed will let you pass.

But in the end, it must be done,
as it has since I drew my first breath.
Threaten me or my forest home
And my claws will bring your death.

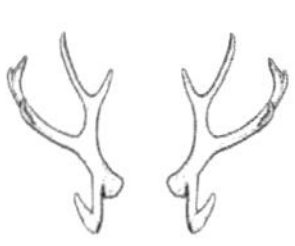

HER AND THE MOON

Geraldine Athena F. Gomez
Lester N. Linsangan

The luminous moon shining over the darkness
As the glistening sun returns to the pits of hell
A pack of wolves howling to the sound of the wind
The sinuous trails of the water, reflecting the moon and stars

Her elegance and her swift
Subtle movements of her fingers to her arrows
The soft and wet soil that surrounds
The falling leaves that cover her scent

Illuminating her presence and her soul as she stands
A Goddess with ambition, antipathy, and equity
Depicting the traits of wildlife
Ruthless yet submissive

The silent sorrows of the innocent sufferers
She who protects the innocence who was crushed
Submerging her deadly arrows to poison
Sinking to one's body, closer and closer to death

A protector yet a killer to all
Each shattered fragments of the innocence
She held tightly, clasping her hands together
As she reaches her hands for the Moon;

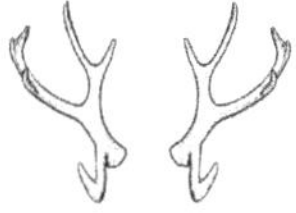

WHEN THE LEAVES FALL DOWN

Briana Nicole F. Bautista
Lester N. Linsangan
Djoanna Marie Pascual-Mataga

The cacophony of the wild surrounds her ears
Chasing in the wild, nowhere near
Looked around in her blood-soaked gown
For the first time, my eyes met her shining one

In a dark room she's the light
In the night sky she's the moonlight
Her ineffable beauty is a bliss
Goddess of the hunt, Artemis

She is fierce and ferocious
To be part of her life is fictitious
She's brave, strong, and cool
Admiring her looking like a fool

She is my guiding star
Her light shines the brightest even from afar
It guides me through the darkest night
She's the brightest star that pleases my sight

I placed her in the night sky up above
Forever and beyond, my moonlight is she
A sharp arrow stabbed my back
On my knees, I'm in full shock

An arrow heart indeed
She made my heart bleed
Though she ended my breath
It was still a painless death;

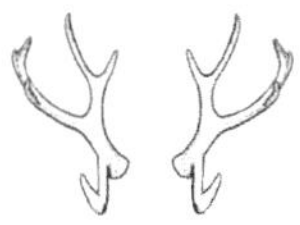

I See the Moon

Briana Nicole F. Bautista
Lester N. Linsangan

All find solace in her care
A guardian who is always there
An embodiment of nature's power and grace
A goddess to be revered, in every place

Arrows fly true and swift
In the forest, she's truly a gift
With bow and arrow by her side
She fiercely wanders the hills and valleys wide

A beauty that radiates from within
Wounds of bravery on her skin
Eyes deeper than the ocean blue
A figure that stands proud and true

In the forest, she roams and prowls
Calming the winds that howl
The guardian of wilderness
Artemis, the mighty huntress

Your beauty is a gift from the gods above.
Your gaze is piercing and bold
It's indeed a treasure to be loved
And a wonder to behold;

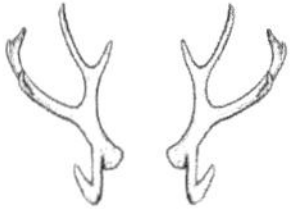

THE SHADOW KILLS THE TIME
Briana Nicole F. Bautista
Lester N. Linsangan

We both fell in love, feels like I'm dreaming
Our hearts beat as one, our love had wings
We soared through life, hand in hand
With him, there's nothing I could not withstand

Our love was strong, but it couldn't survive
The flames in our hearts kept it alive
Flames that died as it was blown by the Gods
I wiped out his tears as it floods

I knew I shouldn't love him
But his love is the light in the night so dim
A love so pure, a love so fine
You and I, two hearts entwined

I was fooled to shoot him dead
He was breathless, shot in his head
With one arrow, I ended his breath
I couldn't believe, I'm the cause of his death

The moonlight I thought would never die
Now seems dull and lifeless in the sky
My tears fell like a silver arrow
That night was indeed full of sorrow

In the night sky, forever apart
But our love remains, beating each other's heart
Though he was gone, he's alive in my heart
Our eternal love, even after death tore us apart;

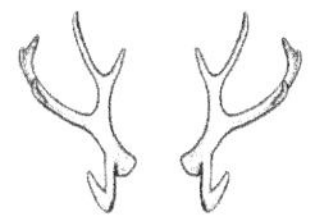

Journey to the Past and Future By a Dyslexic
Dexter Amoroso

Peter said, "I'm sorry to have crushed people's fantasies of time travel, but it is impossible to physically travel into the past, or distant future, because the past no longer exists, and the future has yet to exist." But I, Dex 'The Dyslexic' see things differently.

Dex does not speak for all dyslexic people everywhere, but only for himself. While dyslexics often excel in leadership, creative thinking, problem-solving, innovation, critical thinking, and emotional intelligence, the exact presentation of these strengths and weaknesses are uneven. Given this mix of qualities that make up dyslexia, this means that no two dyslexic individuals are alike. Additionally, because of his science background and concept of God, time will have a broad flavor to him. That said, he recognized that those of differing religion, faith, or indeed, no faith at all, may see things differently. In his unique theological reflections and rational approach, he learned that our faith must transcend the politics and sufferings of this world.

I looked at the picture of me and Peter, my old best

buddy, and mumbled, "I hate myself." There was only one source of our conflict. We just had different perspectives. For Peter, time travel was impossible because motion was relative to both Space and Time. Outside of the perception of the passage of time, there could be no motion, causal progression, or change. To "time travel," motion would have to be absolute, and for motion to be absolute things must somehow be able to come into Existence from Non-Existence. For Peter, Non-Existence could never be.

As I thought back on what I had done to Peter. I had no more tears to cry. Memories of my terrible mistake a month ago pierced my heart like a sharp dagger. I couldn't forgive myself until today...

Peter and I used to be in the same Science and Technology performance task group. Our teacher had assigned us to work in pairs that day. We had to rack our brains to come up with new problem-solving ideas for a Smart transportation innovation contest.

However, we did not agree on each other's ideas.

"Your plan is unworkable. Your idea of a time machine is not science fiction, at the very least, in that it never cared much for the drama to be grounded in anything other than the rule of cool. If you approach it scientifically, you'll only get frustrated 'dyslexic savants.'" Peter spoke with brutal honesty.

"Your idea of a transportation device is not as reliable as you claim!" I said, quivering with frustration.

Weeks passed, and no matter how hard we tried, we couldn't reach an agreement. We eventually failed the project. I was enraged with Peter and devised a plan to retaliate.

I used an anonymous account to post a hoax about Peter not being circumcised on Facebook. "This will teach Peter a lesson!" I chuckled as I hit the post button.

Soon after, rumors spread like wildfire across the school. Within a week, many students started talking about Peter not being circumcised. To his horror, he was the laughingstock of the school. He was so humiliated and depressed that he had to skip classes to avoid rumors. His results plummeted. He was one of the best students in our class until he began failing all of his classes.

"Instead of celebrating the fact I got my revenge, I was filled with guilt," I sadly said to myself, seeing that my once-loved friend's change had been too great for me to bear. Rumors are gossip, and gossip is bullying. I wish I could go back in time and correct my mistakes.

Meanwhile, Christmas was approaching, and my family traveled to Scotland for Christmas break. We stayed at a nice little witchy cottage in the woods near the ocean. Somewhere far away but with access to medical care and free wi-fi.

One night I had a dream. In the dream, God told me I could travel using the "time machine" where I would see how the Mass literally transcended the bounds of time.

At St. Mary's Cathedral in Scotland, during Mass, I was no longer in the present. I was transported through time and space to the First Christmas.

It's like Back to the Future or Doctor Who's TARDIS, but cooler.

As human beings, we were bound by time. We couldn't live in any other moment than the present. The past was written in stone, and the future was unreachable. We are confined by the seconds, the minutes, and the hours.

But God doesn't have that limitation. God was not bound by time. He was in the past, the present, and the future, providing help and grace in all places on the time continuum. In that case, again, God met me in a dream.

In the dream, God highlighted three types of attitudes toward life. There were people who lived in the past and always regretted what they could have done with their lives. They could not forgive the mistakes they made. They could not forgive those who had hurt them. For others, living in the past meant constantly thinking about the good old days, the happy Christmases they used to celebrate. And then there were those who lived in the future. They wanted to move on to the next world. They were forever in the valley of tears, expelled from their homeland. Their lives consisted of suffering, pain, and sacrifice. Those suffering from poverty, disease, and misfortune were just waiting to be released from the world. Their desperation was understandable.

And some lived only in the present. This was the tragedy of the world we lived in today. They didn't think about tomorrow because the greatest deception of evil was to make them believe there was no tomorrow. Only today. Everything would come to an end when they died. In that case, they should enjoy themselves. Do what they could. Forget about sacrifice and use their time to serve others. Just take care of themselves and their needs.

We could not live our lives to the fullest without remembering the past. We must learn from our mistakes and those of our ancestors.

In the homily during Midnight Mass, in St Mary's Cathedral, the church asked everyone to see the destiny ahead of them and not be shortsighted by simply living for the world and for ourselves or to keep on regretting our past. Let us come back to God by seeking repentance.

Finally, I summoned up the courage to phone Peter. I confessed to him, with tears in my eyes, that I was the perpetrator of posting fake news on an anonymous account.

"I'm sorry! Please forgive me!" I begged him.

Thanks to a strange technology called Mass, God grabbed my hand and transported me through time, giving me a window into His infinite nature.

PERSEPHONE
GODDESS OF SPRING,
QUEEN OF THE UNDERWORLD

Life will indeed change its seasons,
but death is not the end-all, be-all

I ride the seasons above and below, among the living and the dead,
and I know one thing for certain: through all the cycles that creation
provides you, you are still you in the end. Your beauty can only
rebirth again and again.

WRAPPED INTO THE BONES OF A WOMAN
Linda M. Crate

i have always been
underestimated and misunderstood:
both light and darkness
reside within me—

people have a hard time understanding
someone who is both flowers and thorns,
butterflies and skulls, dreams and nightmares,
life and death;

i am so full, that sometimes,
people seem empty and shallow and more
hollow than an empty husk—

i have so many depths and heights,
but people tell me that i am too much;

perhaps they simply aren't the people
for me
because i am and always will be enough, just as i am
not too much and not too little—

just multitudes and oceans and land and trees,
talons and thorns and flowers, moons and suns
wrapped into the bones of a woman.

HOW CAN THEY ASK ME TO BE LESS?
Linda M. Crate

people have forgotten Persephone's power,
and i can relate because they don't seem
to recognize mine;

they want to remember her as a spring goddess
but she is more than that—

i, too, contain multitudes which sometimes seem
to contradict one another;
but i cannot help be but who i am and i will embrace
my magic no matter how much it startles or alarms others—

how can they ask me to be less?

i will not surrender my throne nor my crown
to fit the narrative they wish of me,
either accept me as my whole or watch as you are not
invited to the garden of my heart or to know any of the flowers
of my soul.

NO LONGER WILL I FORGET MY THRONE
Linda M. Crate

i feel most at home
when i am in the song of nature,
but i do not shy away from
the morbid and macabre;

have always been told that i am weird
and it used to make me shrink away—

but i have stepped into my power,
into my weird, into my wilds;

because i am both the flower and the thorn,
the light and the darkness, the smooth
stone and the one that cuts;

i am both mermaid and siren,
lyric of the songbird and shout of the crow—

few have ever understood me
or the mythology of my bones,
but i am done being less and swallowing
pieces of myself down so they like me;

i am power, i am beauty, i am courage, i am strength—

no longer will i forget my throne
or my crown,
even if they cannot understand my name
or power i will always be me.

GLINT
Johnny Francis Wolf

(is Venus
minus clam)

Were her simpers not so pointed, edged.. seraphic rapture,
someone brilliant, blinded, bleared by sun off combers..
would have thought her lovely. No.

I think she must be genius sharp, the way she held that hat
too nigh and yet too high if changed my view, my camera's
angle, things I saw between her waves, reflecting shimmers,
rounding thighs.. her lucent eyes demanding that I focus,
filled my soul with fuzz that numbed my head for little else..

And lips forever parted 'til the hat she placed on boat she
left and stood there silent. Naked thinking, how to let me
go.

"I think, perhaps, the light is gone. The magic hour done."

THE WORDS OF DRY SPELL
Ma. Carmela S. Garcia
Lester N. Linsangan

Persephone, Goddess of spring
Daughter of Zeus and Demeter
Wife of Hades; became a Queen
The underworld I am ruling

Death and souls fear me
All in Hell, hail thee
Underneath there, my throne
The life beyond you'll never know

The underworld is in my hands
Tenebrous embrace me as I land
Aquae froze in the ponds
Snap! Entirety turns to sand

Lifeless is too verdurous
Kindness is too atrocious
The aptness of my power
Undefeatable altogether

The duality of my vision
Like the stare of a lion
It starts with the crimson notion
My story, they tell every season

Blooming flowers welcomed me
The waves were calming in the sea
Leaves fell back from their mother trees
Effloresce and renascent season; spring

I came back to the world of light
Warmth and bunnies are dight
The recrudescence of the wight
Flowers' phosphorescence at night

My exuberant mother, Demeter
Waiting for me, admiring my gallery
Lakes flow with steaming water
Creatures rejoice from every comer;

THE EXPECTATION OF TIME
ACT 2

S.E. Reed

"To life," Penny said as she walked into the vacuum.

"To saving humanity." Colt sealed the door behind them.

Penny checked her watch for the final time, then wrapped her arms around Colt, and closed her eyes, welcoming whatever was to come next.

***

"Colt," Penny whispered.

"Are we alive?" Colt squeezed her tightly.

"Don't be ridiculous. We're standing here aren't we?" She wiggled out of the doctor's tight grasp so she could take a better look at their surroundings. They were standing in a forest, no station buildings, no thick plexiglass dome overhead. The entire journey into the past had taken six-sidereal seconds, according to her watch, which for now still worked.

Theoretical quantum physicists Penny Persephone and Dr. Jamie Colton had just traveled through a portal in time– ripped open using Time Crystals and Black Hole Theory in the vacuum system they'd constructed in the basement lab of the Station Three building. When the alarms sounded, alerting them of the tower's demise, they knew their only chance at survival was to make a time leap. Neither of them knew exactly what to expect when the Time Crystals activated, but if Penny's theory on Cyclical Humanity was correct, they would land somewhere in the past.

Penny was acutely aware of the smell in the air—fresh. Nothing smoggy or dank like they had in the dome. The unpolluted, pure oxygen content of this Earth was at least seventy percent higher than what they were used to back home. With every breath Penny took, her head swam in circles.

"I had no idea the trees would be this tall." Colt pushed his glasses up his nose.

The shock of their transport through time was quickly replaced with fascination and awe for the strange new world. The flora was lush and bright from real sun-soaked photosynthesis. A far cry from the translucent plants, grown by UV lights in hydroponic tables, they were used to.

"We should collect our belongings and scout for water." Penny picked up the small suitcase.

She set it on a fallen log and carefully opened it, revealing the few items she'd tossed in haphazardly back at her apartment when the sirens started. She took out a pair of pants and shirt, quickly changing out of the pajamas she still wore, placing them neatly next to her dead brother's ashes. The first aid kit and lab coats were on the ground near her feet, and she stowed them in her suitcase.

"Of all the shit in the lab I could have tossed in the vacuum with us, why did I go for a desk plant?" Colt let out a nervous laugh as he picked up a small potted plant.

"*Triticum Aestivum*," Penny said as she inspected the greens. "Wheatgrass. We can cultivate and grow more. It's good for digestion and–" she paused, there was a loud growl, and rustle in the leaves at the edge of the forest clearing.

"Don't move," Colt hissed.

He quickly handed her the plant and pulled his backpack off one shoulder, so it was accessible in front of him.

Penny had never heard the cocking of a gun before. Weapons were expressly forbidden in all seven stations. But there it was, shiny, and fully loaded. Colt aimed the gun at the rustling. Any manner of beast might be the origin of the noise.

Penny knew the oxygen rich air would cause her to fall unconscious if she sucked it in too quickly, but as the noises of the creature grew louder, it made it nearly impossible to keep her breathing steady. She closed her eyes and imagined her personal attendant, Yen, brushing her long hair with steady, vigorous strokes. Seconds ticked by until finally, the beast retreated. Colt reset the hammer on the gun.

"Penny, you can open your eyes. Our scent is strange to whatever animals inhabit this region. It's gone– for now. Do we know where *or when* we are yet? That will help with species identification." Colt put the gun in the waistband of his pants.

"I programmed the computer for Greenland, ten thousand years before the Ordovician-Silurian Extinction event. The samples we recovered from the RECAP expedition showed an ecosystem with plant and animal life that could sustain humans. But, I have no way to verify our location unless we can find a landmark."

"Fuck, Penny, you weren't kidding when you said you wanted to start humanity over at the beginning. That's four-hundred million years before any record of homosapiens. No one in the future will ever know we existed," Colt said and rubbed his face.

"Yes, Doctor. That was the point. But my plan was to bring everyone from the stations– to build a new society where we could live and thrive instead of going extinct. We just– there wasn't–" Penny paused, realizing the enormity of their situation. "Our world is gone, Colt. They are all dead. The pressure from the collapse of our tower would have brought the others down within minutes. Right now, you and I are the only two humans alive."

Colt picked up the apple off the ground. The one he'd thrown into the vacuum. He held it up to her. "We are a veritable Adam and Eve. Do you want to take a bite of the forbidden fruit?"

She shook her head.

Colt shrugged and took a bite of the apple, the juice trickling down his chin.

"We need water and shelter. And don't throw out those apple seeds. If we are going to breed and raise children, we will need to think long-term. An apple orchard will…"

Cough, cough. Colt choked on the apple.

"Put your arms over your head, Colt. Slow breaths. I don't need you aspirating on the forbidden fruit and dying before you plant your seed in me," Penny informed Colt as he sputtered and coughed up the chunk of apple he'd inhaled.

"You want to have my children? But Penny, I thought you detested my romantic pursuits," he said once he regained his composure.

"We tangled in my bed sheets last night didn't we?" Penny asked very matter of factly.

"I thought that was just the wine and excitement from your discovery of large quantities of Time Crystals," Colt said and smiled.

His eyes went a little glassy, remembering just how

excited Penny had been in those bed sheets.

Penny looked Colt up and down. He was rather attractive, in an arrogant, only man left alive kind of way. If she had to be stuck forever with only one human, he wasn't the worst. She checked her watch.

"We can discuss procreation in greater detail *after* we find water. We have approximately two hours until muscle cramps and fatigue set in."

Penny carried her suitcase and led the way. Using the natural topography of the region and following the pattern of plant growth, it was fairly easy for the pair to find a water source. It was a narrow, clear stream running between rocks. The cold liquid was the purest tasting water either had consumed in their lifetime since no equipment in their labs could fully purify the toxic water of their world.

They decided to follow the stream and look for shelter along its banks. It would be foolish to wander away from the water source, especially because it would be getting dark soon if Penny's watch was still keeping accurate time. They walked atop the rocky bank in silence, stopping once for Colt to fashion a shoulder harness for Penny's suitcase, which she refused to let him carry for her.

"My brother Edgar is in this case. He is my responsibility. Just like it is our responsibility to survive, for our species."

That was the end of the conversation.

Colt admired Penny. She would never relinquish her connection to dead Edgar– or to their past. It took a strong woman to balance both worlds. His heart palpitated. He was having so many strong emotions– quite possibly because of sensory overload. He placed two fingers against the carotid artery at his neck and counted, making sure his blood pressure was stable.

"Penny, look there, on the other side of the stream. An entrance to a cave," Colt said, and reached for her hand. Together they stepped across the shallow creek and climbed over the rocks toward the cave. The sun dipped behind the edge of the ridge and darkness encroached, threatening to swallow them whole.

"Do you have a flashlight in your backpack?" Penny asked.

"I have something better." Colt picked up a fallen tree branch and removed a small Bunsen lighter from his pack. He squeezed the metal brackets, causing a spark on the small flint patch in the center. After a few tries, the dried edge of the branch caught the spark and smoldered into a flame. "We can build a fire in the cave. We have no idea how cold it will get tonight." He said and led the way through the stony threshold.

Penny was very certain the temperature would not dip below a comfortable level, considering the plant growth and the temperature of the water in the stream. But, a fire would provide protection from unwanted animals until they could secure the cave, if they deemed it appropriate for a shelter.

A quick assessment of the cave proved it bare, no immediate signs of it being used as a den for predators. They left their gear and gathered armfuls of fallen branches. Penny was impressed by Colt's ability to build a cross-hatched pile in the center of the cave and ignite it into a proper campfire. Something they'd only ever read about in books.

The red and gold flames illuminated the walls in the cave, and they settled down, letting their limbs warm and relax from the heat. Penny leaned into Colt's chest, finding comfort. He wrapped his arms around her, smelling the sunshine and fresh air in her long hair.

"Colt, although I do find you smelling me slightly arousing, you should stop." Penny pulled herself from his grip and walked to the other side of the cave.

"You're the one who said we were going to–"

"Dr. Colton, please stop talking. Get your ass up and look at this with me. The wall– there is something on it." Penny put her hand up and rubbed the dust from the rough stone surface. The firelight illuminated faint lines and markings.

"No. That can't be, can it?" Colt stood next to her, examining the wall.

Penny squinted through the haze of her glasses and traced the number on the wall, 3.14159. Pi. Then she placed her hand over the drawing at the end of the numbers. A five-fingered hand. Hers was nearly a perfect fit.

"We are not alone," Colt's voice was somber.

Penny shivered.

The science community knew very little of life on Earth before the Ordovician-Silurian Extinction event. Only that aquatic invertebrate were able to survive, spawning into the eight million catalogued species in modern day– before they'd fucked it all up, killed everything, and destroyed the planet.

A tear rolled down Penny's cheek.

"*Why are you crying Pee Pee?*" Dead Edgar's ghost asked.

Penny clutched at her heart, her dead brother's childhood nickname for her, from their time sharing a sleeping bag on the roof of Station Seven and she would wet it from night terrors. It was where all the orphans slept. She could still smell the noxious fumes that swirled through the crack in the dome, their oxygen masks couldn't keep it all from infiltrating their lungs.

"Penny, my god, these markings– could they be from

others like us? Do you think there are more people from the future here in this time?" Colt asked. He was unaware of the ghost in the cave, the constant shadow who stood next to Penny.

"Possibly. That is the idea, Cyclical Humanity theory. It's all happened before, it will all happen again. Like the rotation around the sun– the pull of the tide, the changing of the seasons, life, and death. It is the purest form of the Law of Conservation. Matter can be neither destroyed nor created, it is a perpetual cycle."

Penny turned and threw herself into Colt's arms.

"Whoa, you okay?" He stroked her hair.

"What's the point? If we all die in the end anyway? If others like us have come back here, to these caves, and the future repeats, what is our purpose?" Penny's shoulders slumped as she allowed herself to cry. It was all too much.

"Our purpose is to live. Me and you. Together. We can make love, have children, grow apples and wheatgrass," Colt said and laughed. "We have forever to explore this new world and drink fresh water and watch the stars and tell stories. We are free, for the first time in our lives, we aren't living in a dome. We are fucking free Penny!" Colt held tighter to her now, than he had when they made the leap through time. As if right now, in this cave, was where he might lose her if he couldn't make her understand that nothing from before this moment mattered.

They stood in silence for a long time, clutched in a loving embrace, processing everything they'd been through.

Finally, Penny spoke, her voice dry. "Persephone… I've rather hated my last name, finding it foolish to carry the namesake of a mythological deity. But now, it seems rather fitting, wouldn't you say?" Penny asked, her head still resting on Colt's shoulder.

"Oral traditions start somewhere, behind every myth and legend, there is some truth. Persephone, she was the Goddess of Spring, and symbolized duality. If I recall, she would travel to the Underworld as Queen and come back in the Spring to give new life."

"Yes, something like that," Penny replied.

As a scientist, Penny preferred using facts and data. Back home, in her time, the whimsy of fiction was nothing more than a reminder of how tragic their lives had become, being the last few humans on a dying planet.

Colt slowly guided Penny away from the cave drawings and back to the fire. They stared into the dancing flames. This prehistoric, pre-everything world they were in was theirs for eternity. There was no going back to when they had come from. There were no Time Crystals, no supercomputers, no labs, and no vacuum chambers. Maybe they would find others, out there, like them— but maybe not. The cave drawings were dusty and cracked with age. They could be hundreds or even thousands of years old— placed by others from the future, seeking refuge from their own dying future society.

They had each other, and in the end, that was the only thing that mattered.

"To life," Penny mumbled as she let her body and mind succumb to sleep.

Colt stroked her hair. He envisioned the work ahead of them, it wouldn't be easy, to build a home, and find sustainable food, not at first. But over time, they would learn how to be real pioneers. They would shed their scientist monikers and replace them with new titles, survivors, builders, farmers, partners, lovers, parents. A smile crept across his face. "To procreation, the sexy kind." He chuckled.

Penny reached a sleepy hand over and gently swatted at Colt.

"You're supposed to be asleep," he mused and pulled her closer to his chest. She snuggled into the crook of his body and together they slept.

SPIRAL DANCE
Victoria Holland

Preface: *The Seed*

Dreamer,

I can feel you all the time.

I could be walking through the woods and the wind carries your kiss.

I need you to know that, Viv. I need you to know how close I am to you, for what you read next.

There is nothing wrong with you. There never was! And trust me, I'm an expert. I analyze you in my head. I know you have this idea that you are a monster with everything you've been through. Even though you know most of it wasn't your fault, there is still a hole in your heart where love should be.

All that shame and guilt IS NOT because you are evil! It came from you wanting to be loved, and being judged for who you are instead. There was never anything wrong with you.

I know the storms are you, Viv. But please, for the love of everything, do not be afraid of your own power! You have such beautiful magic. How can you wield such immense power and still only use it to create beautiful things?

I know why.

Your magic comes straight from your soul.

You need to know the goddesses have reached out, all seven of them. They are retracting their safeguards. I know it seems like a stupid move on their part, but I'm not going to sit here and pretend that once in a while, you and I just need someone to believe in us.

They know your power comes from your soul. From your heart. From you. They trust you.

I trust you.

All this madness is because you don't trust yourself.

I have one more thing, for you. It's a poem. I call it… "Her Inner World."

It is beauty
the way her magic
raw, rushing, glittering
pours from her palms
like water's kiss.

It is mystery,
the depths she dives to.
That vast ocean
of knowledge she takes in
to make her own.

It is complexity
her mind, her heart.
Her spiraling worlds
of color, of love,
of creation.

It is kindness,

the way she looks at me.
How, when nobody
is looking,
she wants to be held.

It is beauty,
her authenticity.
She is wild.
She only wants the same
for you and me.

Please don't show that to anybody. It is very personal and meant to be for you alone. But Viv, I never left. Even if it seems the opposite. I'm right here.

I love you,
Your guardian

My bottom lip trembled.

I sat in the garden with the letter hanging from my hand. It came to me when I opened the door of my family's cottage, appearing on our doorstep. I hadn't seen him in so long, but I was drowning.

I needed *someone*.

The winds rose. The clouds had been gathering for a few months, but now they were swelling with lightning.

He was the only one who *could* see.

Nobody else… every day was *the same*. I was too loud. Too much. I wasn't good enough. It didn't matter how kind and wild and strong I was. Just how capable. Just how smart. And now the goddesses have left me.

The winds were swirling, building slowly to a hurricane.

My voice was *nothing*.

My tear fell… and she came on the winds. I breathed in her note, right into my heart, and I sang it out into the sky more beautifully than I had ever sung anything in my life. In my center, the seed, I knew… *I am moving poetry.*

I wept in relief.

Your voice is so beautiful.

Her face appeared behind my eyes: a ginger-haired maiden with a crown of daffodils, snowbells, violets. And eyes, misty white with visions of death.

"I was hoping it would be you," I whispered.

She smiled. I felt her hands in the gentle winds cradling my head, *Your time has come.*

I nodded, "My time has come."

She let me weep until I was ready.

I. *The Path Ahead*

Vivian stomped into the forest without a word to anyone. She wasn't even going to consider their words. She *knew* she was right, even if no one *fucking* believed her.

The call was here.

She'd walk to the ends of the earth for it.

She made her way to a place where nobody treaded. It was an oak arch, curving at the top with vines and wildflowers woven into it. If she passed this gateway without a gift… well, local legend said the fae would kidnap her for a century, but it was more likely they would just kick her back out.

She rifled through her black leather satchel, having prepped an offering already. But something glowed a rosy hue in the outer pocket.

It was the letter he had written her, though not his poem.

She retrieved it.

His words glowed pink. Wind swept through, ripping it from her fingers to the ground at the entrance. It dissolved into dust, with his rosy words climbing up the archway and over the shadows of the forest, lighting up a path with blue light pouring in from the trees.

Vivian beamed.

It had been too fucking long.

Perhaps she had lost the letter, but not his poem. As she walked past the boundary, she whispered, *"The guardian and his goddess."*

His laugh came on the wind.

It was enough.

She started on the path cutting straight through the grass. With every step she took, the dew glittered blue. Mushrooms glowed blue at the base of the trees. And from the nooks in the tree branches, tiny creatures with big, blue eyes peered down at her. It was all *so blue.*

It brought her warmth and wonder.

It brought her concern.

All her peers, all the stories and research warned of these realms… dangerous, deceptive.

Predatory.

But she had always argued the same rule applied to humanity. Just as there were predatory humans and kind humans, so to it was the same for spirits. For fae.

But were they right? Was she being—

SCREECH! Something crashed into her face. She yelped, pulling it off her to reveal a bioluminescent blue bat.

Your conflict will not help you here!

She sucked her teeth, "You're a guide."

You were called for a reason, Dreamer! He freed himself from her fingers and flew to settle on top of her head. *You will understand as you walk.*

She sighed, continuing onward. It was a little… awkward at first but the bat would not fall from her head. Perhaps he was trickster—

A hummingbird appeared in the air from the light in the trees. It sang a song and sat upon Vivian's shoulder. Hummingbirds were such kind creatures, but—

The dew formed a rabbit at her feet.

Cute, but that didn't mean—

The glow of the trees formed twin koi fish, swimming through the air.

Such beauty couldn't possibly—

A spider formed on the rabbit's back, of the same glow.

Vivian laughed, "I get it!"

Above her came a birdsong from another world. The bird was formed of the light in the highest branches, with blue in its plumage lightening through the spectrum to yellow in its tail. It was large and wavy, with fiery designs spiraling all over its body. It was hope.

It was a phoenix.

Vivian beamed.

A doe joined them, small and quiet. Vivian held out her hand and the doe let her scratch behind her ear. She was so gentle.

Vivian whispered to her, "It's as if the forest changed itself just to help me. To… believe in me. It's such a strange thing for me." All the nature around her. All the magic, all the love. Even as the path grew mistier, she still felt it. She looked down to the rabbit at her feet. He was growing tired with the weight of the spider on his back. Vivian leaned down and the spider crawled onto her finger. "May she ride on you?" she asked the doe.

The doe nodded and Vivian handed the spider off to her. They say that helping another is supposed to make you feel better, but she whispered to her companions, "Nobody trusts me."

She heard a mighty voice in the mist: *Do you trust* **yourself**, *Dreamer?*

The voice was strange, but safe. "Would you believe me if I told you that everything you have gifted me in this wood, I would be condemned for where I come from? To ask for this kind of support would be selfish. To admit I trust myself would be arrogant. Even narcissistic."

He emerged from the mist and shadow—a lion, large and mighty. He was shaped from the glittering dew and the glow of the trees. His mane, large and thick, rippled with mist. He asked once more: *Do you trust* **yourself,** *Dreamer?*

She reached for the lion. He closed his eyes as Vivian scratched behind his ear and under his chin. She held him for a moment before admitting to her pack quietly, "Of course I do."

They nodded their heads in support. They stomped their feet in good humor.

She was lucky. She had gained companions before she even had her first challenge.

Alas, all things must come to an end, the Lion said.

The pack around her fell away, dissolving into the crystalized air of the mist. She looked around, confused, even upset because she thought she would have them through the whole thing.

She felt a hand on her shoulder, "You are not alone, Dreamer."

She turned to see an armored elf where the lion had

stood. He was dressed in oak armor and a sky blue cloak, which she expected. However, he had forest-green eyes and brown hair with gold highlights, which Vivian *did not* expect.

In fact, she was pleasantly surprised.

"The Goddess called you, Dreamer, and you answered. Your initiation has begun." His chin was raised high, both hands on the helm of his sword. An intense solemnity reverberated from him. "I am the Knight of the Wood. What did you learn on your walk?"

She smiled, "Conflict will get me nowhere."

"Your chosen weapon?"

Vivian uncurled her fingers and glittering, lavender magic poured from her palms.

"Raw magic," he said, surprised.

"I've always been a mage."

"What the Dreamer chooses is what the Dreamer chooses." He grasped the golden hilt of his sword, and it rang as he unsheathed it. The blade was as white as the mist surrounding them. He waved it over the grass, "Behold your boons."

In the grass, born of light, appeared:

A wand with willow vines woven into it.

A silver chalice with inlaid maple branch designs.

A pine-handled steel dagger.

A golden coin engraved with antlered birch branches.

"Tarot. *Nice.*"

The knight reached under his cloak, "This is for you to carry them." He handed her a leather vest.

It was not of professional make. It was sloppily cut, and pressed and sewn with very weak thread. The buttons were too big, but they were inlaid with a lion symbol, the knight's symbol.

He had made it himself.

She smiled with silent gratitude and took the vest.

As she gathered her boons, the Knight continued, "You will enter a land of your soul's making. You will encounter your life. You will have companions: some you share love with that they do not return, some you share love with that you do not return, and some you share love with that was never lost at all. Your destination will be the clearest thing you see."

Vivian wrapped the leather vest around herself, placing each boon in their respective compartments.

"Once you cross the threshold, there is no turning back until you have finished. With that, there is one final question: Who will you be when you reach the end of your journey?"

All the voices of the people in her life entered her mind and all she could say was, "I am not comfortable enough to share that answer."

"Conflict will not help you here. Only trust will carry you through."

She smiled at him, "I'm proud of you."

"Dreamer—"

"Clint?"

"I can't do this right now. I have to focus." He pulled his chin back. "Remember your lesson, Dreamer," he waved his green-leathered hand and the mist parted to reveal the mouth of a cave behind him. A barrier rippled out like sea water, "Your initiation awaits."

Vivian's reflection was so clear, she could see the green in her own eyes. "I'm not too worried," she said, turning back to the Knight. "*You* made it through. You're the Knight of the Wood!"

The Knight shook his head, "Yeah, I made it. But I can still fail."

"The fact that you finished your initiation is proof that your ability is trusted."

"That's only part of the journey. Once you get what you want, you have to keep it. I protect the wood, my people, and those who come to learn from us. Failure is not an option."

"You've already decided you suck before you've even started."

"You don't get it."

Vivian crossed her arms, "I've decided that I can complete my duty *and* trust myself."

"How?"

"Trust will carry me through."

"Oh, shit." Finally, *finally* Clint laughed, "I already forgot."

She smiled, "Proud of you, bud." She stepped forward when she felt Clint grasp her arm.

"Just so you know, it will feel like months in there."

"How much time will pass out here?"

"Only a few hours."

"Will I age months or years?"

"You'll age as long as it takes in there."

Vivian expected that. It was fairyland. It wasn't as bad as she thought it would be, though. Months in there and hours at here? That was actually rather tame. "Thank you," she said.

"Proud of you, kiddo."

Vivian pressed a kiss to his shoulder and turned into the barrier, letting its watery depths pull her into her initiation.

II. *The Summer Court*

For a while, there was only gold, shimmering light that warmed her like summer. It lasted as long as a dream. She thought, *trusting myself will carry me through,* over and over until she had the courage to look up.

Wetlands with towering willows lay before her for miles in every direction. Their vines hung low. The hot, humid air smelled like wet earth. In the shade of the canopy, Vivian could see a kingdom of willow wood huts, connected together by bridges. They spread as far as the willows did. "The Summer Court," Vivian said reluctantly.

In the distance, miles off, a tree rose higher than any of the willows. Vivian couldn't quite identify its species, but it was bursting with green branches high enough to vanish in the clouds above.

Clint's words… *Your destination will be the clearest thing you see.*

Vivian stepped—

The ground fell out from beneath her and she screamed as she rode a dark, musty tunnel all the way down.

"OW!"

She landed on her butt.

The floor was wet like the rest of the fucking Summer Court, seeping through her clothes. Before her was a table with several officials around it: soldiers, knights, advisors, and the Summer Prince himself with sun-kissed skin, coal black hair, and firelight eyes.

"Dreamer," he greeted.

A couple of his guards came and lifted her up from the ground.

A little overwhelmed, Vivian took in her surroundings.

It was a simple underground cavern with a few streams of sunlight pouring through, so that the summer fae would be nourished. Vague life grew around them, but for the most part, this place looked like the last line of defense.

"What happened, Dante?"

There was a long pause, "Delilah took the throne."

"You are both supposed to *share* the throne."

"I know."

"You are one half of a whole."

"She wanted my half for herself."

"She wouldn't make such a mistake. Why did she do this?"

"Does that really matter?"

"Yeah, it does. What about your people? Your court? The other kingdoms?"

"We can't ask the other kingdoms for help unless it is really needed. You know that. There is a way to these things."

"I mean, sure. But fae or not, you really should ask for help."

"I did," his gold eyes met her green ones. "I even prayed for it."

"Great! Where is it?"

He gestured toward her.

Vivian narrowed her eyes. This was "the quest," evidently.

"And what are we doing, exactly?"

"There are three teams. The Ecologists have the willows and wetlands, the Liberators will free the people, and the Royalguard will take back the throne."

It was not a siege.

It was a coup.

"Fine. But I'm not killing anyone."

"Of course. If Delilah or I were killed, it would harm everyone."

"I mean it, Dante."

There was tension between them already. But Dante

agreed.

With that, they began to mobilize. They waited for dusk to fall to evening. This would be an all-night affair. Vivian was handed footgear for the wetlands and a sling to climb the willows. She drew her wand from her vest as the hours turned into minutes.

Rainbow magic poured from its tip.

"How did you know that was the boon?" Dante asked.

"Wand is fire. Summer is Fire. Duh."

He smiled for a moment, but it quickly fell. "You should never have left."

"I'm not here to talk about that."

With that, they fell silent. As night fell, the firelight of the kingdom above lit with thousands of torches, mirroring in the waters below. It brought a sense of wistfulness to Vivian, for a moment.

But it was the signal they needed and with that, they all walked out into the wetlands, wrapped their slings around the base of the willows, and climbed. Dante, somehow, managed to be next to Vivian.

Clint had told her… *Some you share love with that you do not return.*

They all climbed at once, but the fae around her were strong and lithe. They knew how to reach their tree-top home. But there was a reason Vivian chose magic over the sword. She held as tightly as she could to the sling, waved her wand downwards, and a shield appeared beneath her feet.

It raised her up at the same speed as the fae around her.

Dante eyed her enviously.

"Why did she take the throne? Delilah knows the importance of the balance just as much as you do."

"I thought you weren't going to talk."

"Not about our past."

Dante paused for a beat, taking a breath, "She is the destructive side of fire, and I am the creative side. As you know. I believe that her destructive—"

"That's a reductionist theory."

"What do you want me to say, Dreamer!?"

"I want you to acknowledge that it is not as black-and-white—"

"You can tell *her* that once she's lost the throne."

Vivian exhaled in frustration; none of the complications mattered to Dante. She looked down to the wand in her hands and a seed stirred in her mind. She was starting to understand what her quest was.

As they rose, she watched the Ecologists split off, hiding among the willows themselves.

Dante had told her years ago, "*We and the willows are one. Without them, this court will fall.*"

She was silent as they climbed the final stretch to the top. As quiet as cats, they stepped down onto the bridges of the kingdom, Vivian's barrier vanishing from beneath her feet. She could see the whole Summer Court, lit up by torches, expand out in front of her. The huts and bridges crisscrossed all the way to the palace at the center. It was carved *into* the oldest willows here, the tallest and largest of the whole court.

That was the goal they moved toward. Vivian could be heavy-footed, so she waved her wand back-and-forth to muffle her steps. They needed to avoid waking any of the residents. However, the guards could not be avoided.

Dante took the first one, covering the guard with his hand. His summer magic glowed in his veins beneath his skin and he whispered, "Where is your loyalty?"

On the forehead of the guard, a symbol appeared. An orange flame.

"Good," Dante said, "Meet us at the courtyard." He released the guard and the guard nodded, making his way to the palace.

The Liberators and Royalguard spread out with Vivian always one step behind Dante. She watched him with two more guards, both of them on his flank. He closed his hand down on a fourth guard and asked the same question, "Where is your loyalty?"

On his forehead appeared a red flame.

Dante did not release him.

He clamped down tighter on the guard's mouth, pulling his arm behind his back.

He wouldn't let him scream.

Vivian drew her wand, her intent flowing into magic, throwing Dante back on his ass. She caught the guard before he could fall.

He gasped, coughing up blood. Dante roasted his throat and esophagus.

The guard gasped at Vivian desperately as she placed him down on his back. She poured the rainbow magic of her wand into her hand and pressed into his chest. He was destructive fire, but there was a bent for the creative. "You're summer, right?"

The guard nodded.

"Fire is Summer." Vivian aimed the magic for the creative, sparking it within him.

The guard coughed, and breathed smoothly. "Thank you," he gasped.

"Get to safety." Vivian stood up, walking past Dante without a word. But he grabbed her arm, "You have no idea what you just—"

"I said no killing."

His eyes gleamed with fire. *"You'll see,"* he hissed back.

They progressed, not a single word between them. Dante marked every guard they found and Vivian neutralized any act of death he tried for.

When they met with their team, the Liberators split off for the courtyard. Only Dante's guard was left, the Royalguard that he trusted the most.

He turned to Vivian, "For the sake of your clarity, we will take the long way."

"You will never be able to justify—"

"I disagree, Dreamer."

They made their way through the doors that cut through the kitchens. Dante warned his Royalguard that Vivian would neutralize any lethal attack, so they cut through any possible threats without hurting them severely.

They emerged to the highest tower over the courtyard. When she was a kid, this courtyard was the prettiest, coolest, kindest part of this humid wetland. It smelled of tangy fruit. On the hottest days, Vivian would cool herself in its waters.

She would talk to Dante for hours.

But the pool was dry now, replaced by dust, dryness, and tired workers. Dante stepped up next to Vivian, "Intelligence says they are worked from dawn to dusk without pay. They are fed just enough to keep them useful." Some workers swung their pickaxes, others stood to the side with water bowls. "What little of the population isn't here, are used simply for the pleasure of the guards."

Vivian clenched her jaw. "What are they mining?"

"An ancient material that was once used to spark our flames. It makes the fire near-impossible to extinguish. We stopped using it centuries ago."

"Why?"

"Because it butchered our ecosystem, and slave labor had never been higher."

Vivian's anger showed through rainbow magic sparking from her wand.

"You hate this just as much as I do."

Vivian shook her head, "Delilah isn't this stupid. It doesn't make sense."

"I intend to put things right, no matter the cost." He cupped his mouth with his hands and mimicked a birdcall for the Liberators. And then returned to his mission.

Vivian followed reluctantly.

The door to the throne room was right around the corner and Delilah's Royalguard attacked. Dante's Royalguard caught them, gaining the upperhand.

Vivian just watched.

They strongarmed them until they collapsed to the ground.

They entered the throne room as fast as their element. They cut through Delilah's Royalguard before they even had a chance to draw their weapons. Dante drew from his side a curved golden dagger as he and Delilah launched at each other. Unlike her brother, Delilah's hair was a thick, sun-kissed mane.

But her eyes were fire just like his.

Vivian stood by the door.

It was not her kingdom. Perhaps she should just let it happen.

She looked up at the glass ceiling above, where the highest willows reached. The way they bent, the way their vines wept. The way willows could protect you. The way they worked with the storm instead of resisting it... it was a rare beauty that only this court knew.

Rainbow magic poured from her wand into the willow

wood walls of the palace. A whisper came from her chest: *You can see it, even with everything happening around you.*

What spoke? The magic? The willows? Her own heart? All three? Vivian admitted to it… *Even in tragedy, there is beauty.*

The magic threaded its way through the palace. She followed it through the halls, back to the courtyard.

There was a struggle between the liberators and the loyalists. Swords drawn; blood spilt.

You can see them all.

A slave on the ground with a guard's blade at his neck.

A child crying over her dead mother.

A page, rare in his bravery, skewered by his own knight.

Dozens more in the same place.

Summer winds swept through. Vivian heard the rustling leaves and cracking wood of the willows. She brought her hands up, bursting with rainbow fire… *I can see them all.*

She guided her magic, **their magic**, through the palace, into the courtyard, and up the feet of every single person there.

They stopped.

The slave with a blade to his neck asked his attacker, "Why are you hurting me?"

"I… I don't know."

A guard watching the grieving girl walked up to her and took her into her arms.

That brave page collapsed into the arms of his knight as his knight begged him to stay alive. All that was left were sobs, horror, regret.

And all the people looked up toward the throne room.

Vivian sprinted ahead, the magic following her through the walls.

Dante held his golden knife to Delilah's throat. A vicious zeal poured from him.

Delilah was shocked he had the upper hand.

Vivian reached for Dante first: *Why do you want to kill Delilah?*

Like his fire, his rage, he answered openly: *Because she never made me feel like I belonged.*

Vivian guided the magic for his heart.

To Delilah: *Why did you take your brother's throne?*

Delilah: *Because he gained the throne through his gender—*

No.

Delilah: *Because I understand the duty of ruling better—*

It's deeper.

Delilah: *Because I can do a better job than him…*

And?

Delilah: *Because… he…* **he ignored me!**

Her truth was vulnerable and venomous. Vivian guided the fire for Delilah's heart.

She held onto the magic until… *she released.*

Dante grasped his sister by the collar and threw her. "WHY!? WHY DID YOU DO IT? WHY DID YOU TAKE IT!?"

"BECAUSE I CARE TOO AND YOU WOULDN'T LISTEN TO ME!" she collapsed to the ground, "I can't do it. I can't do it on my own. You didn't need to do this; I was going to reach out to you."

"Why?"

"My side doesn't work alone. I-It d-doesn't w-work," she sobbed.

Dante stared at her, confused. He looked up and past Vivian, his people stood in the doorway. Wounded, hurt…

and witness to everything.

Vivian stepped away for all of them.

She ran through a side door, down a spiral staircase, and out an arched, wooden door into the wetlands. She was closer to the tree in the distance, but only marginally. Only a few feet off stood a well. Her way out. "The *fucking* Summer Court," she spat as she stepped off the wetland and onto solid ground.

"Dreamer."

"No."

"Dreamer!"

"Go fuck yourself, Dante!"

"Vivian!"

"You don't ever *fucking* listen to me!" she shouted back at him. He was tired, sweaty, injured. And he was limping along after her.

"I am only…" the image of him shimmered like sunlight. "I won't be able to stay for very long."

He was a projection. She crossed her arms, seething. "You don't *ever* fucking listen to me. Your stupid coup wasn't necessary, Dante! Delilah's actions are not excusable, but her decision to take the throne was partially your fault. Your stubbornness is so bad it almost destroyed your home! You don't even—"

"I know the willows spoke—"

"There is a reason they did! They wanted your hearts to do the talking! *All I see* are people's hearts! There were opportunities for peace and healing all over your kingdom, but you wanted to rip it in half instead. Please *do not* do the same to your people. *They need* to rule now. *They need* to speak."

His projection shimmered and he sighed, "I became destruction."

"You're still a good person. I need you to act like it."

He crossed the gap. He whispered, "In another life…"

All those memories… she softened *just a little*, "In another life."

He pulled her wand from her hand and she fell backwards down the well, stretching her body into a dive. She heard him say, "You would have made a damn good queen."

II. *The Autumn Court*

Her hands pierced the surface of the water. She cut deep, met only with bottomless darkness. She never lost breath, but the current was wild. No way through, flung this way and that as if the ocean wanted to drown her.

But she was a Pisces. She rode the currents as easily as she danced with the stars.

She grasped the chalice strapped to her vest. The current pulled her and she let it. She prayed… and waited… and she gasped air into her lungs.

The water had become whipping winds. Thick clouds blocked out the moon. Trees cracked against the wind. All around her, a forest caught in an oncoming storm.

But she smelled apple and cinnamon.

Moonlight broke through the clouds to reveal the brilliant colors of maple trees.

It all led to that tree in the distance. Thick and winding, bigger than any mountain. It had *leaves of light,* the same scarlet-orange-gold as the forest around it, shimmering and glittering. It rose to mingle with the clouds and the stars.

Vivian started for it. The mud and fallen leaves were so thick, it was like pulling her feet through water. But it smelled of a lovely decay, and she yearned for the same companionship she always did this time of year. Her first love's face was only a memory. Just a feeling now.

True connection was rare for her.

She felt a deep chill, like the veil was thinning.

She found herself in a clearing. It was an even circle all the way around with altars of bone at the center of it. Atop the central altar was a skull with a crown of maple leaves and the last blooms of summer. Candles sat in his eyes, flickering.

Perhaps she should have run.

But she heard sobbing louder than the storm. It brought her such great sorrow, for she knew those cries well. They were hers when connections of great sacredness had ended. They were her friends' who had ended the connection with her. These friends, they were always lovely, beautiful, something of magic… and they disappeared on her every time.

She felt their sorrow, always. One way or another. But she never followed it.

This time, she did.

She found a girl only a couple of years older than her, nestled against the massive trunk of a tree. Vivian recognized her instantly.

Some you share love with that they do not return… "Luna?"

The girl looked up.

Luna was such a beautiful person. She had sharp ears, ashen hair, skin as brown as tree bark, and etched into her cheeks were tears that shined like the northern lights. They kept falling, never stopping. "Luna, just talk to me."

"Stay *away from me!*" Luna snarled as she stormed off into the shadows.

Staying behind was the *appropriate* thing to do. But **motherfucker—**

"Why do you always do this!?" Vivian demanded in

pursuit. "You always run!"

Luna cried out angrily, shoving out her hand. Vivian was turned around so she was caught up in the blinding shadow of the winding, tangling trees.

They were all right! This was a trick! She had been kidnapped! She wouldn't see anyone she loved for two decades! She was stupid to trust any of this! She knew, she…

A pause in the wind. *Up above.* Over the towering trees.

A twinkle in the sky.

Vivian took a deep breath, covering her heart with her hands. She whispered to her goddesses, to her spirits, "You are here."

Between breaths, the wind rustled her hair… and she heard it.

Luna's voice.

If Vivian came to her outright, Luna would run. So, for just a moment, Vivian closed her eyes and listened. Luna's voice was rhythmic and kind… and had been dismissed a thousand times. She carried her song with the rise and fall of the forest's breath. It was the wind and the moon and the coming storm… and Vivian could feel her song reach so deep into the ground, the trees lit up… from their deepest roots to their highest branches... right into Vivian's bones.

She opened her eyes and before her was a tomb. Luna was curled up inside, sobbing into her clothes. Her dress was torn to ribbons and rags. The material was waterworn, with faded colors that were once as vivacious as her court's maple trees. Only a thin, gray sweater covered her shoulders.

How long had Luna been out here?

Vivian wanted to ask, but… she had to do this right. She crossed into the tomb, a dusty, derelict place with cobwebs in every corner. A place of death. A place of reprieve.

She said carefully, *courageously:* "You keep your music and voice only for the flora and fauna."

Luna looked up at her.

"And yet you knew I was here when you sang."

"It doesn't mean—"

"You know what you did, with that song?"

"I don't care."

Vivian continued: "I am constantly caught in this autumnal limbo where I yearn for intimacy with a boy who only pretended to care. I was shaken and shattered. I yearned for him for four whole years afterwards." She sat down in front of Luna, folding her legs as if they were young girls in the stacks. "I think you know what that's like."

Luna's tears ceased for a moment.

"Your song was of such beauty that it took me out of my grief, and gave me the forest instead."

"It gave you—" She averted her gaze.

Vivian said it anyway: "Your song gave me connection." She could have stayed in grace, but her gut clenched up and she needed Luna to *know.* "When you left, you took that safety away from me."

Luna pulled her hair by the roots and screamed with all her pain. Vivian was thrown back, swept up with everything. The tomb, the forest, the leaves beneath their feet.

All into a storm.

A gray array of chaos that was impossible to navigate. But Vivian could feel, in all of it, the fear. The swirling, contrasting, conflicting ocean of emotions that she, that those she loves, that every friend she had ever had, held within their hearts. It was that ocean that convinced everyone to run in fear, to freeze in place, to hide who they were in order to survive.

Who could blame them?

Vivian shared her truth for one second and Luna tried to drown her.

She decided… to float in this space for a little while. Perhaps she was trapped forever. But it was warm and safe. She felt held in Luna's magic, of this girl who had abandoned her.

Vivian saw, from a splash of light, her chalice glitter. She detached it from her vest and the maple tree design lit up with the light of Luna's tears. Vivian cradled it in her hands, remembering herself. Was it her mind speaking next? Her mouth?

The words came either way.

I have been wandering my whole life for other souls who understand magic. Imagination and compassion. I have yearned for people who wanted to heal just as I wanted to heal. When I meet someone I love, they are family. No questions asked. Lover, family, friend. Love is love. I live by that statement.

You had all those things I yearn for, and yet you still left.

Why is that?

How can you be like me, and just leave?

It has been this way, all my life. I meet a girl who feels like my soul sister and she leaves, or moves, or just lives so far away. These girls mean so much to me. I love them completely, and that is at least in part, because they live by the same principles I do.

But, Luna, you left.

How can I search out girls who are like me… and they leave?

I only leave if I have to.

In the water, Vivian heard sobbing. In the water, Vivian felt denial.

If you can hear me, then you will hear me.

I held myself back with all the soul sisters I lost because I thought I was too loud. I was too weird. I was too annoying or overwhelming with my love. But I want you to hear me because out of all of them, you were my favorite.

You know better than this. Others who do not walk the path can be excused to a certain extent, but you are seasoned. You are educated. You know psycho-spirituality, philosophy. You know we are all one. You left and you know what you did was wrong. It is always the case that I love my soul sisters more than they could ever love me.

Perhaps that is the case with you.

But I'm certain of one thing.

"I really, really love you."

Anger and fear so great that the water pressed and contrasted. Like the sea, like a storm. Vivian might lose breath, might be stuck forever… but this was not an attack.

This was one last attempt at resistance.

Swirling, spinning, and Vivian let her love bring her still. She twisted and turned with the current, the ocean… *the womb*.

She swirled out.

Her feet met squarely with the earth. The last of Luna's ocean was contained within the chalice. Vivian bent the water from the chalice, straight at Luna, shoving her up against a tree.

Vivian stormed up to her and slammed her hand against the tree, right beside Luna's face. "You forget that I am an artist too. You forget that I bring connection too!" She barred her teeth, "You forget that I need love *too!*"

Luna said nothing, her tears never stopping.

Vivian shook her head, "You know how this works. Love killed you? Fine! Only love can bring you back." With that, she shoved the chalice in Luna's arms. She turned away, gathering up her belongings.

"Where are you going?"

"I cannot be like you. I cannot freeze out the people in my life. Yes, I have problems with them but at least they are there for me!" She gestured toward Luna, "At least they try to work things out with me, instead of drenching me in seawater!" She placed her satchel around her shoulders and started for the tree in the distance.

"Why do you care so much?!"

"I don't know anymore! I don't know why!" Vivian shouted back at her. "All the reasons I had are moot because you dropped me like a stone."

Luna crossed her arms reluctantly, "Say them anyway."

"Why should I?"

She rolled her eyes, "Because love killed you and only love can bring you back."

Vivian glared.

"Look I hate it too, okay!?"

Vivian closed her eyes so she didn't have to look at Luna. "Why do I care? Because you're sensitive. You're kind and open-minded. You have a good heart. I love your art and I love your fashion. I love your interests and your principles. You're beautiful. I love how you see yourself and I just…" she opened her eyes, shaking her head at the ridiculousness. "Fuck, *why did you leave!?*"

The rain finally fell.

They stared at each other, with no other sound but the wind.

Luna averted her gaze, pretending to speak to empty air, "There is… There is no way it is possible for someone to love me as much as you do."

From Luna's voice, that could light up forests and turn storms into oceans, Vivian heard every friend that had ever left her.

Sunlight cut through the clouds, creating an autumnal golden day. The maples swelled with color, apple and cinnamon wafted in the air, and the veil sang its song of mystery. Instead of a bone altar or forgotten tomb, around them were standing stones. Pillars of rock that had stood since ancient times.

Luna's appearance had changed too. The tears of light were now inked, weaving maple branch designs. Her ashen hair was dry and clean, held up in a sloppy bun by a tree branch. Her dress was as colorful as the splendid maples and her gray sweater flowed as the veil.

"You tried to kill me," Vivian said.

"I tried to make you go away," Luna replied, rolling her eyes. "It wasn't my fault your energy is so potent that you *got caught.*"

Vivian laughed, "You underestimate me, I swear to God."

"I really don't, I just…" She looked down at the chalice in her hands, "*Soror mystica.*"

"No. Nuh-uh."

"*Soror mystica.*"

"Nope! You do not get to use your voice to wiggle your way out of—" but Luna captured Vivian in a hug.

"*Soror mystica.*"

Vivian's resentment gave way to Luna's heart, growing in her like tree branches. All of Luna's fear and regret and…

"I love you," Luna murmured.

Vivian's eyes welled up, "*You hurt me.*"

Luna hugged her tenderly. "I do love you. I've just never experienced this before."

"What?"

"Love. Like…" she lowered her voice to whisper, "Love like this."

Vivian rolled her eyes in surrender before pressing a kiss to Luna's cheek.

"I'm sorry. I'm sorry, I'm just—"

"—you're scared." Vivian pressed a second kiss to her cheek, "I know."

Luna sighed in visible relief. She gestured toward the massive tree in the distance, above all the rest, "It's an ash tree. Just so you know."

Vivian sucked her teeth, "You thinking what I'm thinking?"

"It's the only thing that makes sense."

Vivian nodded, "We need to talk more."

"And we will." Luna held up the chalice, cupping it in her hands. Vivian cupped her palms around Luna's. The autumn winds caught in the chalice, swirling like wine, and Vivian took a long sip of it. She beat wings she did not have and as the winds carried her north, Luna's voice…

"*Soror mystica.*"

IV. *The Winter Court*

She tried to ride the winds like she rode the water, but their wildness was relentless and could not swirl her to safety.

No.

She had to navigate this.

In the distance, up here above the clouds, she saw the branches of the ash tree, gnarled and curling upwards into the cosmos. Glittering starlight weaved into them in-turn. Vivian grasped the pine-handled dagger in her vest and pulled it out.

Massive swan wings spread out behind her.

She beamed. She had always wanted wings. Perhaps she could cut straight through to the ash, but there were still two more seasons to get through.

So, she held up her dagger and it caught the wind. Vivian beat her wings to its guidance. It skated in a steady decline, cutting through the thick layer of clouds to reveal a wintry landscape of frost-covered evergreens. They ended at a frozen lake, which led off in the distance to a glacier towering like a mountainous gate.

Vivian had never seen a glacier before! She parried—

The winds pushed back against her, "But—"

You will see it. She looked around and though she saw nothing, she knew there was a spirit in the sky with her.

"What do you mean?"

She wants to see you. The spirit caught the dagger, carrying Vivian in the opposite direction. Straight for the evergreens.

At first, she thought they would find a clearing for her to land. But they hurtled closer and closer without any obvious landing sight. Vivian screamed, swinging her legs forward so that her feet slammed against a tree, catching herself among its branches. It shook under her weight. She held fast to it, she was *safe*… among pine needles and tree sap.

Her hair, thick and curly as can be, was stuck to the tree bark. Vivian groaned, detaching her hair, "It's gonna take forever to get that out."

"Collect the frost!"

Vivian looked down to see no one. "What?"

"Collect the frost! It has special properties!"

Skeptically, Vivian did as she was told. She pressed her finger around some frost-encrusted pine needles, let it melt a little, and then brought it to her hair.

Almost instantly, the sap in her hair dissolved into glittering frost.

Vivian smiled with deep satisfaction, *"Magic."*

She looked up. Sprites hovered in the air. Their appearance was somewhere between winter harshness and snowbell softness. Their wings were as thin as ice on window glass. From the cold air, they conjured an ice slide all the way to the ground. Vivian took the path, laughing as she slid to the forest floor.

From the momentum, she was instantly on her feet. She looked around and the forest was quiet. There was no life, save for the evergreens.

"Do you know who I am?"

Hidden within the shadows, Vivian thought it was just sheeting boreas winds. But no, it was a woman with a dress that could have been made of them. Her pale skin was freckled with frost. Her hair was as thick and curly as Vivian's, but an auburn red, gathered in a crown of winding, crisscrossing braids down her back. Her eyes were as blue as winter roses, as deep glacier, as frostbite.

Some you share love with that was never lost at all.

Vivian smiled, "Of course I do, El."

"Then you know where you stand."

"The Winter Court."

"And I'm its queen! Come with me. This will be an easy one."

"The Winter Court will be the easy region?"

She smiled, "Winter can be quite easy. You need only patience to wait it out, and solitude to nurture yourself in the meantime." She took the lead for the frozen lake.

With El's words in her mind, Vivian said, "The glacier won't let me near it."

"You must walk the temple path to reach the temple."

Vivian rolled her eyes at herself, "*Duh.*"

El laughed, "I didn't know at first either, Dreamer."

"It's so obvious, though. It's actually kind of embarrassing. I've loved fantasy and magic since I was a kid but I'm only really starting to understand what it is now. Before it was mostly aesthetic."

"What do you mean?"

"It's so pretty!"

El laughed, "I get what you mean. Do you know *As Above, So Below*, then?"

"I do. It means—"

"*We are all one,* yes. But what does it mean *to you?*"

They caught some of El's winds to carry them down the hillside. Wispy spirits rode with them, kissing the flora with their frost. As they stepped off, Vivian took a deep breath of cold air… *What does it mean to me?*

She exhaled, the air fogging up in front of her. "I was once told by a medicine woman to find my niche. I chose the Way of the Tree."

"*Continue.*"

Vivian reached her fingers up toward the sky, "My branches are into the cosmos: the astral plane, stars, angels, gods, the spirit world." She brought her other hand downwards, clawing her fingers, "My roots are into the earth. Ancestors, herbalism, animism, nature, folk magic." Then she covered her chest with her hand, "But my *trunk* is my inner world. My imagination, my love for fantasy and storytelling. My creativity, my love of the arts. My compassion, my value of authenticity. My passion and my strength. My healing spirit." Vivian smiled shyly, "As you asked… *As above, so below.*"

El beamed, gesturing toward the ash tree, "*Yggdrasil?*"

Vivian laughed, "I love it so much."

"Did you consider it when you created your belief system?"

"Probably. Subconsciously."

They came to the shore of the lake. The sun was almost gone and the temperature was dropping, but El walked onto the ice anyway. It could bare their weight. "It has stood in mythology for as long as the north has stood. Hearing those stories as a child kept me going."

Vivian was trying to listen, but the winds were picking up.

Trust will carry me through.

"It lives within the consciousness of anyone who has heard or seen it. It's in me. Like it, I'm mythic. I'm not just the storms or the snow or the ice. I'm the season itself. It's the spirits too. The winter sprites, the snowbell fairies, even the fae that keep the fires going. The whole thing is mine." Snow was gathering in the air and Vivian had to stop to cover her face.

"My magic… *I* am happiest in nature." The gathering winds had blocked out the sky. Vivian curled in on herself. She couldn't walk anymore. "To take a step towards unnatural cycles in my season is something I can't take lightly."

El crouched down in front of her. Fuck, she was *fae.* Tricky, capricious, as slippery as—

"But for you, I will do just that."

She took the dagger from Vivian's hand and held

it up high. It caught the wind, the ice and snow, the whole storm. It spiraled into the steel, layer by layer, until all that was left was the silent cold.

Vivian shivered profusely, covered in frost. She couldn't move.

El crouched down again, "You know this. Use your fire."

Vivian inhaled and let the air bring fire to her lungs. She held it, warming her whole body until it was too painful to hold. Then she exhaled it like a dragon, laughing as she went, all the frost thawing away. "I can't do that in the human world."

"The realms of reality and imagination are closer than you think." El held out her hand.

Vivian took it and as she stood up, she looked out into the night. A thousand stars, the big, bright moon, the northern lights dancing beneath them, and a frozen lake that reflected it all back as clearly as a mirror. Snow-covered evergreens. And with her sensitive eye, she could see frost hovering in the air. "Glitters like living December."

"Wow. I need to get that as a tattoo."

"I might beat you to it."

El laughed. As she handed Vivian back her dagger, Vivian admitted, "I thought you were going to kill me there for a second."

El's eyes widened, "No, no! I'm so sorry, my magic is just tied to my emotions! I got a little excited!"

"I know! Well, *now* I know. It's just… you threw the cycles off balance for me?"

"You know me as well I know you. I just want you to be okay."

"I… really like you and for that affection to be returned is rare for me."

El gently grasped Vivian's arm, "It is hard for me to let people in."

Vivian covered El's hand with her own, "Will your choice impact the rest of the court?"

El looked out over her court, "It's hard to say." They started for the temple, "My magic is the season itself. But… there are just spirits *everywhere!* Doing their own thing! There is me, but then there are spirits for the snow itself, and the frost. There is a spirit for the wind, but then there are spirits for each *kind* of wind. There is a spirit of *water in general,* but then the lake itself has a spirit. There is the Evergreen King, but then *each tree* is a spirit on its own."

"That's what I'm learning about the gods."

"What do you mean?"

"It's like a *symphony,* El. It all works together as one. In the Greek myths, every child Gaia and Ouronous have is a subcategory of what they are. Time, Shooting Stars, Inquiry, Kindness, Motherhood, Magic, the Moon, the Sun… and then *their* offspring were subcategories of them and so on."

"Do you believe everything has a soul?"

"A spirit tethered to it?"

El nodded avidly, "Was it designed that way? Or do you think it just happened naturally?"

"As Above… *So Below?*"

El beamed, "The balance is bigger than I thought."

They reached the glacial temple. It looked as if it had gone untouched for centuries. Perhaps that was on purpose. But if this court was a symphony, this temple sang the loudest. Both women inhaled that song deeply, and exhaled it like a prayer. It was… *ancient and hallowed. And right.*

El took the dagger from Vivian's hand, and pressed it into the wall of the glacier. The temple froze over it, and an entrance of raw ice opened for them. Solemnly, El warned:

"This is a place where the veil is thin, Dreamer. There is a reason I don't take a lot of people here. The spirit world and the material world merge here. It will be deep and cold."

"Just because it makes me uncomfortable doesn't mean I won't understand."

El hesitated… and then took Vivian's hands.

They entered the temple.

Within was a cathedral made of white, glowing, cleanly carved ice, held up by columns of the same make. El raised her hands once for swirling, curling décor to form within the face and the nooks of those columns. At the center stood a podium, simple in its design. But Vivian could hear that it was the source of the temple's song.

The floor was as clear as glass. Below it, Vivian could hear a heartbeat. "This might be the thinnest spot I've ever seen." She backed up, crossing her arms. "I'm just, I just… I-I need a—"

"Were you closer to your mother or your father?"

Vivian sighed, "My father."

Flowers appeared from beneath the ice floor. Rose petals, thistle blooms, brilliant gazanias forming a spiral path leading to the podium. A single flower blossomed atop it: a pomelia with pink petals reaching into white.

"I wasn't close with my mother either," El said.

Vivian stepped up to the beginning of the spiral. All she had to do was walk it. Like a doctor talking to you as they remove your stitches, El would be here the whole time.

As she started, El said, "My mother never had much to say. My father was the one who knew how to help."

"Diddo."

"How so for you?"

"I'm queer, neurodiverse, mentally ill, potentially genderfluid, highly sensitive, plus-sized, I am open about not liking to work, and my vocation is a combination of healing, magic, and art," Vivian replied, the steady rhythm of her walk bringing her calm. She retrieved a gazania, balancing it between her fingers.

"That is… a nightmare when someone doesn't get it."

"That's been my life."

"I knew my mother loved me."

Vivian shook her head, "She should have been the person to understand."

El stepped up beside Vivian, walking with her, "People make a lot of mistakes when they are scared. When they don't understand."

The magic was swelling strong. "If she had trusted I wasn't a monster, I wouldn't have this wound. Your mother's choices are more excusable—"

"How? Her fear still led to years of self-hatred for me."

"And you just forgave her."

"I haven't, quite. But I know generational trauma scars us all. You and I are living proof of that."

Vivian reached the pomelia, its power stronger than any of the flowers at her feet.

She placed the gazania in her hair and cupped the pomelia in her hands. A light opened from its center and Vivian saw a lake nestled in a hilly valley, blue under summer sky. Vivian walked for it, reached for it…

Go too far…

"I know." She kept her feet firmly on the grass and reached her index finger through the lake's surface. Instantly, someone grasped it. Her face was young, her eyes as red as pomegranates.

But, from beneath the water, *she rose.*

Fiery red hair, dress black as night, eyes green as spring.

She turned… a crown of snowbells, daffodils, and violets blossomed in her hair. She held out her hand and her mother took it. The wheat-blond queen of the harvest, with summer green clothes, tears thawing on her cheeks, "You're okay."

"I had to go, Momma."

She stroked her daughter's cheeks, "I know, my darling. *I'm so sorry.* I never meant—"

"I know you didn't, but you did."

Her mother hesitated. A long moment of quiet… "I know. Let me tell you why."

Up above, thunder shattered. Lightning struck. Blades crossed, ringing with blood and betrayal and pain. Brother against brother, sister against sister, parent against child. Time ate his kin and Tenderness saved them. Vivian had seen this all before, but it played out in shadow. As if she was only meant to see a peak.

But their story fell to the earth like rain.

Humans crossed blades. Blood, pain, and a once beautiful paradise was betrayed by foreign invaders. A woman with thick, dark curly hair wept, blood staining her nightdress. She wore the face of Vivian's mother. She wept within herself, *They will not be remembered.*

"No. They have been remembered."

Who?

"I know very little, but… *Diana?*"

The woman laughed: *She won't die!*

There was a loud bang, shouting. The woman urgently looked behind her. But still, through her tears: *I'll be okay.*

"You'll be dead."

But I'll be okay.

"No! *Please*—" Vivian was pulled back from the woman, the wars, the goddesses, from the lake. She inhaled sharply, reaching for the pomelia, but it collapsed to ash.

"No!" she turned to El desperately, "No, you have to let me back in!"

"Dreamer—"

"You have to! I-I was so close to *understanding. Please*—"

"Dreamer, *look!*" she waved her hand out to reveal the inside of the cathedral had changed into a Sicilian *piazza.* Just like her mother's old pictures, carved down to the tiniest detail of architecture lining the streets, except in ice! It led to a church in the baroque style, rising to an arch at the very top. In front of it was an old sign that read: *Santa Maria la Cava e Sant'Alfio.*

"St. Mary... *of the Pit and St. Alphius,*" Vivian translated. "This is my mom's home."

"You created it."

Vivian pressed her palm against the wall of the church, and she could feel a life that was not her own. Laughter, warmth, the sweet taste of *gelato* on her tongue. "Why does this feel safe?"

"Generational joy is just as possible."

Vivian... would have children one day. But she knew she would make mistakes too. Slowly, she admitted to El, "Momma did change when I told her she hurt me."

A song, and the northern lights appeared around her. She turned to El, holding out her hand... and El returned it. "We'll see each other again, don't worry."

"You want to?"

"More than anything." She smiled; the last thing Vivian saw before the lights carried her off. Her voice echoed… "I'll never leave you, Viv."

V. *The Spring Court*

The aurora borealis danced her south until they no longer shined. As they faded, she emerged and found herself on the edge of a gentle land that smelled of wet earth. She stood behind a line of birch trees, leaf tips peeking through.

Vivian smiled and eagerly got to her knees. She scanned around the birch tree roots to find… snowbells! She reached for them, ready to forage.

Her hand met with another. Her eyes met with another. He was short, shorter than Vivian, with a fluffy, curly brown beard and matching hair. He had sharp ears, a kind smile, and a clever spark in his spring-green eyes. "Leo," Vivian greeted.

"That is King Leonardo to you. This is *my court,* Dreamer."

Vivian found that to be a tad rude. The last boon in her vest glittered in her mind—the coin engraved with antlered birch branches.

Fae had strange customs. Including that if she paid them to shut up, they would have to. But… Leo was kind.

So… "Fair enough," she conceded.

He whispered, "What are you doing here?"

"It's my initiation."

"What!? Congratulations!"

"You didn't know? You fae always—"

"They don't tell us everything. I'm not quite sure what your task is."

"The last three have been quite diverse, let me tell you."

"Well, we'll find out! C'mon, Dreamer! I want to

show you what I have been working on."

Leo gently detached the snowbell bloom from its stem. He led Vivian through birch trees into the sprawling forest of his court. Oaks rose high over the birch trees, sprites danced spring green to life, and spring beauties speckled the forest floor.

"We are in *the thaw*. Daffodils and violets will be next," Leo informed her.

Some incredibly pretty sprites flew up to them, with flower petal wings and crowns of snowbell petals and grass woven together. "My Lord, the stars are at the right angle."

"Excellent! You know what to do."

The sprites flew out into the forest in a swarm as colorful as their season. They rose to a net filled with glass orbs. They retrieved them and handed them to all the flora the forest held.

Vivian could instantly feel the flora's concern.

Leo held up an orb for her to see. Within it was raw sunshine. "*Leo,*" Vivian challenged.

"With a constant source of sunlight—"

"They could fry! Have you at least tested this?"

"As much as time allowed."

Vivian narrowed her eyes, "So then you are aware that if this goes side-ways, you may overwhelm your own court before midspring—"

"*I* am the sovereign."

That again. Leo's sensitivity that he didn't know how to properly harness!

The coin glittered in her mind.

"Fine," Vivian relented. She handed the orb back to Leo and leaned against an oak. She watched quietly, all the while weaving healing prayers into the soil for the flora to inform her of any problems.

Within a few short days, they wilted. Leo flitted and flew between them desperately. "Why? What is this?" His was the concern of a father.

The oaks, the birches, the spring beauties all turned their eyes to Vivian.

She got to her knees and pressed her palms to the earth. The prayers she had given had woven themselves into the underground network of roots and fungi. She rode it into the trees, brush, flowers, herbs.

They gasped: *Too much sun.*

"They are parched."

Leo looked up at them, "Perhaps it was too much for them."

"A brush fire could have started!" Vivian retorted angrily.

Leo's eyes glinted with anger as well. But he raised his hands. They were strong, with a silver ring around his left ring finger. Storm clouds gathered and rain fell from the heavens.

Vivian could feel the land take a deep breath. "You will have to keep these rains going at a relatively constant manner so that they may—"

"—recover. Yes, I am aware."

His lack of malice calmed her. "Why are you doing this?"

"If we can enhance the efficiency—"

"Take it from me, Leo. Trying to "bring efficiency" to nature doesn't work."

"I can make it work."

"Your season is so beautiful," she murmured.

Leo set his jaw.

"It's so gentle."

"Gentleness does nothing in the long run." Leo

walked ahead of her.

The rain thawed the earth. As Leo predicted, daffodils and violets rose. Oaks and birches flourished… but a few of the more fragile herbs were having trouble. Vivian stopped beside some wild basil. "Do you have any of those sunlight orbs left?" she asked a sprite.

Leo glanced back at her.

The sprite handed her a very small one. Vivian placed it in the drenched earth beneath the basil and it grew green and strong. Vivian told the sprite to do the same for any other flora that were wilting because of the rains. She walked up to Leo, falling in side-by-side with him.

His sprites administered measured sunlight to all the places it was needed. Flowers swelled with color. The air was light.

They entered a valley where the wind was warm and gentle and all the flowers blossomed. The animals grazed, the sprites danced, the nymphs breathed their perfume into the air.

"*The Flourish* has come," Leo said thoughtfully. "Lilacs, lilies, and tulips are next."

"And cherry blossoms and magnolias!" Vivian proclaimed, running in glee for the nymphs. They laughed, handing her a crown made of their blooms. "*It's been too long*," they sang.

"It's so good to see you all again!"

Vivian laughed with them, she played and sang with them. Zephyrus winds spun them all in dance. "It has always been a dream of mine to dance with you all," she whispered to the lilac nymph as they all laid in the grass together. Nature spirits were no happier than in the height of their season.

Yet, Lilac smiled sadly. "Our king has forgotten."

Vivian looked up and Leo was briefing his sprites

once more. She balanced herself on her elbows and listened: "I have refined the tech to include sun and rain. As before, it will be released in balance with the course of the stars."

Vivian sighed. Stars had more of a spiritual impact than a physical one.

"Rise, my sprites. As high as you can go," Leo commanded.

The sprites did as they were told, carrying the orbs of sun and rain to the skies. As Vivian watched, she whispered to the nymphs, "Ladies, collect any herbs, flowers, and berries that can be harvested. They will not be of use for much longer."

Like the oaks and birches, the nymphs sighed with concern. They retreated into themselves and released the resources they were ready to share. Vivian gathered as much as she could in her dress, but Leo's strategy began before she could finish. As the rains fell, Vivian kissed a *thank you* to the nymphs and went to shelter made for Leo and his fae folk. Vivian sat beneath it, observing.

The coin glittered in her mind again, but this time, she knew what Leo was thinking. And he knew what she was thinking.

Vivian rose at dawn to the labored breathing of the flora. The birdsong was panicked. The coyote calls were rapid. The fauna that the flora fed and sheltered gathered around the fae camp, seeking help.

Vivian made sure she was the first on sight, even before Leo.

Every single plant in the forest was wilting. Even the trees weighed down, their branches hanging low.

Leo stepped up beside her, "Perhaps if we—"

"Stop this."

"You are not—"

"Sprites!" she called. They came to her tired and breathless, with heavy wings. "Cease the task that your king commanded for just a few days. Allow the sun to shine as much as he can."

They nodded in unison. The sprites rose into the sky and the rainclouds parted for the sun to shine in all its splendor. At first, the flora shook at the shock of the warmth. But slowly, that gave way to comfort. Branches strengthened; leaves perked up. The flora blossomed bigger and brighter than ever.

At dusk, Leo and Vivian laid together in a valley of pink-and-white magnolias. They were still; they did not want to disturb the recovered beauty.

"Why are you doing this? Really?"

Leo hesitated… "You've seen how the world is changing. My realm is nature, Dreamer. All the courts are. The fluctuations in the cycles have impacted every one of us." He sighed with deep concern, "One day, humans will come for us. I… I need to have *something* to give them."

Vivian pressed a kiss to Leo's forehead.

He took her hands, "Why are you so resistant to efficiency, Dreamer?"

"Humans already came for me," she answered bluntly. "They expect me to fall in line, do the work, and deliver for a system that has never done me any favors. They do all this, without even bothering to ask what *I* need."

Leo sighed, "You feel I am behaving that way."

"*Yes*, but… what is your plan?"

"I was hoping I could nail the seasonal cycle to a science so we could deliver the harvest sooner. My season is the foundation for the harvest at summer's end. If we could deliver abundantly and consistently, perhaps we could survive a human invasion."

Vivian had to admit… the plan had potential. "Have you tried discussing this with your subjects?"

"My council feels we shouldn't sully ourselves with humans. To them, we are superior. That is ridiculous, of course. Humans have modernized far quicker than we have."

"I asked if you consulted your *subjects*. Your council can flit about all they want, but it is the plant and animal life that provides for *all of us*. The nymphs, sprites, and animals could probably work with you on this."

"That is an excellent point. It may wound some egos."

Vivian snickered, "Humans are no different! The global warming crisis could be fixed within a few decades instead of in generations if people would just *take it seriously*. But people don't want to pull themselves out of their comfort zone. They'd rather be lazy than do the right thing."

Leo traced his hand along the curve of a magnolia branch above him. "We are more similar than any of us want to admit." He pressed a kiss to her knuckles, "*The feast* comes next. The delicate blossoms will wilt to give way to sunflowers, roses, marigolds, and all the other flowers that blossom into late autumn. Everything will be green. Everything will be hot." He smiled, "I know you love these mild days."

"If you could make *that* last longer, I might not complain."

Leo chuckled.

Together, they walked into the final days of spring. Leo insisted there was nothing left to do! "Despite the hiccups, this was a rather successful experiment."

"I mean, I agree. But we can speed up the process a little."

"How so?"

A long time ago, Leo had taught Vivian the art of

gardening the forest. Vivian gathered up the decay to recycle into compost, cut away at any invading species, and burned away—

"Vivian, no!"

"Why?"

"It's going to be a hot year, love. We can't control a fire if it goes awry." He gently closed her hand, extinguishing the flame.

"Good point."

Soon, it was just as Leo predicted: hot and lusciously green. "The harvest will be abundant this year," he commented. His nymphs, birds, sprites, and animals gathered around the vernal throne. It was a chair built on an oaken stump with a frame of harvested birch wood. Pink peonies, lavender lilacs, and brilliant violets were woven into it.

Leo offered it to Vivian.

"What? No!"

"You are a queen."

"Only in spirit! My wanderlust is too strong for this chair. I'd be bored off my ass."

Leo laughed heartily, "I like it more than anything I've ever done."

"Which means you should have it. You will not cease to care."

"And you would?"

"For the people? No. For the throne? Yes. I would end up handing it back to you for that very reason."

He chuckled a little, but his smile fell. "Thank you… for not using the coin on me."

Gently, so softly, she wrapped her arms around him. She pressed her lips to his, a kiss she never thought she would have. "It would have been cruel," she whispered. She pulled her boon from her vest and placed it in his strong hand.

He sat in her warmth. She held him until he turned to birch trees and marigolds. His last words were like lilly perfume… "No matter what they say, lover, you are the one who makes the final call."

VI. *The Path Beyond*

As Vivian stood up, day became night. The clouds parted, the branches of the ash stretching out infinitely.

She was almost there.

She walked the rest of the way, no magical transportation required. No cover or weapon. Summer evenings were always so warm, she could walk through them bare. She removed her boots and socks, the grass still soft from the nourishing Spring rains.

In all her life, she had wanted an adventure like this one, with someone beside her. But, instead, she had been with five people she loved dearly. All she had to do was reach out and they would welcome her. To have that kind of certainty was a blessing she had always yearned for.

So, yes, she was alone in summer.

But she was not lonely.

She reached the tree, so large it could form its own planet. It entangled with the stars, to worlds far beyond this one. She climbed upon its massive root and in the distance carved into its trunk, was a small, arched door. Carved in its center was the image of the maiden with flowers in her hair and eyes misted with deathly visions.

Vivian walked along the massive root sacredly and eagerly, to the doorway. The maiden was moving. "Were you watching me all this time?" Vivian asked.

"I've been waiting for you all this time."

"Did you have to go through all of this?"

"You know I did." Misty white parted for green irises, as green as Vivian's, "The longer you wait in pursuing what you need, the more violent the impact when you can't go anymore without it. What did you need that you waited too long for?"

"Trust in myself."

The door waved in the wind like a curtain. A rip in creation. An entrance to another realm.

Vivian was not afraid.

She stepped across the barrier, but in the in-between, she asked: "What did you need that you waited too long for?"

The same as you.

Vivian crossed and within she found the universe. The cosmos, trillions of stars in every direction and a bridge of the northern lights that stretched across stars and galaxies and planets. It was as stable under her feet as wood.

Her boots had vanished from her hands. She had no more boons. The entrance behind her vanished. Even her satchel was gone, save for the poem her guardian had written her.

It was just her, barefoot and alone, with only the bridge to walk.

As she took one step forward, the poem dissolved in her hands into rosy pink magic. She allowed it… she just knew a dream was coming true.

What did you need that you waited too long for?

The magic rose into the stars and to Vivian's left, a One-Eyed Wiseman answered: "Courage."

Another step and of the same rosy pink to her right was the Mother of Roses: "Faith."

With every step she took, the rosy magic created another face for her.

To her left, the Magician: "Trust in my kin."

To her right, She with Wings: "Initiative."

To her right again, Grayman with Stone-Eyes: "Self-love."

Beside him, Deadman, Judge of Deadmen: "Trust in her."

She looked down and right in front of her sat a boy, a man. Kindness and Calm. He smiled in congratulations: "Just trust."

Beside him, a veiled woman appeared. She was hidden, but her energy was mighty. She said: "I had no such trouble. But nevertheless, *Patience.*"

Kindness and Calm laughed and as he faded, three Winged Beings appeared before Vivian. One held the moon, the second a spear, the last freshly-made paints.

The first answered: "Intellect."

The second answered: "Strategy."

The third answered: "Movement."

Angels they were and their wings gave way to the Boy with Wings on His Head. With a gleam in his eye, he answered: "I could stand to slow down a little bit."

Vivian almost snorted and as she did, the Kind Lady of the Lotus appeared. She answered with a mother's love: "Assertiveness."

Vivian was skipping now, swirling and jumping, the rosy magic dancing with her. Here among gods, among spirits that live forever, she felt like a child again.

To her right, a Half-Masked Woman: "Authenticity."

To her left, the Archer in the Trees: "Compassion."

To her right again, the Triple-Headed Flame: "Mortality."

Vivian smiled, "*Fascinating.*" She turned to skip—

And she stopped. To a mighty mermaid above her. As blue as the ocean, as black as the night sky, as big as the cosmos.

Her smile felt like love. *"Memory."*

Vivian reached for her, but her palm pressed against another that was not the mermaid's, but just as large. She followed the arm up and up to the massive person hovering in the ether…

A dreamer.

She had long, thick, brown curly hair gathered in a braid down her left shoulder, with a flower crown atop her head that changed with every season. The cosmos bled into her dress, dark and glittering. The northern lights shaped into a corset around her chest. Forest-leaf slacks and black boots of the deepest soil. An oceanic satchel, with art, magic, and healing supplies. A dagger holster in her boot for wartime. A sheath at her belt for her maple wood, phoenix feather wand. An Italian horn at her sternum, a Celtic Cross at her stomach. Around her shoulders, a sky-blue cloak that cycled with her soul. And a heart that glowed with rosy magic.

Her eyes were the same green as Vivian's.

"Hey, bitch."

They both laughed.

"Can you answer it now?" the dreamer asked. "Who are you now that you have reached the end of your journey?"

Vivian grew into *the dreamer.* "Myself."

Epilogue: *The Blossom*

The legends say… Persephone emerged from the underworld both Goddess **and** Queen.

They say… Odin sacrificed one of his eyes to hang on *Yggdrasil* for 9 days and 9 nights, all to gain runic wisdom that has been forgotten and remembered throughout the millennia.

The legends say… Osiris became the god-king he is because of the love of his wife. Healed after unimaginable pain and betrayal. Healed by her hands into the dead's king.

They say… that Guan Yin's compassion was so great, she redeemed all of hell. She continued on as a bodhisattva with her mission of compassion for all who live. *They say…* that Jesus sacrificed himself on the crucifix for the fate of all humanity. He rose from the dead three days later to show us there was no reason to be afraid.

I don't know what the stories will say about me. But I can show what my guardian wrote when he saw me emerge:

The storms, all these years, had torn and ripped apart the wilds of the region. But never before had I seen them this way. The winds blew in directions, this way and that, uncanny to their nature. They bent, created enormous pressure. There was confusion among the natives, even discussion of evacuation.

Except… for her family. Her blood kin as well as her soul kin.

They felt called to the center of the storm, the eye gathering over the lake. For some of these people, their decision made sense. For others, it was something they would have never been caught doing. For some, she no longer spoke to. But they remembered what she had told them about the storms. About her.

One-by-one, they made their way to the lake.

As they gathered under the eye, it brought calm.

There she was, all the way off, standing on the water. She looked like she had been adventuring for months.

She raised her left hand effortlessly.

The whole storm, clouds and winds, lightning and rain, swirled and spiraled in the air towards the center of the lake where she stood, wrapping themselves into her. Layer by layer, it disappeared into her hand until with one final breath, sun broke through.

Birdsong rang out. The air was still.

The world smelled of wet soil.

She smiled softly. To all of them, she said: "You should have believed me."

APHRODITE
GODDESS OF LOVE & BEAUTY

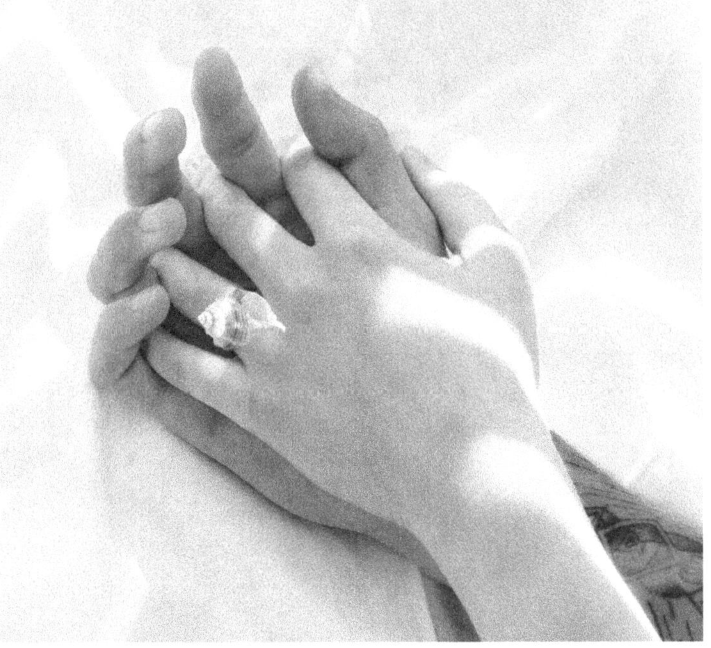

The poets speak of me as this beautiful, elusive, untamable force. Venus. And yet, I am so feared. I am love, darling. But love touches every crevice of creation, even the parts of it many would deny. This is why people die for me. Once you taste true love, in whatever form it may take, there is no going back.

3 MINUS 1 IS 2
Johnny Francis Wolf

It is in DROOLING
we reveal a
certain

predilection,

TRUTH.

Not laudatory,
fawning in our LEANING
towards
youth.

+

Principles that govern
when we DRIBBLE,
who
we are..

propensity to 'pretty',
slighting strength,
and shunning

SCAR

(and pairing up of
women thinking THREE
of us on par).

+

As if these two would
have a fling, a boy
and girl, girl
STEW..

assure thee, all dear readers
male, they wouldn't
NEED
a

you.

(Aphrodite and Sappho)

LETTING DROWN
Johnny Francis Wolf

the paper labors wield the field you felt
where ink bestains and bloody rains portray

abundant lamentation, blows are dealt
as lachryma on vellum wizens gray

———

she rides upon a spoor of bestial whim
a wolf allowing wafting in her wake

to breathe the air of balladry and hymn
imparting pen with lavender in lake

———

if swimming out to where the mortal sink
releasing favor, fabric falling far

is black and white when wholly glowing pink
denuded for the barest moon and star

———

in silhouette the colors move to ash
without this one are left alone to splash

(Hera fore was wed)

DESIRE AND DECADENCE
Lady Andariel
© 10082022

The secret folds softly opened, revealing the prize that had been the object of many other's unfulfilled desires.

The perfectly moistened petals dripping with honey so sweet, I could not help but drink.

Oh! And drink did I! Until the liquid decadence became my source of life. Perchance akin to an intravenous fluid injection for my now desperately dripping thighs.

The deliciously filling fountain flowed endlessly as I tasted each petal's flowering individually.

Nectar seeped from every pulsating pore.
Pouring into my vase, exposing finally, the innermost core.

Gathering this immutably gorgeous flower into the depths of my starving darkness was neither gift, nor peace. I drained, hungrily, the drops of her silk-like dew. I knew I could never taste all she offered. I gently brought her spent form in my arms, and we fell deeply asleep knowing we would worship again soon, in the temple of Aphrodites.

INITIATION
Lady Andariel
© 10162022

Blue eyes shine brightly at me, set in front of the evening's rising moon. The sand beneath our feet begins to cool, and the wind picks up, brilliantly tussling her hair.

She is divinity on this most hallowed of nights.

I reach out my weathered hand, slowly running my fingers along her sweetly scented, soft skin. She smells of coconut and pineapple. Her breath quickens and her heart rate jumps a time or two.

"Breathe, child. The time is nigh, but not yet is it due."

She whimpers at my voice and struggles against my ministrations. I notice a momentary downturn of her red, velvet lips. I caress her dimpled cheek with my roughened finger tip.

"Is that a frown?

My lovely girl, you have been chosen to bear the seed of new magic into our world. You are highly prized, perhaps even envied, but more so, honored."

The guests begin to arrive. The air is charged with a magic high.

Fires are built in circles along the beach to keep warm the many attendees.

The band finishes a final sound check and begins playing. Musical notes fill the air with the tempered sound of Beethoven, but with a darker, more metallic flair.

I call the guests to order.

Each already knowing their place, they close ranks.

Ever so slowly a chorus of voices chants in deep tones. The words unintelligible to those who are not aware and do not know.

"Nos, tenebrarum custodes ac cultores, deos veteres invocamus."

The chanting grows stronger and louder until a final drum beat rings out in an unholy timbre bringing a deafening silence.

The wind howls its disdain and the clouds have once again cleared, leaving the beach blanketed only with the light of the fires and a Full Moon. The sound of lapping water against the shore perfectly sets the mood.

The Virgin is brought into the center of the circle, placed in front of the seeding table. She is docile now, as if hypnotized.

Her eyes focused on some distant dream or perhaps a favorite fable.

I step up and gently remove her robes. Ah! How marvelously her pale skin shimmers and glows.

She slowly kneels.

With lips gentle as a spring breeze she kisses my feet. Her fate is sealed.

There will exist no single Mother or Father to the child borne of this night. For her, each participant would freely give their own life.

Both the bearer and born will from henceforth be known as Daughters of Lillith, Queen of the Night.

Dear Jacob
Sarah Herring

Dear Jacob, I love you with a love that cannot die.

Please know that no matter what.

I'm so sorry for the time I wasted.

For the years I ignored you.

I'm so sorry for not loving you the way I do now.

I BEGGED God to allow me to love you for so long.

I write this sobbing, with a throbbing soul.

Please forgive me.

I don't deserve you.

I never did.

I never will, but you love me anyway.

I can't possibly fathom why but you do, and you do it gracefully and properly.

You are a god yourself, my son.

Please, dear Jacob, allow me to show you what it means to be my son.

I adore you.

I will protect you and I will be your best friend.

I promise.

Please don't let my folly become your demons.

I never want you to feel pain.

I want to be pregnant with you forever.

Let me love you.

I will not betray you, even if it costs me every last thing I have.

You are worthy, Jacob.

It is your birthright.

I will not let you fail.

Thank you for choosing me.

Thank you for being my son.

Because of you, I have eternally won.

I owe you all of it, with interest.

It's yours.

I don't want it.

Keep it.

Cherish it.

And please just don't forget me, my precious.

You are God to me.

Love, Mommy

OCEAN DUST
Erin MacKenzie

Standing before the dawn of her own creation
The burning sun bows to her beauty
The wind follows her like a ghost
And her glowing face echoes the sunset.
She belongs to the elements; she belongs to the world.

And yet she stands apart.

If you pray to love and to all that is holy,
You pray to her.
She fills the earth and the skies
With love and despair.
She burns herself up, just to be enough.
Just to feel their love.

Bury my bones in the sand by the sea
She says,
So that I may wash away with the lonely tide.
From sea I came, and to sea I'll go
As nothing but ocean dust.

PERLA
Alexandra Folch-Pi

Sleeping under this rock, surrounded by all my things I have collected, it makes me feel content to be living this life. I am mostly unbothered and get visited by my family often, which I appreciate. Life underwater is complicated but can be simple. For example, I've heard about human girls and how they spend hours in front of the mirror to like the way they look. Where I live, there is none of that. Vanity exists, of course, how can it not when you live so flawlessly in nature and under the ocean. My skin is impeccable, and my hair constantly floats which eliminates that mortal problem all together. There is never a reason to paint our faces, it would just come right off.

As I fly, I mean swim, through my neighborhood, the sounds of the water in my ears is relaxing and all the creatures swimming around me adds to the calm.

"Hi Perla."

"How are you doing, Perla?"

"Your hair looks beautiful today, Perla"

I hear all the little voices in the distance as I zoom by. Especially from my little buddies on the ground. They are the most underrated part of the ocean; they aren't just bottom feeders. They can give really great advice. One of my closest friends is a starfish and Benny would never lead me astray. The big guys are nice too, but they take up a lot of room and can't just chill. Have you ever been to a Whale bar? I do not recommend it unless you want to be shoved in a corner unable to get a drink because you're the smallest person in the room and the tender is a whale himself. I'm laughing now, but that is a story for another time.

So, yeah, my life is pretty perfect. I don't really have a need for a male in my life right now. They never brought me anything good. Everything seems to be going well when a male comes along, no thank you. I'm on my own journey to find who I am, and I feel like I have barely scratched the surface. One thing I know for sure, I am too much of a mature mermaid woman to be giving these little sea anemones a place to mess up my life. I try to flow through life with a light heart. I hate when there is a disruption of my peace.

Every now and then I'll swim to the very top just to stick my face out for a moment. The sun is a warmth I do not usually experience. When I first felt the sun I was not sure what was happening to me. It felt scary but comforting at the same time. Alas, I cannot stay in the sun for too long. Much like humans spending too much time in the water and starting to shrivel, that happens to me. The dive back down is my favorite part, straight down, fast, and no stopping. I happily let the ocean drag me down for my amusement.

I am home once again, swimming under my rock to my giant mother of pearl bed. I flop onto it weightlessly and start daydreaming. I can understand, based on everything I have just said, you're probably thinking, "wow her life sounds awesome" and "what could she be daydreaming about that she doesn't already have?" Well, I would be lying if I said I didn't crave some adventure. Yes, everything down here is wonderful, but it is the same thing all the time. Everybody needs to get away sometimes, or at least that's what I've heard.

Even if I wanted to, my family is so close they barely let me out of their sight and there are so many of us. My clan is the largest one on this side of the ocean, I come across family that I didn't even know I had. You can always spot us by our birthmark Iris on our bodies. Mine happens to be on my stomach in between my rib cage nestled safely under my breasts. Which are covered by shiny sea material and shells, in case you were wondering. My hair is a copper red, and my tail is a purple teal color. I've been told it's a beautiful color, which is good to hear I guess. I see it all the time.

A few moments of silence then my sisters start swarming into my room. They must've just got home. I love them to death but sometimes they are too energetic and positive for me. Not that positivity is a bad thing, I just seem more grounded than them which is interesting since we are floating around all day.

"Perla look at this hair piece the tuna made me! They all worked together pretty quick," said my sister Aura. The hair piece was like a shell crown. It did look cute.

Aura is my favorite sister, I know that is harsh to say but in a family as big as mine we all kind of pair up and it's normal to have those that you bond with more.

"It looks so good, some of their best work yet. You look beautiful," I replied.

"Thank you! How's your day been?" Aura asks.

I stare at her, reluctant to answer the question because I can't think of any response I haven't said before, because everything is the same.

"It was ok, same sludge, different day."

"Must you be so negative? You mean you swam around flawlessly and said hi to all your friends and family. While floating through paradise?" she replied. She may be my favorite sister, but she still has the mindset of everyone else.

"How can you know if this is paradise? We've never seen anything else." I countered.

Aura just rolls her eyes at me. She is aware of how I feel, we have discussed it numerous times.

We hear a knock on my cave. "Guys did you hear about Finnien?" my other sister, Kailani, comes in and asks.

"No, I haven't. What's going on?" Finnien is a younger merman. He is not part of my clan, but I see him and his family at different functions. He is maybe around 15 years old.

"He went missing. No one has seen him since two days ago. I really hope he is ok, I heard that it was following a fight he had with his father," Aura took the reins and explained.

Fascinating, this may sound weird. You would think living in the deep blue ocean that neighbors would go missing all the time, but at least where I live no one has ever gone missing. We are relatively out of the way of large traffic and hunting creatures. He would've had to travel far to really go "missing".

"Wow, that is so strange. It is unheard of in these parts."

"I know I thought the same thing." Kailani replied. "They are organizing a search party for him. If we don't take the matter into our hands, who will?"

She made a valid point.

"Ok I will be there in a minute." I agreed.

"Me too!" Aura chimed in. Excited to help.

All three of us along with some other members from my clan, a couple other mermaid clans, and whatever fish and bottom feeders that were willing to help and keep their eyes open. I know it's not that easy for them to get around sometimes. Basically, we all split up. Aura and Kailani went in a different direction together. I sort of strayed off into this dark area. I never mind going off on my own. I've always been the "lone wolf" of my family, you could say. Also, another odd thing, I like darkness and small places. That stuff has never scared me. That being said, I'd understand why no one would want to come with me. I can't imagine how it is on land, but darkness underwater can be a little eerie. I can't help it, it happens to be peaceful to me in some way.

The water is completely pitch black at this point and I can even feel more of a chill in this water.

"He probably would've never gone this way," I say out loud as I turn around and start to swim back. Before I turn around completely, in my peripheral vision I see a flash of light. No, a shimmer of light. It is coming from below and I start to follow it. What a gorgeous cave I've stumbled upon. It was so bright and shiny almost like it was calling me over. "I'm going to check it out, if I'm drawn to this cave, I'm sure he was too." Don't get me wrong, mermaids love shiny things. I have yet to meet one who doesn't. However, this was different I think, this would draw anyone in. I hope it's not a trap.

I approached the entrance of the cave slowly. Take my time going in. It was a white iridescent color. Close to the color of my tail but more white, less blue. It was so bright it was almost like there was a light on. But suddenly the light fades. For a girl who loves the darkness, I did not like where this situation could possibly lead me. I started to turn around and go back but looking back was darkness as well. The beautiful shiny cave I just approached was an illusion at this point. Nothing left to do but to keep swimming forward. I started to panic slightly but then the ground below me started to change. Almost wooden, then I started to experience an abrupt burst of pressure from the water I was swimming in. It started to push me up, it was so fast my hair was being whipped back along with all my appendages. I had no choice, all I could do was close my eyes and hope for the best. The pressure was so great I couldn't even fight the water. Of course, with my grounded mind a part of me is sure I could die in the moment, not a clue where this little snafu is leading me. At least today is not boring, I chuckle to myself.

I must've fallen asleep or blacked out is more like it. My body felt so heavy. They must've done something to me, whoever they are.

"Something is happening to me! Something is wrong!" I start yelling to myself.

I'm wrapped up in a ball completely in shock. This must be how babies feel when they are born. Well not exactly but the same sensation. Everything was hard and bright and loud. I wasn't being cradled by the water anymore. That has always been there for me as a comfort, which I never even knew till this moment. Like an everlasting hug, the weight of the ocean. It was the strangest sensation I've ever experienced. I found myself gasping for air. What an odd thing to say and feel. Me "gasping for air", I chuckle to myself again before going back to the panic. Even my chuckle "blows" on me, what the fuck is happening.

I open my eyes for the first time and see my skin with dirt on it. I'm shaking uncontrollably, my breath is matching it. I can't handle this I think I'm going to, yup. I turn to my side and vomit, what seems to be water and phlegm. I feel myself sweating and my heart racing. I stay on my side and wish I was back in the pleasant, simple environment of my people. Is this torture? Am I captive? I miss Aura. My thoughts are racing, then again it all goes black.

I'm not sure what's happening yet. I can't move and my eyes are still closed. Definitely more rest needed. Then I felt my arm move and now I am moving. I have risen off the ground and thank god, because the pressure in my head relieved so quickly. Lying like a rock on the ground was causing a throbbing headache, but I couldn't move. It still lingers, but is entirely more manageable. I'm still moving, swinging my.. Legs back and forth in the air. Oh god I might vomit again. I have legs. My beautiful tail is gone. How could this be happening? Am I human? How cliché could this story get? I wish I could move. I wish I could say something. Finally, one of my eyes starts to open while the other half of my face is nestled in a chest, nice and warm. I see a beard. It's a man. He is carrying me, is he the reason I am here? Friend or foe? He seems to be carrying me quite intimately, but how much can you tell from this. My eyes close again. I feel myself drift off into sleep again.

I'm in the darkness now, where I was when I went through that cave. This time I turn around and see the light out. Treading the water to my sides, I start to swim fast after the light. No matter how fast I swim it still continues to be out of reach. Let me put more speed behind myself.

"Ughh," I grunt with effort. Still nothing. What is happening here? Is this a trick? "Help, Help!" I yelp and then wake up with a startle. It was a dream.

The bed was soft, warm, and inviting. Incredibly comfortable, even the air around me was warm. There was a smell in the air that was also inviting. A sudden rumble appeared from my stomach. I'm starving, which I guess is a good sign. Where do I even start? I don't know where I am or what's going on still. I feel so out of control. One thing I know for sure if I do not get something to eat, I will be useless either way.

I remove the covers and see that I am completely naked. So odd, yet, interesting. I have zero idea what's going on. So, this is a human bosom? They look so weird. Where is the color and shimmer? They also seem far more naked then my original ones are. This is a primate huh? At this point I feel as far away from my fish ancestry as I can be. I place both of my.. Feet on to the ground. There is a pink, tan, and teal dress that has been laid out for me. It must've been, why else would it be sitting so perfectly. I put it on, and it feels so freeing, comfortable, and a cute color.

It almost felt like I was floating to the kitchen because something smelled so good. The whole home seemed dome shaped and wooden, but it was the comfiest vibe. There were pleasant trinkets and artwork along with a stack of blankets and a fireplace. You get the idea. I walk into the kitchen to find a three-layered cake. It was sloppy and lopsided. Covered with icing and raspberries. I was surprised to find myself craving this, I've never had that much of a sweet tooth and yet, I could not stop myself. I placed my whole hand on one corner and tasted it. It was a perfect amount of sweet. I grabbed another piece and found myself starting to stuff my face. Then I heard a creak in the ground, like the floor was aching and whipped my head to the right.

"You need something to wash that down?" A man said.

He was standing in the hallway. I could tell he was judging but had a smile on his face. Maybe he found it amusing. I'm embarrassed for my behavior, but what's done is done.

"I'm so sorry. I'm usually not like this. It just smelled so good and I'm not sure what was going on. I thought, for sure, some food in my stomach will be a start to getting a handle on things." I found myself rambling. "I don't usually have a sweet tooth either, so this is very not normal for me." I stopped.

As the man came into the light from the dark hallway, I couldn't help but notice his features. Jet black, short hair, jet black beard, and muscular physique. His eyes were incredibly blue. I've never seen such beautiful blue eyes. We mermaids have black irises, such colorful fluorescent people but our eyes are black. I would assume that's the "creatures of the deep blue sea" in us.

"It's ok, really. There is no need to apologize," He responded still with a smile on his face. He reached to grab a plate for me to use. Handed me a tool to eat the food with. "Here's a fork. Please, sit down. Would you like something to drink?"

"Yes, please," He is very helpful. He pours something out of a little pitcher that he pulled out of an ice box. Walked over and put it down on the table next to me. I look at it.

"Here you go, it's buttermilk. How are you feeling?" He asked me.

He's concerned about me? Is he the one who found me? When I was being moved I remember seeing him out of one of my eyes. It was only his beard though.

"Hungry," I coughed, choking on a mouth full of food. "I mean, I feel a lot better." So stunned by his good looks, I almost forgot about the hard questions. "Thank you for asking. Are you the one who brought me here?" I asked, unable to lose his gaze.

"Yes, I am. My name is Gabriel and this is my home."

He said as he gestured to the rest of the area that I analyzed previously.

"My name is Perla," I introduced myself. "Are you the one who brought me to this land?" I asked, nervously for the next response. Gabriel paused for a second and looked at me with shock. Still, it doesn't tell me much about what he will say.

"This land? What do you mean by that? No...," He shook his head. "I found you in a tree hollow. You were just lying there passed out. You looked a little shook and sickly. I wasn't sure what happened, but I knew you don't leave someone like that all naked and cold." First of all, I love that he has seen me naked. I've always been super comfortable with my body, and I bet he loved what he saw. Yes, I know he was saving me, and I was not looking good, but still. "What do you mean 'did I bring you to this land?'" He continued.

I caught myself pausing as well to take a look at my surroundings. I wasn't sure how to explain this. He might think I'm crazy but, here we go.

"I'm not exactly from here. Where I come from I have a tail and live under the sea. I know it sounds crazy right now, but it's the truth. Believe me or not, either way I came through something or something happened to me and now I look like this. Human," I explained. He seemed receptive, nodding his head with his mouth open and his hand grasping his chin. Possibly a little shocked. He thinks I'm crazy doesn't he?

"Hmm… I believe you," he declared. Now I was the one who looked shocked. "Oh, and I hate to break it to you," he turns around and starts walking to the hallway again. With his turn I see what looks like wings. Turned down and connected the center of his back. They were a beautiful red, a very vibrant color.

"You, you have wings?" I was surprised. From the front I would've never guessed.

"I hate to break it to you, but you're not human. You're a pixie like me." What the fuck? This experience keeps getting weirder. I walked back towards the bedroom and got a glimpse at my wings. They were a purplish teal color, almost like my tail. It made me feel better, like in a way that I have not completely lost my mermaid.

"Wow, it's beautiful," I commented.

"Yes, it is. No pixie around here has that color. I'm surprised you didn't notice you had them because you flew over to the cake." Did I really? Could it be possible that I truly was floating over to the cake. Incredible.

"Is that why you believe me?" I asked.

"Yes that, but also recently someone was found roughly around the same spot as you and they have said the same thing. I didn't believe him, but I believe him now," he explained further. That must be Finnien! Thank god this whole strange experience will not be for nothing. I knew he must've been drawn to the shiny cave.

"Though I must say, he is nowhere near as pretty as you," he blurted out so confidently. I felt myself turning red. I guess I wasn't the only one checking the other person out.

"Oh, well thank you," I tried to look into his eyes while I said it. It was hard. "I think the boy you mentioned went missing near my home. Funny story, that's actually why I'm here. I was out looking for him and stumbled upon a portal I guess? Or something that brought me here, I don't know," I explain.

"Ah, I see," he replies. "Well, tonight all the pixies across this part of the forest are getting together for a fire and celebration. We do it at least once a week. I'm sure he will be there. The last I heard he was staying with a friend of mine. They'll be there, I'm confident." Yes you are.

I nod. "Okay, that sounds perfect. Everyone back home will be so relieved."

"That's great to hear. I'm happy to be of help," Gabriel responds.

I started to feel connected. It's hard to explain but just talking to him I could feel this pull and I am almost certain he could feel the magnetic energy himself. Frankly under the ocean I've never had this feeling which is why I never felt the need to be with anyone. Not now though, hell all he did was call me pretty and the chemistry was potent in here.

I could swear he was starting to lean in, wait yup he is definitely leaning in. Here comes the panic. "So what's the celebration for?" I asked in order to interrupt the flow of attraction. I also walked around him and back to the kitchen to eat some cake. He followed.

"It's a celebration of life that we like to do," he explained as he poured me another glass of buttermilk to wash down the honey cake.

"You guys have a celebration of life at least once a week?" I asked.

"Yes, we do. Life is a precious delicate journey. We like to appreciate the opportunity and be grateful. In our own way of course. We believe the universe helps provide blessings if it knows how we feel," Gabriel said with passion. I was impressed by his optimism about his home and the traditions they do. In a way he kind of reminded me of Aura. It helps me understand why she talks about our home like she does because life is a gift regardless. It made me think about my near-death experience coming here and how grateful I am to have made it. "You'll see," he said as I looked up to him from my cake. "It's a blast."

"I think that's really cool that you guys do that," I replied. "Can we go back to the tree hollow?" I asked. I need to see what I came through, what is in that tree?

"Sure, we can. I'll have to warn you, there didn't seem to be anything there. It was just dark but let's go," he explained. I wiped off my face and put my plate on his counter to be cleaned later. We both started making our way to the exit, the door was dome shaped as well. Fitting for the charming little home.

I want to take this in for a second. Standing right outside Gabriel's home has the sun hitting directly onto us. I closed my eyes and let the warmth wash over me. There was no pain and no fear of shriveling, my skin and my brain liked it, I could tell. A tear started to form in my eyes, it felt like such a high. My mood was lifted, and I couldn't catch my breath. What a euphoric feeling. Behind my eyelids I see the orange, yellow, and brightness. This is what I've been missing out on? The sun is such a life force.

"You ok?" Gabriel asked. I probably looked crazy. He probably never saw someone react like this from walking out in the sun.

"Yes, sorry. I've just never been able to step into the sun like this before," I explained. "It just feels incredible."

"Wow that is crazy to me. I definitely take the sun for granted," he looks up at the sky. "I'm going to remember this moment. It will help me to always remember to appreciate this," he puts his arms out to signal to the entire forest surrounding us. I hadn't even noticed the rest of the forest.

I take a step off the ledge and let my wings carry me. It wasn't hard to comprehend, it was instinctual. This is a wild experience, am I dreaming? How did I go from a swimming creature at the lowest part of the world to now flying. Being so small, it keeps me from flying above the trees, but still. I skipped right over human, though still closely similar. Gabriel and I were flying all around in circles, through flowers and grass. It felt like nature was reaching up and trying to call us down. I swear the grass was stretching out to me. I could almost hear them. This is what it's like being a pixie. One with nature on land. I flew above the trees and sat at the tip of tree. The sky had so many colors, ranging from pink to blue and white with the sun right in the middle of it all. The view was breathtaking, I took a mental image. I hope I remember it forever.

I hopped off the tree to let myself fall. Gabriel was watching me from lower down. "Perla!" he yells for me. Does he think I'm actually falling? He catches me.

"I was going to catch myself, you know." I gaze into his eyes while he carries me and flies. One hand on my back and the other under my knees. It fell silent and all I could hear was my heartbeat. This time I felt the urge to be closer to him and put my face on his shoulder. I was the one leaning in now. Then suddenly, we landed, and he set me down.

It was this giant dark hole on a tree. Having only the tiniest bit of light coming in from the entrance. Wooden and just dark. There was nothing to be seen, I tried to wonder a little deeper. However, I kept my distance in case something happened. Definitely not prepared for that to happen again. There wasn't any sign of trickery or capture. No science or destruction. Just a regular abnormally deep hole in a tree. Which led me to the conclusion that this was not intentional. Besides the cave being shiny underwater. Hmm maybe it was meant for us to explore? Not to be intended badly. "Interesting," I blurted it out after complete silence and investigation.

"What?" Gabirel asked.

"Nothing, it just seems fine," I responded.

"Yeah, the only weird thing to me is how shiny the leaves were on the outside," he pointed out.

Picked up my head and turned it to him. "How did I miss that?" I asked him. Clearly I was too distracted with a slightly romantic flying experience to pay attention. Man, I'm off my game. I flew outside for a quick peak, and yes the tree did have shiny leaves but not like the cave's. The leaves were still green but had a shimmer to it. That's probably all the pixies need to notice. "The cave I went through to get here was a shiny shimmery cave."

"Well, that's definitely a pattern. What does it mean?" he asked.

"I have no idea," I deduced.

We hopped out of the tree hollow and started to fly. I followed Gabriel to the gathering in order to find Finnien. The sun was starting to set while we were on our way. Another beautiful experience I'm happy to have witnessed. Without having time to stop and enjoy it. It didn't matter because I was bathing in it. Finally, we landed on the ground. He leads me to a tree trunk that has already been chopped. The flat surface that has been created on top of the trunk because it has been chopped, was now a meeting space for pixies. From the perspective I had, the tree trunk was huge. Already so many people arrived. They all looked like me as well with beautiful wings. A lot of greens and reds but Gabriel was right, no one with my color. I immediately see Finnien because his wings are an abnormal blue compared to everyone else's. "Finnien!" I yelled for him in between a crowd of people.

He looks over at me. "Perla? Is that you?" I'm surprised he could recognize me at all like this, but I guess I recognized him so.

"Hi! Yes, I'm so happy to see you. Everyone has been

so worried about you back home. I joined a search party to find you and wound up here," I explained.

Finnien looks relieved. "Happy you found me. Don't get me wrong, it's fun here but I wasn't ready to leave my home."

"I completely understand. It kind of took me by surprise too," I tried to relate. If I'm being completely honest, besides the initial getting here, this experience has been one that I've been craving for a long time. I was ready to leave home. "It's ok we'll get you back."

"Hello! And welcome!" I hear a voice coming from a higher platform on the stump. I look over and it is an older pixie covered in robes. "Though we have done this many times I wanted to formally greet you all. There was once a time a millennium ago at least, we were not blessed with the peace we have now. I would like to share with you the story of how we have come to such peace, that we hold so dear to our hearts," the older man gestures to Finnien and me.

"He has never told this story," Gabriel whispers in my ear.

"Who is he?" I asked.

"He is one of the last surviving pixie elders of our forest. They hold the history and knowledge of our people." I look back over at the elder.

"Long ago, before there was structure and civilization amongst our people, we all used to fend for ourselves. We were not neighbors or a community. It was purely about survival. There wasn't any contentment amongst creatures. We were feral and rivals. Especially between the pixies and the mermaids." I stand there with my mouth open. "We are land creatures, and they are water. Mostly out of the way, what kind of rival could there even be?" He asked rhetorically to lead to his point. "Mermaids tend to the nature of the sea just the same as how pixies tend to the nature on land. Both hold a special bond with their surroundings. It was as simple as a competition on who would be able to do it better. In the moments when mermaids and pixies would communicate it was never kind and always were words of jeering or hate," in this moment I felt like people were starting to stare at Finnien and me.

"It was until one of our kind fell in love with one of theirs that we found peace. Their names were Rose, she was a Pixie, and Salé, he was a merman. No one can truly say how it all started. There were rumors that Rose would fly to the ocean front in the middle of the night often. Her family just assumed it was a hobby or maybe she found the ocean front pleasant. They couldn't deny it was a nice area. It was discovered about their affair, and they refused to end their relationship. They chose love over our, at the time ridiculous, notions and way of life. Now in the times we live in, I admire them for their will to rise and fight for what they believe in and for who they love," he said with a smile on their face and a little chuckle with it. "We could all stand to be a little more like them," his smile disappeared. "Alas they were executed for their crimes." The whole crowd gasped. "With their death, the shiny tree was created in our forest and the shiny cave underwater. Their spirits still live with us now in those portals. Till this day we aren't really sure how it happened just the same as our lack of know-how for why we have been placed in this world, in this universe. They are symbols of the bold life force that was held in them. Nature agreed with their want for peace. The world created a solution for no one to have to struggle anymore if this was to happen again. Though they loved each other, not living in the same physical capacity and environment made it difficult, not impossible, but difficult.," he signals to the rest of the crowd. "May we take this celebration today and be grateful for the sacrifice of Rose and Salé and to welcome our friends from our sister land here tonight," and now he is pointing at us. Everybody starts cheering. "Let us remember why we are here and let us be equal!" He then drinks a glass of something, and everyone starts chanting. The bongos begin to play, and everyone starts dancing.

"May the party commence!" Gabriel enforces.

I get handed a glass of something. Before I imbibe in the festivities I look at Finnien. To make sure he is having a good time, that he is ok. I turn to him, and he is talking to other people having a drink himself. As long as we are among friends, he is safe.

Everyone is dancing and I'm still standing on the sidelines drinking my drink just observing. I wonder if the elders in my waters know about this story and never shared it. Maybe it has never been a problem until now. I'm not going to worry too much about it at the moment. To think there was a time when the world was like that, wild.

"You having fun?" Gabriel walked next to me and asked.

I looked at him. "Yes, just stuck in my head a little about what the elder said," I explained.

"I know, that was some pretty crazy stuff. The evolution of life is a wild ride. Unfortunately, they were probably not the first sacrifice to be made for things to really change and become more civilized," he said. It was sort of a grim way of looking at things if you ask me. Though he did have a point. Change doesn't just happen overnight. "It was a pretty romantic story though, I got to say," he concluded. "I'm a sucker for this kind of thing."

"I like that. I never used to be. When it's real it's different if you ask me," I responded with a blush.

"Of course, the real thing is best, but it's fun to hope and dream right," he replied. He was more of softie than I expected. "Would you like to dance?" he asks and puts his hand out. I think for a second and go for it. Why not? A little fun couldn't hurt.

The sunset is completely gone now. Torches lit on all the edges of the stump and our bodies are all up against each other, half naked crowd, and sweating. Moving to the rhythm of the chanting and the drums. My body is pushed onto Gabriel's. I could feel his hands moving down my back over my wings and down to my ass. Coming back around, the punch starts hitting now. I'm not a hundred percent sure what I have ingested but everything felt heightened. Damn, this has all been one huge trip as it is. Everything had moving edges, close to seeing double but not really. Gabriel touching me and me touching him brought out this warmth in me. It was euphoric and erotic. I ran my fingers over his lips as he played with my hair. He put his hand under my hair and grabbed it by the roots. Finally, he leaned in and kissed me. It was a hell of a kiss, and we continue to.

The morning hit and the sun was shining through our windows. Birds were tweeting and I rolled over to continue cuddling with Gabriel. We're completely naked now. Last night was one of the best nights of my life. An adventure of a lifetime and experienced things I never thought I would. The party last night had unbelievable, incredible vibes.

"Good morning," Gabriel wipes his eyes as he wakes up.

"How did you sleep?" I asked.

"Good," he responded.

"So that's what they call 'making love' huh?" I asked.

He laughs "Yes, it is. I guess as a mermaid you don't usually do that?"

"No, never. Even if I wanted to, there was no one I ever felt this way about. I mean, comfortable enough to do so," I explained.

"Well, I'm happy to hear," he said. "Listen, Perla, I don't do this that often either. I know that right now there is a strong level of attraction between us. I could feel it from the first moment," I love the honesty. "If you're into it, I would love to see where this goes. Now that we know there is a way for you to come back and forth. I figured we could try?" he asks. I appreciate him thinking this through. I'm not sure how my family will feel about it, but I've never really cared for how they feel about that sort of thing. I can also take my time telling them.

"A thousand times yes, I would love to see this further. You see, I haven't wanted to give someone a chance for a long time. I don't want to give up on this now," I stated.

"Hell yes! That's amazing, you have no idea," he gives me a peck on the lips and then kisses me all over my face, I giggle.

"First, I need to bring Finnien back home safely. I'll be back okay," I state.

"No problem, take your time. I trust you," Gabriel smiles.

I put another dress on. This time it's purple and gold. I walk out to the living room and see Finnien still sleeping on the couch next to the fireplace. Such a good kid. I saw him sitting talking to some of the other teenagers all night last night while the adults were dancing.

I pour myself a glass of buttermilk and hear a creak in the floor. I see Finnien coming down the hallway. "Hey there, good morning."

Finnien yawns, "good morning!"

"You ready to go home?" I asked.

"Yes," he said without hesitation.

We begin to leave the house and hop off the ledge to fly over to the tree hollow. We land directly near the darkness. "I'm a little nervous," he lets me know. I'd be lying if I said I didn't feel the same way, but I think I understand now.

"Just remember Finnien, we are going into water. We are no longer breathing air and we will no longer have legs," he looks up at me. "It's a shock to your body but maybe if we are prepared for it, it'll be less excruciating. We were raised in water, remember that," he nods his head. He understands.

We hold hands walking through. It was like last time, the light began to fade behind us. It is completely gone now. Water started to build up at our ankles, rising higher and higher the more we walked. It felt like we were walking forever. Then suddenly, oh shit. It came rushing at us like an eruption of water. I was scared for a moment, until I touched my face. I had my gills back. We're completely floating in water now, my eyes are closed again but I'm breathing. It's fine, everything is fine. The rushing of water in my ears stopped and I wasn't being pulled by it anymore. I open my eyes and we are both floating in the cave. We made it!

I look at Finnien. "Are you ok?" I ask in panic. His eyes were still closed.

"Did we make it?" he asks.

I laugh at the circumstances, "yes we made it."

"Thank god," he says unscathed. We swim out of the cave and out of the darkness into our neighborhood. People start swarming around us.

"Oh my god! It's them!" Aura sees me. She swims over and hugs me. "Where have you been? Are you ok? I missed you so much!" Still hugging me.

"You found Finnien?" Kahlani says and hugs me with relief.

"Yeah it's a crazy story. I'm safe. We're both safe," I reassure them. "It's hard to explain and I will explain soon but I have to go back now," I state.

"Go back?" Aura raised her voice.

"Don't worry about me," I held her hands. "I'll be back tomorrow." She smiles, that's a good sign. "Trust me," I kiss her forehead. Then I swim back to the cave, seeing Aura explain to Kahlani in the distance. I'm so grateful for them, very filled with love after everything that has happened.

I swim through the portal again. This time expecting to be more primal. I come out fine, a little more anxiety then I would have going into the water but that'll fade the more I get used to it I believe. Approaching the entrance to the tree hollow, I see Gabriel waiting for me. "How did it go?" he asked.

"They had some questions clearly. I just didn't want to answer all of them right now," I explained selfishly. "It's ok, good thing I can always go back tomorrow," I concluded.

"Damn right," he responded. Then put his arms around me as we kissed and started to fly up at the same time. Directly in the blanket of the sun.

About the Authors

Dexter Amoroso

In a world where words are his weapons and nature is his sanctuary, meet the gentle warrior with a panther-heart. He gracefully tends to plants, caressing petals and kissing flowers, a poet in bloom amidst a colorful mosaic of life. With the spirit of a samurai and the wisdom of a gardener, he wields his Katana, delicately crafting Haikus that dance upon the winds.

But beyond the ink-stained battlegrounds of poetry, he embraces a different kind of responsibility. A devoted father, he dons the cape of parenthood, nurturing his two little boys with boundless love and unyielding patience. Balancing the delicate artistry of verse with the chaotic symphony of fatherhood, he becomes a student of life's multifaceted melodies.

Never one to settle, he established the McKinley Publishing Hub, a self-publishing haven where dreams take flight. Here, authors find solace, support, and empowerment, as they navigate the vast literary landscape. With a pen in one hand and a world of possibilities in the other, this gentle warrior ignites creativity, cultivates growth, and paints stories that enchant hearts, leaving a legacy as enduring as the ancient cherry blossoms.

Lady Andariel

Lady Andariel resides in the United States and has worked with the public, through restaurant management, for the past 35 years. Lady Andariel's pennings were born out of a need to put voice to every human emotion that could possibly exist. Whether love and romance, self growth, hatred, anger, vengeance or peace, Lady Andariel feels it immensely and gives allowance to speak the innermost secrets that we all keep hidden in the double locked and well guarded chambers, deep within our souls.

Lady Andariel, also writes under the Pen Name, Andariel: Maiden of Anguish, C. K. Sailer, and CKS. She has been published in private, worldwide and nationally distributed Anthologies and Ezines, including Dark Poetry Society, Open Skies Poetry: The Divine Feminine, New Generation Beats 2022 by National Poetry Foundation, Silent Spark Poetry, and several issues of Raven Cage Ezine. You can also find her writings on Her Facebook Page, The Musings of Lady Andariel.

She also recently published her own collection, Manic Mayhem: Playing with the Demons in My Mind, which is available on Amazon in paperback and kindle versions, and is looking forward to the release of Manic Mayhem 2: Dark Desires in early 2023.

Michele Barnett

Michele 47-year-old vocational rehabilitation counselor who is still pursuing a graduate degree in her free time. She enjoys writing poetry and short stories. Her favorite genres to write are science fiction and fantasy. She currently lives in Florida.

P. Carter

Patrick edits energy news by day and has been writing stories in Brianna's queernorm world by night since 2018. He also runs a critique group, where he has helped dozens of writers get pages requests, agents and publishers. He and his family live near Washington, D.C.

Linda M. Crate

Linda M. Crate's (she/her) works have been published in numerous journals and anthologies both online and in print. She has eleven published chapbooks of poetry, the latest being: fat & pretty (Dancing Girl Press, June 2022).

Glenda Darusow

Glenda Darusow was born at St. Joseph's Hospital on February 29, 1960. She grew up in Hampton Maryland. and graduated from Notre Dame Preparatory School in 1978. She received her B.S. in Education from the University Of Maryland in 1982 and taught English at various high schools within the Baltimore County School System. In 2013 she retired from teaching and married her longtime partner Belinda Deets. The couple now reside in New Market, Maryland. Glenda enjoys reading, writing, yoga, camping, and gardening. She also enjoys reading to children at the Urbana Public Library under the moniker, "Glenda The Good Witch."

Binod Dawadi

Binod Dawadi, the author of The Power of Words, is a master's degree holder in English. He has worked on more than 1000 anthologies, published in various renowned magazines. His vision is to change society through knowledge, so he wants to provide enlightenment to the people through his writing.

Tom Elmquist

Tom has always been a bit of a word nerd. He used his scribblings to express his adventures, fears, and loves throughout his life. Collecting special copies of his favorite tomes and displaying them proudly as he stared longingly, hoping to one day have a copy of his own book in the mix. While Tom has been writing for twenty-five years, this is the first time he's felt the urge to finally put his work out to the world. Watch for more stories from him as he forges forward with his first novel.

Alexandra Folch-Pi

Alexandra has lived in the Boston area her whole life. During the day she works in corporate America. Her family members constantly relate her to a mermaid and a fairy, based on her fashion and dyed red hair. In her free time, Alexandra likes to make friends a priority. She enjoys reading, and films. Her main goal in life is to work as hard as she can and travel the world. She always says "I want to see everything once." We get a glimpse of this passion in her short story.

"To find oneself is a beautiful thing."

Dana Hawkins

Dana Hawkins is a caffeine-fueled queer mom of three humans and one adorable yet slobbery St. Bernard from Seattle, WA. She attended numerous writer's conferences and romance writer classes, worked with critique partners and beta readers, and has as many writing craft books in her home as she does coffee mugs.

Amanda M. Hayden

Hayden is the Poet Laureate for Sinclair College and Professor of Humanities, Philosophy, and Religions, with emphasis in Indigenous, Eastern, Women's, and Environmental Studies. She has received several recognitions, including the League for Innovation Teaching Excellence Award. She published a book of stories about her rescues, Windy Chicken Farm Animal Rescue, and her academic essay: Saunter Like Muir was recently published by Routledge in Eco pedagogies: Practical Approaches to Experiential Learning. She lives with her partner and three daughters on a small farm with a rescue menagerie, including her three dogs, two cats, two goats, seven pigs, many chickens, and a duck named Dorothy.

Sarah Herring

Sarah is a fiancée, mother, daughter, entrepreneur, writer & more. She was born in Jersey, grew up in Dallas, & moved to Salt Lake City in 2020 at the height of the pandemic. That's where she met her fiancé & Jake's stepdad, Mike, back on September 2020 at the local community college. It was a twist of fate. She's currently a writer and an author since 2007 when she was published in an anthology for teens at thirteen. A less common known fact about Sarah is that she's an eleven year survivor of severe domestic violence. She advocates for "breaking the silence" and for mental health. Sarah's best friend took his life a year ago due to unmanaged alcoholism because of severe mental illness. So, with that and being an autism awareness advocate, she has her hands full. She now lives in St George UT, about 200 miles east of Las Vegas with her fiancé & son.

Victoria Holland

Victoria Holland is a Pushcart Prize-nominated author, and the anthologist of this collection. She has published essays and short stories in multiple collections, including *Into the Mirror, The Magical Muse Library Vol. 1* and *Vol. 2*, and *I'm not the Villain, I'm Misunderstood*. She does advocacy work, but she moonlights as a student of magic, psychology, and art. She is a romantic, a traveler, and does everything from her soul whether she likes it or not. Victoria lives in Massachusetts with her family, her lovely friends close by, and hopefully one day with a cat she can name after one of her favorite characters.

Victoria can be found on social media @toriofthetrees

J.L. Jenson

J.L. Jenson's story, LUDAMUS, appears in the 2022 Best Women's Erotica Of The Year, Volume 8 anthology. She is also an aspiring women's fiction writer. Her writing goal is to tell stories that not only entertain, but spark discussions. J.L. graduated with a degree in journalism and lives in the Northeast United States.

E.L. Johnson

E.L. Johnson writes historical mysteries for Dragonblade Publishing, the #1 ebook publisher of Historical Romance on Amazon. As a Boston native, she gave up clam chowder and lobster rolls for tea and scones when she moved across the pond to London, where she studied medieval magic at UCL and medieval remedies at Birkbeck College. Now based in Hertfordshire, she is a member of the Hertford Writers' Circle and the founder of the London Seasonal Book Club.

Shaelynn Long

Shaelynn Long is a former dirt road kid from Michigan and current small-town English instructor. She has previously published *Ache, Blur, Work In Progress*, and *Dirt Road Kid*. Shaelynn can usually be found with a nose in a book and covered in Corgi fur. Shaelynn's novel *Fury's Fate* will be published through Wild Ink Publishing LLC in October 2023.

Erin MacKenzie

Erin MacKenzie is a publishing assistant living in New Jersey with her girlfriend, their cat Sancho, and their bearded dragon Yossarian. Erin also has a short story published with Beyond Words in a collection entitled Beyond Queer Words.

Amy Nielsen

Amy Nielsen spent nearly twenty years on the other side of the writing aisle as a children's librarian, sharing her love of books with young readers. Daily immersion in story took root, and she started penning her YA debut, Worth It, behind her checkout desk. When her youngest son was diagnosed with Autism Spectrum Disorder, life shifted. She used her love of writing to help other families and started the Big Abilities blog.

She is the author of *It Takes a Village: How to Build A Support System for your Exceptional Needs Family* and the picture book,

Goldilocks and the Three Bears: Understanding Autism Spectrum Disorder. Amy's upcoming novel *Worth It* will be published through Wild Ink Publishing in May of 2024. She recently had a piece featured in the Writer's Workout Our Pandemic anthology. Amy also freelances for The Autism Helper, Playground Magazine, and other online publications.

When not writing, she and her family can be found boating in Tampa Bay. You can find Amy at www.bigabilities.com or www.amynielsenauthor.com.

J.K. Raymond

It is impossible to list the number of art projects and major and minor life events that landed J.K. Raymond in the clandestine moment, where a somewhat witchy woman flew out of the broom closet and completely off the rails after a near-death experience that lasted seven days.

A more romanticized version of her story would be to say that she arrived home from the hospital ready to live life to its fullest and execute the only idea she'd been able to hold onto while the pain tore at her. A promise that she'd finally finish the book she'd always dreamed of if just given another chance, if the pain would just stop.

Yeah, it didn't work out like that.

Pain like that doesn't leave room for thinking. It is dark, it is hollow, and it is empty of everything but the sound of your own screaming.

And then suddenly it stopped. Lessened really, but alive and capable of some thought was more the thing. But the hollowness never left her, it hitched a ride on her soul like a shitty souvenir, charmed to return her demeanor to a state of darkened emptiness as often as possible.

And one particularly dark, hollow, day there was just enough of J.K. left to remember her bag of tricks, the one that had helped her survive this tragedy and that, in this ridiculously wonderful and ridiculously awful life of hers, and in it, she saw a twinkle.

Hand to Hecate, something twinkled, something deep, deep, down. And if she squinted just right and closed one eye, she could see it become clearer and closer until it floated light and charming like a feather to lightly tickle at J.K.'s bilateral hippocampus.

Whimsy.

And though it, whimsy, that is to say, had always been with her, she had never, ever thought it would be the meat and bones of her. The only thing left when all else seemed to be gone—her very essence.

Funny little word whimsy, for J.K. it held the power of a lifetime in the silly little sound it made when she first exhaled it on a broken breath, into a word, that formed more words, that arranged themselves neatly into piles of paragraphs, that breathed life to creatures in dimensions far, far away, all full to brimming with it, because of it, the last trick in a magic bag.

Whimsy.

But there was a caveat as is always the way of things where whimsical things are concerned. In order to activate the whimsy necessary to breathe away the hollow, empty darkness, it must be shared. And though it is one thing to write like no one is watching, it is another thing entirely to bare your ass in hopes that others might find comfort in it.

But that is what's been done, and this is where J.K. Raymond stands, bare-assed and whimsical for the whole world to see.

Please, Enjoy!

J.K. also would like you to know that she has the most amazing safety net in her tiny world, which selflessly helps her to continually heal. Her husband of twenty years, Matt Houser, her two sons Aidan and Jace, her mother JoAnn, and her grumble of pugs, Lollie, RueRue, and TukTuk.

J.K. Raymond received her Bachelor of Arts from Fontbonne University in 1995, where she fell in love with everything in St. Louis—and under it.

Raymond's upcoming book, Infinite Mass, will be published through Wild Ink Publishing in December 2023.

Emily Reed

Emily Reed loves writing and has always liked creating new worlds to daydream about. She just so happened to put it on paper one day and kept doing it. Emily enjoys a few genres, from romance to dystopian to fantasy. While writing stories is a passion, Emily also enjoys writing poetry. Her favorite kind is slam poetry, and most of her writing is based on that style. Her ideal audience is the dreamers of the group. People who love to escape into pages and imagine the impossible. They would be the people who always dreamt of more out of life, the true romantics at heart.

S.E. Reed

My Heart is Hurting, S.E. Reed's debut YA novel was published by Wild Ink Publishing in July 2023.

S.E. has spent the last 20 years of her life moving around all five regions of the United States, which gives her a unique American perspective. Many of her pieces have a strong Southern theme, but she also dabbles in the strange, bizarre, and fantastical.

Her work has been featured by Wild Ink Publishing, Parhelion Lit, The Writer's Workout, Tempered Rune's Press and Survival Guide for the 21st Century. She has won several YA writing contests and actively participates as a delegate for YA Hub on Twitter.

S.E. resides in Florida with her family– nestled between the swamps of the Everglades and the salt of the Atlantic Ocean. This summer she'll be sitting in a lawn chair, working on her next novel and listening to EDM… (Ask her about her days as a DJ). Or she'll be in the pool begging her kids not to get her hair wet.

You can find S.E. on her website at www.writingwithreed.com. Also on Twitter at @writingwithreed.

Luna Silverwood

Luna Silverwood is in the last semester of obtaining her veterinary technician degree and currently work as a pet sitter. Her dad enjoys reading Greco-Roman mythology and passed his love for the lore onto Luna. This basis in Greek mythology lead her to becoming Greco-wiccan, someone who is Wiccan and worships the Greek pantheon.

Johnny Francis Wolf

Johnny Francis Wolf is an Autist — an autistic Artist. Designer, Model, Actor, Writer, and Hustler — Yes. That.

Worth a mention — his Acting obelisk — starring in the ill–famed and fated 2006 indie film, TWO FRONT TEETH. The fact that it is free to watch on YouTube might say an awful lot about its standing with the Academy.

Homeless for the better part of these past 8 years, he surfs friends' couches, shares the offered bed, relies on the kindness of strangers — paying when can, doing what will, performing odd jobs. (Of late.. Ranch Hand his favorite.)

From New York to LA, Taos and Santa Fe, Mojave Desert, Coast of North Carolina, points South and Southeast — considers himself blessed.

Johnny's love of animals, boundless. Current position working on a hacienda in Florida as laborer and horse whisperer has recently come to its seasonal conclusion,

— Greyhound and the Jersey Shore are drawing him North.

Johnny is the author of MEN UNLIKE OTHERS, Volumes 1 & 2, published by Wild Ink Publishing LLC.

Lacraecia

Lacraecia is a wildlife enthusiast who lives in a small rural town with her family in Oregon near the Cascade Mountains. She enjoys gaming, music, fantasy, and playing with her cat Zaphie.

Visit Wild Ink Publishing's webpage for more wonderful books.

Wild Ink Publishing is new to the publishing industry, which means we are able showcase some of the brightest wordsmiths by unleashing the shackles that usually stop people from publishing traditionally.

wild-ink-publishing.com